MW01196303

THE GIRL IN THE WINDOW

DIANA WILKINSON

Boldwood

First published in Great Britain in 2024 by Boldwood Books Ltd.

Copyright © Diana Wilkinson, 2024

Cover Design by Head Design

Cover Images: iStock

The moral right of Diana Wilkinson to be identified as the author of this work has been asserted in accordance with the Copyright, Designs and Patents Act 1988.

All rights reserved. No part of this book may be reproduced in any form or by any electronic or mechanical means, including information storage and retrieval systems, without written permission from the author, except for the use of brief quotations in a book review. This book is a work of fiction and, except in the case of historical fact, any resemblance to actual persons, living or dead, is purely coincidental.

Every effort has been made to obtain the necessary permissions with reference to copyright material, both illustrative and quoted. We apologise for any omissions in this respect and will be pleased to make the appropriate acknowledgements in any future edition.

A CIP catalogue record for this book is available from the British Library.

Paperback ISBN 978-1-83603-316-5

Large Print ISBN 978-1-83603-315-8

Hardback ISBN 978-1-83603-314-1

Ebook ISBN 978-1-83603-317-2

Kindle ISBN 978-1-83603-318-9

Audio CD ISBN 978-1-83603-309-7

MP3 CD ISBN 978-1-83603-310-3

Digital audio download ISBN 978-1-83603-311-0

This book is printed on certified sustainable paper. Boldwood Books is dedicated to putting sustainability at the heart of our business. For more information please visit https://www.boldwoodbooks.com/about-us/sustainability/

Boldwood Books Ltd, 23 Bowerdean Street, London, SW6 3TN

www.boldwoodbooks.com

To all the staff at Joey's Brunch in Hitchin. The best coffee, the best service, and the best views in town.

Children begin by loving their parents; as they grow older they judge them; sometimes they forgive them.

— OSCAR WILDE

Remember when you judge your parents that they were children once... Understanding will help lighten the load. Forgiveness will set you free.

— THE AUTHOR

1

I can't wait to be settled in the corner of Angelo's, my favourite café in all the world. It's nothing to do with the ambience, or even the owner's effusive personality. It's all to do with location. Although the Robusta coffee is strong, and sends my mind skyrocketing, it sets me up for the day. I'm a real coffee addict.

I always come first thing in the morning as I have a noise phobia. I crave silence, it's what I know best, and I'm only really comfortable in quiet places. If coffee was served alongside books, I'd probably spend all day in a library.

When I first found Angelo's, I didn't know that the silence and addictive coffee might soon not be the most important reasons for being here. Things changed pretty quickly.

It's exactly 7.30 a.m. and the doors are already open. It's usually Angelo himself who waves me in with a sweeping gesture and a tired, 'Buongiorno,' but today it's Candy, the perky young waitress dressed in her trademark fluffy pink. She's young, only sixteen or seventeen. Fresh out of school.

I plop my bag by the window, and follow her up to the counter. This morning she looks tired, eyes red and puffy, and not yet brimming with energy. I tap my card on the reader, and she nudges the drink my way. She smiles, but her eyes have that faraway look.

Soon I'm snuggling into position in the corner by the window, both hands wrapped around the enormous toasty mug of comfort. My first frothy cappuccino of the day. Heaven. I take a sip, before turning my attention outside. This is when my anxiety ratchets up.

The scene on the street is like the set of a long-running soap opera with a steady cast of regulars. I've been coming here, same time, same seat, for nearly three months now. It's like watching a silent black-and-white movie, where the images are vague, and you have to concentrate hard to work out what's going on.

I often wonder if people know I'm staring out at them. Maybe someone might also have me in their sights. I could be a seedy voyeur for all they know, although I'd hate to think someone was watching me every day.

At least I've got cover.

I'm camouflaged behind a huge three-tier flower planter which is plonked on the pavement, directly outside the window. In the summer it's a riotous sea of colour, but today, mid-November, waxen bushes and hardy evergreens provide scant cover.

My paranoia at needing camouflage is a bit extreme. Most passers-by don't even look my way. Glancing through the café window is the last thing on their minds as they shuffle past. At least my own view, as I look up, is clear enough.

I'm especially riveted by the activity in an apartment diagonally across the street, the one above the chemist's shop. It's where a pretty redhead comes and goes. I try to imagine things about her. Her age. Her life. Her background. Things that make her tick. Her name. Mel? Emily? Taylor? I can't decide what might suit her best.

At least once a week, a man in cycling gear rings on her front doorbell (7.45 sharp), after he's padlocked his bike outside the health food shop. She cracks the door, looks up and down the street, and tugs him sharply inside. Sometimes he kisses her lightly on the cheek, nothing slobbery, as she pulls her dressing gown tight. The door is swiftly closed, and he follows her up the stairs. Occasionally, I think she looks my way, picking me out behind the café window. But I can't be sure.

I've been lost in thought for the past fifteen minutes, when the man suddenly appears. I was in danger of relaxing, but no chance now. I watch, bereft, as the couple disappear inside, and I start imagining all sorts of things. My mind ticks quietly, incessantly, in my anxious imaginary world. I could be under the bed again, listening, waiting, and hoping. Hoping for the slightest sound which never comes, and mumbling silent prayers.

But I can't tear my eyes away. By the time my second cappuccino arrives, I'm wide awake, on the jittery side of alert. My heart is already racing.

Candy's sudden appearance makes me jump. She sets down a second mug in front of me. I always pay for two cappuccinos at the same time, and Candy brings the refill when she thinks I'm ready. Although it's a daily ritual, I'm so engrossed in staring across the road that she still manages to give me a start.

'Enjoy,' she says.

'Thanks.'

Candy's sparkly name tag, attached to her fluffy pink jumper, is a magnet for conversation. Luckily, like me, she's reticent to chat. She has that sullen teenage half-asleep look, and blushes at the slightest interaction. Despite our age difference, we're not dissimilar. I dread having to make small talk, a skill I've never mastered, whereas Candy's reticence is likely youthful lack of confidence. Or her mind is elsewhere.

She does know my name though. By mistake, one morning I left a copy of the magazine I work for, *Echoes of London*, on the counter. Next day, when she gave it back, she presented it opened at my column page, and pointed.

'Is that you?' she asked. Her cheeks reddened, as she indicated with a long pink nail the portrait head and shoulders shot, her eyes agog. I could have been an A-list celebrity.

'Bella's not my real name. It's Izzy, but yes, that's me. The agony aunt.' I rolled my eyes, assuming she might think it a weird job.

'Wow. That's amazing.'

She was about to ask a question, but, unwilling to engage, I got up to leave. With a fleeting smile, I left her to it.

It hasn't stopped me wondering if she might now regularly read my column, having found out who I am. But I won't be asking. I rarely let myself ask questions, of anyone. Not just of Candy.

My father's words are etched on my soul: *Do not ask questions. The devil deals with nosy gossips.*

I used to lie under the bed in the dark, petrified of making a noise.

'Good night, Izzy.' Dad would rap at the door. He was allowed to talk, but Mum and I had to live like Carmelite nuns.

When I was ten, the day after my birthday, Dad handed Mum and me two separate pieces of paper. They both said the same thing. I was excited, thinking it was a game. A treasure hunt perhaps, or a random bit of fun. Forgetting, as a ten-year-old might, that Dad didn't do fun.

From now on, there will be no talking in the house. We will communicate by note. God has advised this is the way forward for our family to live. Father Padraic O'Malley.

Dad was the respected parish priest, we the exemplary family unit.

I think even Mum at first thought it was a joke. But no. For the next four years I crept around, daring only to whisper in Mum's ear when he wasn't around. It didn't stop the smacks (on my backside) and the welts across Mum's face when he heard the slightest sound.

Under the rusting bedsprings, I built an imaginary den. Surrounded myself with books, using torchlight to get lost in my own world. I would wet myself when his feet appeared by the bed. I couldn't breathe, and my whole body trembled. He'd stand there for what seemed like an eternity. Every night for four years and 216 days.

Did I get used to it? Did the silence become bearable? I can't even remember, other than it became a way of life. I was allowed to talk at school, although Dad advised against it.

'Only if necessary, and only if you're asked a question.'

I'd simply nod. And that was it. When the teacher, Mrs Melon, asked if I'd anything I'd like to add, or ask, I'd shake my head.

The worst was the other kids laughing at me. Bony fingers, dirty ragged nails pointed at me, as I slunk across the playground. The only communication I knew was through books, and that's how I learned how other people behaved. Normal people, that is.

Then one day I exploded. Mum tried to calm me down, pleading for me to stop, but I couldn't. I yelled until I was hoarse, raking the skin off the back of my throat. Four-plus years of pent-up anger spewed out in that one moment. The one moment that changed our lives forever.

'Izzy, it's for our own good that we stay quiet,' Mum cried.

Well, it certainly wasn't for our own good. Dad relished our discomfort, and even though Mum had never spoken in the house again after the notes, he still beat her black and blue. He guzzled the communion wine and undid his belt, whipping her like the infidel he said she was.

Teagan, my cousin, and my only friend, even now assures

me, over and over, that talking is good. Asking questions is good. Facing up to people is good. It all sounds very good, but all the therapy in the world can't knock back the habits. The fear. I still wet the bed when the terrors return.

But Jed has always understood. He listened, horrified at my story. He tells me none of it was my fault, hugs me close. Nothing I could ever tell him would stop him loving me.

You know what? I believed him.

Sometimes I fiddle on my phone while I wait for the cyclist to reappear. Try to take my mind off things. I play Wordle, and a series of other wordy games, and often WhatsApp with Teagan. But today for some reason I'm overly anxious, and can only sit and ruminate. I twiddle my hair, go over things. Jed is always on my mind.

Last night he and I had a rare argument. He was glued to the telly, watching gruesome reports on Ukraine. I snapped.

'Turn it off. Stop watching it, please,' I yelled, over and over. Recently it's been the only way to get his attention. I rarely raise my voice, but I've been like a pressure cooker, desperate to let off steam. I scare myself when I explode.

Jed is quiet, predictable, and amazingly calm when stressed. It's hard to read his moods though, as his tone is always measured.

Although he's certainly not as relaxed as he used to be. His body has stiffened, and he's constantly fidgeting. I'm petrified he's moving away from me, and that he might disappear forever. I fear he no longer loves me. Not the way he once did.

He never shouts back, even when I push and push. He tries to understand me, and waits patiently for me to calm down. But these days I feel like I'm walking on eggshells.

Last night, after my outburst, he didn't even comment. He simply changed channels, and was soon concentrating on a Netflix movie.

'Is this better?' he asked.

Despite all my doubts, he acts in a way to keep me happy. He tells me constantly that he loves me, texts me incessantly, and leaves me loving notes all around the house. Yet I know he's locking me out of a secret world he's inhabiting, a place I'm not supposed to know about.

Teagan repeats that I should ask if I have my doubts. Perhaps I will, one day soon, but I'm much too scared to hear the truth. I couldn't live without him.

Lost in thought, time passes, and soon it's nearly 8.30: the time the man reappears onto the street.

On the dot, he exits the front door.

I sit up straighter, my heart racing from both caffeine and nerves. I lean to the right, and crane my neck for a better view. He pauses for a moment and waves back up.

The lady, whatever her name is, looks lovingly down from the first-floor window. I think it's lovingly, it's hard to be sure, but that's what I'm imagining. Even with my hawk-like vision, the window is small, and her features indistinct. She trills her fingers, and hovers behind the cloudy glass until the cyclist disappears from view.

I start the countdown, set the timer on my smart watch. Five minutes, give or take a few seconds, she'll step out onto the street herself. Yep. Thirty-four seconds early. Here she comes.

She's more flustered than usual, and her hair more flyaway. The little boy, two years old at least, clings tightly to her hand.

His light blue blazer, and gold embroidered cap, tell me where they're heading. The little Montessori nursery on the other side of town.

Then suddenly I rock back in horror. Holy shit.

Something dreadful has just happened. My mouth gapes, and my heart smashes against my chest. Despite the shock, I can't help noticing that the lady doesn't look round.

She hasn't realised that her visitor has been hit by a car.

Her visitor.

My husband.

4

If Starbucks hadn't closed for a refurb, I'd never have come to Angelo's. If I'd told Jed that I'd changed my early-morning coffee haunt, he'd probably have been more careful. Especially if I told him I sat by the window.

He has no idea I'm on to him. I've confided in no one, not even Teagan. I tell her I have doubts about what Jed is up to, but don't embellish on the detail. I guess I should, as she's the only person, apart from Jed, who knows my story.

She was the first person to get a word out of me after my parents died. Her dad was Mum's brother, and I moved in with them after Mum's suicide. Teagan was like an older sister, best friend, and mother all rolled into one. Jed doesn't encourage our friendship, wondering why I need her now I've got him.

'It wasn't your fault.' Teagan still repeats the words on a loop.

But it was my fault. If I hadn't exploded, started yelling at Dad, telling him I was fed up being quiet, none of it would have happened. I saw red, and all the bottled-up silence exploded in a vent of fury. I can still hear the screams.

I trust Teagan with all my heart, but can't bring myself to tell her what I've seen through the café window. If I did confide, she'd insist I have it out with Jed, and leave him if he is cheating. Move on, she'd say, telling me the world is a big place, full of opportunities. It might be for her, but not for me. Jed is my whole world, and I can't imagine life without him.

I loved Angelo's when I first came, and soon decided that I might not go back to Starbucks once it reopened. It would have been a toss-up, but then one morning I saw him.

Jed, my husband, parking his bicycle outside the health food shop, and sauntering across the street to ring on a doorbell.

That first time, I sat bolt upright, thinking I'd maybe pop outside and surprise him. He was supposed to be on the way to work, cycling as always to the station. I watched, half-expecting him to push something through the letterbox. Why else would he be there? My heart pumped, and I had to grip the tabletop to steady myself, even though I was sitting down. I came over dizzy, as if suffering from seasickness.

The last thing I expected was for him to go inside. But when the lady leaned over and kissed him... was it on the lips? I can't remember clearly that first time, but all I do know is that I began to shake. As if I was having a minor fit.

I still wonder what would have happened if I'd gone straight across the road and accosted him then and there. But I'll never know, as it's much too late for that.

I sat and stared at the front door. A whole lifetime flashed before my eyes. What was Jed doing? He couldn't be having an affair. Surely not? Not my Jed.

After he left, got on his bicycle and presumably rode on to the station, I remember I still couldn't move. A text from him pinged onto my phone shortly after, maybe only fifteen minutes later, telling me he had arrived safely at the office. This was the first lie of many, as he could only have been on the train, and his office at King's Cross is thirty-five minutes away.

It was about two weeks later that things got even worse. I was at my lookout post, rigid, anxious, and nauseous, waiting for the next episode. I couldn't imagine things getting any worse. But one morning, after he appeared and rang the bell, a little boy hurtled through the front door squealing.

Squealing at Jed. I couldn't hear the noise, but excitement was etched on the boy's little features. He jumped up and down, arms thrown wide. Jed bent down, his skinny cyclist's arms hoisting the lad up in the air. He then swung him round and round, and I can still hear the shrieks of joy in my head.

Night after night I lie in the dark while Jed gently snores, and imagine the laughter. I can see the kisses, feel the hugs. The little lad wouldn't let go, even as Jed tried to prise his fingers free.

I'm still not sure which is worse. The fact that Jed might have a mistress, or that he has a son. I'm convinced the boy must be his son, otherwise why would they be so close?

I've no idea what to do. I feel as if I'm buried alive, and have been struck dumb like I was all those years ago. Of course I should ask him what's going on, that's what a normal person would do.

But then I'm not like other people.

5

My hands fly to my face, slap against my cheeks. An involuntary scream escapes, and I look round the café to see if anyone else is looking. There's only Candy, and one other customer – the estate agent with the *clicky-clacky* footwear whom she flirts with every morning. Her eyes light up when he strides across the wooden floorboards in his hard-soled leather brogues, as she coyly teases her hair. But today, I've no interest whatsoever in their interaction. I stare aghast through the window.

Jed, my husband, who moments ago remounted his bike, and was filtering into the traffic lane, has been catapulted into the air, and is now lying on the pavement. Oh my God. He's contorted, lying on his side with his green helmet askew. At least he's moving. He's trying to get up, but despite the effort can barely raise an arm even a centimetre off the ground.

My heart is pumping hard, and I'm glued to the spot, staring at the horror. The soap opera that is my morning viewing has taken a dreadful twist. The predictability of the scene has turned into one of carnage. A small group stop and stare. One lady drops a four-drink holder, and chocolate-coloured liquid explodes over the pavement. I can lipread her expletive.

Candy rushes along the length of the café, and gasps.

'Oh, no. Izzy, what happened? Is he okay?' she asks, eyes like saucers.

'He's moving,' is all I say. I'm not sure how I'm supposed to know if he's okay or not. Perhaps I look like a nurse.

'Thank God.' Candy's cheeks are flushed, as she hurries out through the open doors onto the street.

The small group of onlookers is growing by the second. Everyone wears deep furrowed worried masks, mouths down-turned, but it's hard not to sense the relief that the misfortune isn't theirs, or that of someone they know.

The temperature in the café seems to have rocketed, even though the doors are thrown wide, but I'm so hot I can hardly breathe. What if Jed is seriously injured? What if he dies? I can't do anything but watch. There's nothing I can do, and I'm too scared to go out. At least there are lots of people round him.

I try to stand up, but my legs are seriously wobbly, and my hand shakes as I carry my coffee cup back to the counter. It's nearly 9 a.m., but there's no one at all now behind the counter. Candy has all but abandoned ship.

My insides have turned to liquid, so I scoot to the toilet. My fingers are so damp, it's hard to slide the bolt across. I slump onto the toilet seat and hang my head, willing my heart to calm down. I've heard how people, when they witness fatal accidents, need therapy for PTSD. This must be how the trauma starts.

I freeze when there's a rattle at the toilet door.

'Are you in there, Izzy?' It's Candy. Her voice is shaky, high-pitched and excited all at the same time.

'Yes. Won't be long.' My words come out in a hoarse whisper.

'Oh, you should see what's happening.' Her words are loud

and clear, as if she's pressed her lips against the door. She's desperate to share the drama.

'Give me a minute,' I croak, willing her to go away. I could do with staying here for a couple of hours. I need to play for time, let things calm down. Then I'll sneak off. I don't want to be a witness, and have to give a lengthy statement to the police.

I can't face questioning in case I crack.

6

'Shall I get you another coffee?' It's Candy, again. It can't have been more than five minutes since she last knocked, but I need her to go away. She's desperate for me to engage, and share the horror, and is screaming through the door.

I wonder if she's taken photographs, and selfies alongside the glum bystanders to post on Instagram, with the caption underneath: *I was there.* No doubt she'll embellish the tale for regulars, telling them she was in the thick of it. It'll make a change from sharing the daily tedium of the job. She dreams one day of owning her own café, telling us this when Angelo is out of earshot.

I hold my breath, willing her to go, when the sudden wail of an ambulance siren breaks through. Even behind the locked toilet door the noise makes my stomach churn.

Candy's footsteps finally retreat, and I guess she's on her way back outside to join the other watchers. An emergency certainly brings people together.

I picture the stretcher being carried out, and the cyclist being gingerly lifted up, and manoeuvred into the vehicle. The blue light will keep flashing until the ambulance moves away. The hee-haw noise, alerting traffic to an emergency, will only carry on if there's a threat to life.

A few minutes pass until I brace myself, take a few deep breaths, and slip back out into the café. There's quite a queue now for coffee, or more likely for camomile tea to calm the nerves. The drama has certainly been good for business. Ted, the young guy who usually works alongside Candy, has appeared, and he's heating paninis up in the toaster. Candy is fussing with intent, taking orders with the grim face of a mourner.

It's an excuse for all these people to take time out. Delay getting to work, or facing the challenges of their own lives. I check my watch. It's now ten past nine.

I need to get cracking. I promised Jed I wouldn't be late popping round to see his mother, as she'll be watching out for me. Likely peering through the caked-in-grime net curtains of her soon-to-be-demolished mid-terrace deathtrap. Jed wouldn't be too happy if I didn't call round, and I certainly don't want to upset him. I have to believe he'll be okay.

Before I step out onto the street, I watch for another couple of minutes. The siren is flashing, but quietly. There's no warning wail of death. It must be a good sign, surely. I breathe more easily when I think Jed must still be alive. I bet the lady with the little boy will be relieved, that's for sure. Although she probably doesn't know yet, as she never saw what happened.

I shiver, pull my collar up, and sling my bag over my shoulder, twisting my neck for a last look towards the counter. Candy's not looking my way. Much too busy taking care of business, and reliving the horror with each new customer.

A final glance through the window, and I nearly jump out of

my skin. An old man with a white stick has his faced pressed up against the window. Is he staring at me?

I need to get out of here, and as far away as possible. No one knows Jed, the cyclist lying on the ground, is my husband, but I feel all eyes are on me.

7

I scurry through the market, up the steep hill by the castle, until I reach my car. My heart hammers from the effort.

My hands are shaking so badly, I drop the key a couple of times before I manage to un-zap the lock. The door of my bashed-up black Ford Fiesta cranks open, and I slip through the rusty gap. My phone is at the bottom of my bag, but I need to text Jed. I usually respond promptly to all his messages, and don't want to change the pattern. He propped a note up against the toaster this morning saying he didn't want to wake me when he left.

Text me once you've been to Mum's and let me know all okay.
Love you. XXXX

Before I start the car, I key in a message.

> Hope you caught your train okay. Let me know when you reach Edinburgh. Got delayed getting to your mum's, but on my way. Will soon be there. Talk later XX

Leaving kisses, with everything that's going on, doesn't come easily. Watching him visit another woman has been eating away at me. But I don't want him wondering what might be wrong if I leave them out. The more normal things seem, and the more regular our routine, the easier it'll be to cope. I'm trying to hide behind a seemingly normal façade, constantly trying to hide the worry, anxiety and doubts. He has no idea what I'm going through, and the dreadful thoughts I'm having.

Today he was supposed to be on his way up to Edinburgh on business. I doubt he'll make it after what's happened, but I'll carry on as if nothing's changed. I have to sit it out. Maybe the accident will be the thing that pushes him to finally tell me what's been going on. I feel sick thinking about it, but for now, all I care about is that he'll be okay.

Going round to see Blanche will at least keep me busy, take my mind off things. It'll give me something to do while I wait for news.

Whenever I go and check on his mother, Jed phones her first to let her know what time I'll be there. He wants us all to get on, and works hard at cementing cordial relations. He talks about how lucky he is to have the perfect family. Me and Blanche are all he needs.

Funny though, he leaves most of the minding of his mother up to me these days, despite his proclamations of devotion. I can't remember the last time he called round. My stomach knots when I think about it all.

The car rattles, shakes, and judders as black smoke billows from the exhaust. I pull out into the steady stream of traffic, and Google Maps tells me I'm only ten minutes away. At least the roadworks have finished. I'd like to drive faster, but no such luck. I'm grateful when my rust bucket starts, let alone picks up speed.

I'm soon pulling into Miners' Terrace, which I've nicknamed

Rotten Row. It's beyond depressing, with newly erected scaffolding around the properties at both ends. The windows of these properties have already been bricked up, the residents long gone. They were the first to leave. The bulldozers are ready and waiting. The mid-terrace houses are just as grim with blackened brickwork and rotting door frames.

Blanche is the last resident in occupancy. The developers are desperate for her to give up the fight, and move out, as she's the only person still living there. But the developers will have a long wait, as she's determined to die in Pantry Cottage, the cosy name attached to her crumbling deathtrap of a home. The name might evoke cosy country images, but the reality is something else entirely. Pantry Cottage is a one-up-one-down nineteenth-century mid-terrace minefield. The walls are crumbling, and the loosened cement between the brickwork rains down if anyone so much as breathes on it.

I kill the ignition, and the car does a shivery death rattle. I'm wondering why Blanche hasn't one foot on the doorstep, the other still planted firmly inside, like she normally does when I pull up. Or why she isn't twitching behind the moth-eaten net curtains. Today there's no sign of her.

Generally, if she's not in sight, she's hovering inside by the handset which is attached to the green flowery wallpaper. She waits for the bell to ring so she can speak into it and greet guests in a loud imperious voice. That said, Jed and I have been her only guests for months now.

I check my watch. I'm only ten minutes late, and wonder if Blanche has already tried to contact her son to find out where I've got to. The thought makes me even more anxious than I am already.

As I approach the gates, a man in a yellow hard hat appears out of nowhere, and heads my way. He's wearing heavy-duty Caterpillar boots, and gripping a field-trip-type clipboard.

'Hi.' He smiles, all dazzling teeth and crinkly eyes, and offers an outstretched hand. I wonder who he thinks I am, as I haven't seen him before.

'Hi.' I ignore the hand, and lean mine instead atop the metal gate.

'Are you visiting Mrs Hardcastle?'

This guy is smoothly handsome, and with his manicured nails and flawless tan is certainly not one of the on-site labourers. More San Tropez than Home Counties weather-beaten. His hard hat teases at a jaunty angle. He's like a kid battling the embarrassment of wearing a cycling helmet.

'Yes. Why? Is there a problem?'

'No. I'm just keen to speak to her.' He smiles again, perfect teeth glinting in the sunlight. Jed tells me Blanche won't answer the door to anyone except him, me, and the postman. I'm under strict instructions not to let anyone near her.

'Sorry. I can't help.' I look away, and start walking the few steps to the front door. I wonder if Blanche is watching what's going on, as this guy's appearance might explain why she's keeping well hidden.

'Shall I hang around? Maybe you'd ask her if I could have a quick word?'

He's not easily getting the message, and I'm desperate to get inside before he starts asking more questions. I'm already flustered.

'I can ask her.' I'm not sure if he hears me, but he's still lingering. Blanche will definitely not want a quick word, and I need him to go away. His proximity makes me uneasy.

I wait until he's moved off, proceed to the front door, and rap gently with the brass knocker. Flakes of rotting paint drizzle to the ground. I peer in through the small glass panel to one side, shielding my eyes against the sun. There doesn't seem to be any movement downstairs. I step back, and look up, but still no sign of life.

My heart picks up, as I get a sense something's not right. Blanche is always waiting eagerly for me to turn up.

Mr Hunky Foreman is watching from a few houses down. I dig out Blanche's spare key from my bag, desperate now to get inside. If there's something wrong, or Blanche has had a fall, or worse, and I can't get hold of Jed...

I dread to think that far ahead.

8

The unopened mail has been stacked neatly on the hall table. The sight gives me momentary comfort.

'Blanche? Blanche? Are you here?'

I close the door tightly behind me, and pull the bolt across. Just in case.

My voice quavers in the quietness. The house is like a morgue.

I peek into the lounge, which looks surprisingly tidy. It's also had a recent coat of polish over the mahogany surfaces. I cough when the cleaning abrasives hit the back of my throat.

'Blanche?'

The kitchen is even more spotless than the lounge. There isn't a dish, cup or single piece of cutlery sitting out, and the stainless-steel sink is sparkling. It's like an advert for Mr Muscle.

Blanche isn't slovenly, far from it, but she's not the tidiest either. She snaps at Jed, tells him to stop fussing when he tries to start the dishwasher. She only switches it on when it's loaded to the brim.

I doubt she'll be in the utility room, and even less likely in the cellar. I brace myself to have a look. The stone stairs to the basement are treacherous, even for Jed and me. Let alone Blanche. A quick scan, and there's still no sign of her.

She must still be in bed, and as I head up the stairs creak. An unusual sickly scent of air freshener sets my cough off again. There's no hint of the usual musty damp smell.

'Blanche?'

I push open her bedroom door, and although the curtains aren't closed all the way, the room is morbidly dark. The windows are so small that light battles to get in even with the curtains open. But today it's almost pitch black.

Blanche is slumped on the bed, barely visible under her flimsy bedding. She's lying at a really awkward angle, white bony toes poking out from under the off-white sheet. At least her eyes are open.

'Izzy.' Her voice is even hoarser than mine. 'Is that you?'

I pull back the curtains so I can see her. She looks dreadful, like a corpse.

'Yes, it's me. You're okay, I'm here now.'

I take her hand which is deathly cold, yet her forehead is dripping in sweat.

'Blanche. You're not well. I need to call a doctor,' I say.

She tugs back her hand, and snaps, 'No doctors. I'm fine,' her voice like a foghorn.

She looks far from fine. Perhaps she's got Covid. Or flu. Or worse. I've no idea what to do.

'Let me call Jed.' I know I'm unlikely to get hold of him, but I can't think of anyone else to call. Apart from an ambulance.

Blanche's eyes are like a hawk's as I key in his number, but it goes to voicemail. I was hoping he might pick up. Who am I kidding? He's more likely lying unconscious in a hospital bed.

I leave a message anyway, so that Blanche can hear me. My words are shaky.

'Jed. Get back to me, please. Blanche isn't well, and I don't know what to do.'

She stares at me, listening intently to what I say. She slumps back against her pillow once I've hung up.

'Can I get you anything? Tea? A soft drink? Some toast perhaps?'

'There's soup in the fridge. Could you heat me some up?' she whispers, as if the earlier snapping has sapped all her energy.

'Of course.'

'It's home-made.' Blanche's voice is weak, but clear.

'Oh. When did you make it?' I ask, suspecting the soup might be well past its sell-by date.

'I didn't make it,' Blanche says, then puffs out a weak laugh. 'It was Madison.'

'Madison?'

Who the heck is Madison? I get an uneasy feeling. Jed hasn't mentioned anyone called Madison. Although, come to think of it, he did mention a few weeks ago that he might get his mother a regular cleaner.

Why didn't he tell me? He might have forgotten, but I'm not convinced. It feels like a deliberate oversight. He used to tell me everything, without me ever having to ask. He knows I don't like to ask questions.

My stomach somersaults, and I come over nauseous. The overload of coffee, lack of food, and shock are not a good mix.

'My new cleaner. She does a great job.' Blanche wheezes, breathless from talking. 'Didn't Jed tell you about her?'

Her croak follows me out the door, and back down the stairs.

9

I feed Blanche a small dish of chicken soup, wash her face and neck, and make sure she's comfortable, before I tiptoe out of her room. A gentle rhythmic vibration of her lips tells me she's sleeping. I've no idea what else I can do.

According to Blanche, the cleaner, Madison (whoever she is) is due back tomorrow morning. Hopefully, Blanche will be okay until then.

When I step back out into the glare of the sunlight, thankfully there's no sign of Mr Hard Hat. I spread my fingers across my forehead to shield my eyes, and scour the street. It's the first time I notice a large hoarding attached to the scaffolding at one end of the terrace. I'm not sure if it's been erected since I was inside, or if it was already there. My mind is all over the place.

Bailey Finch Construction

My first thought is to wonder if Mr Hard Hat might be Bailey or Finch.

Despite the heat, I'm shivering when I climb into my car. It does its usual choking splutter before kicking into gear.

It's already midday by the time I get home. My head is pounding and anxiety is hitting me in waves. There's still been nothing from Jed. No messages, no calls, and the image of the accident plays in a loop in my head. I've no idea how to get it to stop.

While I'm waiting for news, the best thing I can do is work. The day is almost half over and I haven't even started on my weekly column. I don't know how I'll concentrate, but I have to try.

I'm not hungry, but know I need to eat. I cut up some cold chicken, and throw it between two doughy slices of bread. Hopefully it'll settle my stomach, and help sop up the coffee. I'm beyond jittery.

I carry the sandwich and a bottle of water through to the study, and close the curtains before trying to settle into the darkened space. A single lamp keeps me company.

My den is kitted out like a mini-library. Jed helped me put up shelving, floor to ceiling, on the three walls that don't have windows. They're stacked high with all manner of books. The sight is like an oasis, and when I close the door, lock myself in, my mind slowly calms.

Every few minutes I check my phone for messages. There's still nothing. Not even a love heart or coffee cup emoji. Usually when Jed travels up to Edinburgh he sends so many texts that I've no time to reply before another one arrives. He starts texting even before his train has pulled out of King's Cross.

After what happened this morning, I'm not expecting anything, but it doesn't stop me checking. The blank screen makes my imagination run riot, and I'm imagining all sorts.

What if something really bad has happened? What if he can't walk again? Or worse still. What happens if...? I can't allow myself to think of the worst-case scenario. Life wouldn't be worth living without Jed.

I open my laptop, knowing that I need to gear my brain for work, take my mind off things. But it's too tempting to google local news before I start.

The accident replays on a loop in my mind, as if in slow motion. There must have been a resounding thump on the pavement when he landed, but I heard nothing through the window. Did he scream before he hit the ground?

I scroll through Twitter feeds, articles, recent news, local updates, but nothing. The bicycle accident might not be top priority, but surely there would be something if it really was that serious. No news must be good news, right? If Jed had died, surely it would already have got out. Candy would have spread the word through the local grapevine, and, a prolific poster, on all her social media feeds. I check her Instagram story and posts, but so far nothing.

When I can't find any news about the accident, I tackle the sandwich. I chew each bite a dozen times before I can swallow. It takes the whole bottle of water to get it down.

Curiosity has got the better of me, and I do a final bit of googling before I tackle my email mountain.

Bailey Finch Construction isn't hard to find. And there he is, Mr Hard Hat, MD, smiling for the camera with photo-shoot perfection. Minus the headwear, dark luscious hair swirls across his forehead. His trimmed beard is shadowy, and adds to the machismo and mystery. He is handsome, attractive in an obvious way. His name is Adam Finch, and after a few more minutes' googling I find him on Facebook, and LinkedIn. He's single, which strikes me as odd, as he's the sort I imagine getting snapped up fast. Adam Finch is the type of guy Jed hates. Arrogant, and too good-looking by half.

Whenever someone like Adam crosses our path, Jed grips my hand more tightly, and it makes me love him even more.

10

I finally open up my agony column emails. There's another fifty-four letters. People are desperate to get things off their chest, and sharing in public seems to help. That said, I don't believe a lot of what they tell me. There's always a rich smattering of stories involving bondage, handcuffs and police truncheons.

When we first got together, Jed devoured my columns, as if hoping to learn something new about me every week. I can't remember when his interest waned, but then I can't remember when he became a completely different person. My Jed. My soulmate. Where did he go?

I have a list of content that I'm not allowed to use on my *Dear Bella* agony column. Ever. Swearing, anything remotely pornographic, racist, or anything hinting at violence. Grayson Peacock, editor of *Echoes of London* (an ageing sugar-daddy with a lecherous grin) vets everything before it goes to print. Every week, in advance, he asks what's on the agenda for the next issue. He's constantly pushing for more saucy content, especially in relation to extramarital affairs. Cheating sells good copy.

I'm surprised that this is his favourite angle, as he must be wary that I might include content relating to his seedy goings-on. I think he's a latent voyeur, the kind who smacks his lips when talking about *ménages à trois*. I've been tempted, more than once, to ask if he's got any personal angles he'd like included. But I like my job, and don't think winding him up would be a good idea.

I'm sharp at picking out genuine emails, and it doesn't take me long to come up with measured responses that will look good in print. If there are no particularly interesting emails, no letters with sufficient bite, or at least with a modicum of risqué content, Grayson gives me artistic licence. He encourages me to come up with more daring angles. Make things up.

'Use your imagination. Something meaty. You know what I mean, Izzy.'

Grayson leers through the screen, and winks. Small comfort that he's far away. When we Zoom, his eyes bore through me, and I think of Dad, minus the dog collar. It's the knowing, threatening stare that keeps me quiet, defying any challenge. The memories eat me up.

I don't verbally engage with Grayson, only when absolutely necessary, but I've got his measure. That's the thing about being shy, and not being a talker, your senses are on high alert. I read people well. I listen, and I watch. These are my tools for understanding.

Working from home suits me. It's not the library, but it's the next best thing. I love the quiet cosiness of my little den, and I'm like a private detective in my own little world.

Coming up with something new for my column each week isn't easy. The list of taboo subjects is so long, but I like a challenge.

I try to settle, for a couple of hours at least, and slowly, methodically run through the email mountain. Then I see it. The letter that catches my attention. As I read on, the last corner of sandwich crust lodges in my throat. For a couple of seconds I can't catch my breath, until I manage to cough it up. I shove the plate aside, and dare to look back at the screen.

I read, reread the letter, go back to the beginning and read it again. It's an omen. I know I need to use it. I bite the inside of my cheek, draw blood, and with shaky fingers I get to work.

11

Dear Bella,

I don't know where to start. But I've been married for twenty years, and have just discovered my husband has a whole other family! I'm completely devastated and have no idea what to do.

My husband, Ricky (this isn't his real name of course), travels a lot. I've always enjoyed the peace and quiet when he goes off on his monthly trips. I get the house to myself, and invite the girls round for cocktails.

Ricky is very handsome, arrogant, and controlling. But he's always been so in love with me. Or so he told me, and still does. I believed the bastard. Can you imagine?

Well, I found out recently that not only does he have a teenage son by me, but he also has a set of nine-year-old twins (a boy and a girl) with another woman called Cassandra.

I've no idea what to do. I'm beyond furious. I haven't told him yet that I know about this other family, but wondered if you could offer up some advice. Anything. Anything at all. I

need to plan out my future. Both financially, and also personally. You see, I think I'm losing my marbles.

I'm even more scared that I might kill the bastard.

Yours,

Fuming

* * *

Dear Fuming,

How absolutely awful for you. You have my complete
sympathy, as well as that of most of our readers, no doubt.

Not only has your husband been unfaithful, he has lied to
you... and carried on the pretence over the last ten years at
least.

My advice? Well, he's not the man for you. Or for anyone
for that matter who wants a stable, happy home. I must ask
myself, and perhaps you can let us all know, if this Cassandra
knows about you? You might be tempted to keep her in the
loop.

What to do next? Well, that's up to you to decide. Personally, if it was me, I would pack his bags and throw him out.
One thing I have learnt from doing this column for so long is
that people repeat patterns. If he's coolly conned you so that
he can have the best of both worlds, I suspect he might also
have conned Cassandra.

The one thing I definitely wouldn't recommend though is
causing him harm. This is not the way forward. Revenge is
best served cold, as they say. If Cassandra doesn't want to
be with him, he might soon have nowhere else to go.

All the very best and keep us posted as to what you
decide.

Bella

It takes me ages to compose the response. I mean, what can I say? I get up, wander round the house, up and down the stairs, and try to calm my racing thoughts.

The letter is so real, I could have written it myself. Although I now suspect (am almost certain in fact) that Jed is having an affair, and also that he has a son, it's small comfort that he hasn't been cheating for as long as the reader's husband.

My reply is logical, and measured. I reread it several times, before I'm brave enough to fire off to Grayson for approval. But first, I take out the reader's reference to 'killing' and the word 'bastard', and tone down the content.

Maybe she should go ahead and *kill the bastard*, but then what? She'd suffer even more. Also, there are the children. But I'm sensing something else. Deep down, I suspect she might still love her husband. Love just doesn't go away. I haven't packed Jed's bags, and feel sympathy for the reader. I'm not sure I could ever leave him.

She's angry, wants to vent, but perhaps that's all she wants to do. Perhaps, like me, she has no one else she wants to tell, or is too embarrassed to share the shame.

Second families. It's a new subject for readers, and it'll be a long wait until Saturday before I get feedback.

Maybe someone will help me decide what I should do.

12
_____

I manage to keep working well into the afternoon, reading, sifting, and picking out random letters from the pile.

For a few hours I get lost in other people's worlds until my own doesn't seem quite so bad. I choose a minimum of two letters each week for my column, and then come up with measured responses.

As the minutes tick by, my concentration starts to wane. I check my phone every few minutes, but there's still no word from Jed. The screen is blank, and I get more and more panicky waiting for the comforting ping of texts. But there's nothing. Only complete silence. The silence should be comforting, as a knock on the door would be worse; the police with something to tell me.

It's nearly five o'clock when I finally give up, and close down my laptop. I end up lifting out a chilled bottle of white wine from the fridge, and pour out a meagre mouthful. I'm hoping a couple of sips might take the edge off the paranoia.

I wander into the lounge, turn on the TV, and flick through channels. Backwards and forwards, and then I start all over again. Six o'clock chimes from the clock in the hall. It was an early heirloom from Blanche. Her face pops into my mind every time it sounds, but this time Jed's mother is the least of my worries.

I put on a light-hearted romcom, letting it play quietly in the background, but it's hopeless trying to concentrate. The images of Jed's accident are still going round and round, and my head spins from constant rewind.

Jed regularly travels to Edinburgh to meet with clients, and he should have arrived hours ago. He usually phones, or texts at least, when he gets to the hotel. His messages are always loaded with kisses, smiley faces, and love-heart emojis. He never forgets.

Soon after we got married, Jed began to travel away on business. He was reluctant at first to leave me, but we soon fell into a routine. After he'd been gone a few days, I was desperate for him to return. It's his presence I miss, more than dynamic conversation or wild passionate sex. I miss his warmth, the cuddles, the security. He promises he'll never leave me, and that's all I've ever needed to hear.

Jed works in financial investments, for a small company called MoneyMart. He advises people on products. Mortgages, pensions, and suchlike. He works out of a small office round the back of King's Cross, and one of the perks of the job is that he gets a healthy travel allowance. With clients all around the British Isles, first-class travel and stopovers in smart hotels are part of the package.

'You could come with me,' he suggested when the trips became more frequent.

I'd love to, but we never have any spare cash. Until recently, I'd no idea where the money went. That aside, blowing what little is left each month would be crazy, especially as I'm desperate for a new car before my Fiesta completely conks out.

'Don't worry. I'll be fine on my own,' I told him. It was a lie, as I'm never fine.

'I'll pay for you,' he replied, thinking I didn't want to waste my own savings.

We keep two separate accounts. His and hers. We agreed I should have some independence. Now I wonder if he wanted his own account so I couldn't see where his money went, and what he was spending it on.

Whenever I used to mention lack of money, he would mumble something about unwise investments. He apologised, kissed me over and over, and promised to be more careful. I know not to pry, and until recently, trusted him to make things better. He promised, after all. But every time he leaves, he mumbles, with a hangdog expression, that he wishes I were going with him.

'Maybe next time.' I always say this as I wave him off.

Two years have passed, as well as many 'next times'. He works longer hours, but nothing's got any better. His shoes are scuffed, his shirts worn around the collars, and eating out has become a long-forgotten treat. For a while I suspected he might be an addict. Drugs. Gambling. Drink. Thinking one day he'd own up, and we'd work through it all together. But now I know it's worse, much worse than I imagined, and I've no idea how he'll ever make things right.

At least I have my job. Okay, it's only part-time, and my salary isn't much, but it's mine. I've saved a little nest egg for the future, which might come round sooner than I thought.

I keep trying his phone, but it only goes to voicemail. Around nine, I give in, turn off the TV and downstairs lights, and trudge upstairs. I'm exhausted from worry, and despite three cups of camomile tea, my mind is racing.

I crawl into bed, praying for a few hours' sleep, and pull the duvet round me. In the morbid silence of the darkened bedroom, I send a final text.

> Jed. Please let me know you've arrived safely. I'm starting to really worry. XXXXXX

I overdo the kisses. Jed hates when I leave out the XXXs, asking me if I don't love him any more.

'Even a love-heart emoji would do,' he suggests, his face puckered with worry.

I tell him I forget, I've been so busy. It's a lie because I would never forget. It's just it's become harder and harder, as the weeks go by, and I watch him from the café window, to leave kisses.

But tonight I'm desperate for a response. I want him to know I'm here, waiting for him. I need him home, and I'm so worried about what might have happened. If he had been really badly hurt, or worse, I'd have heard. Wouldn't I? I'd be on his recent list of calls.

I keep my eyes on the screen for several minutes. The message doesn't seem to go through. I can't tell when Jed was last on his phone, as he blocks everyone from seeing when he was last online.

Even I'm blocked from his activity.

13

I toss and turn all night. Nightmares and flashbacks are gruesome company.

I wake from fitful sleep around 5 a.m., drenched in sweat, feeling hot one minute and shivery the next. Shortly before six I give in and crawl out of bed. There's still no word from Jed. Every time I opened my eyes in the night, I checked, but there's been nothing. Not even the usual thumbs up and red hearts.

Deciding to go jogging while the rest of the world wakes up, I drag on an old sweatshirt and tracksuit bottoms. A quick pound round the park, a shower, and hopefully I'll feel more like myself. More able to cope with whatever is to come, and I can still be at the café by 7.30.

Even though I'm not expecting Jed to turn up today, I aim to be at the café as soon as it opens. It's become a masochistic ritual. Even when Jed doesn't appear, I'm drawn to watch the woman and the boy. It's as if their routine might tell me something, give me clues as to how my husband is involved. It sounds crazy, but it's an obsession.

An hour and a quarter later, I'm killing time by waiting on

the wooden bench by the NatWest bank. The branch is directly opposite the health food shop, and diagonally across from the café.

Sitting at home, checking for messages every couple of minutes would have done my head in. Thoughts swirl round and round, and I use logic to try to make sense of everything, and to put my mind at rest. But it's futile. I'm unable to climb down from the heights of anxiety. Even though I'm sitting in a different location, I'm desperate to know what's happened. If I don't hear anything today, I'll have no choice but to start phoning round hospitals tomorrow.

At least four regulars, whom I watch every morning from the café window, pass me by. There's an old lady with a shopping trolley who wheezes as she shuffles along. She's got a blanket slung over a shoulder which makes me think she's been sleeping under the butcher's awning again.

A couple of teenage girls, skirts like curtain pelmets, are giggling at something on their phones. A few pouting selfies, and they wander on past.

Then I see the old man who stared at me through the window yesterday. I realise, from his white stick, that he's blind. He pokes and prods the pavement, and walks past. I breathe more easily when I realise his stares had nothing to do with me.

I can't believe the accident was only yesterday. My mind has been in turmoil, and the nightmares last night were horrific. I dreamt there was a bright yellow notice at the scene, with a telephone number in bold black lettering asking witnesses to come forward. The type of notice you see on the roadside, where bunches of flowers and photographs appear shortly afterwards. Notices linked to death.

But on the street outside the café there are no signs that anything out of the ordinary took place. I look up and see

Angelo across the street struggling with the breakfast board. It's still only 7.27, but he's never late.

I take a few deep breaths, and brace myself for going into the café. I'm not up to talking to Angelo, to Candy, or to anyone about what happened yesterday.

I just need to sit quietly, and look out the window.

14

As well as seeing Jed through the café window, I've started watching him at home.

I focus on the small, seemingly insignificant things. There's nothing major staring me in the face but there are tell-tale signs that things have changed. Even if I hadn't seen him from the café, I'd know something was up. His body language tells a story of its own, and his habits vary when they were once so predictable.

For starters, he looks anywhere but at me when I ask a question. He knows I was brainwashed by my father not to pry, but he's bizarrely edgy if I dare ask the simplest thing. It's as if he's bracing for a taxing inquisition.

A few days ago, I asked him where he'd left the keys to the safe. He raised his eyes to the heavens, pursed his lips, as if trying to remember. When I query anything at all, his eyes skirt around my face, avoiding all contact. If I ask anything vaguely contentious, he walks away. Heads for the fridge, lifts out a beer, and plays for time. He hates confrontation, as much as I do, so I know not to push. But his behaviour is distinctly odd.

Last week when he got home late, my first question, as I sipped a lukewarm tea and stole my gaze away from the daily crossword grid, was 'How was work?'

'Fine.' This has become his default reply to everything. *How are you feeling? Everything okay? How's your grumbling back?* 'Fine,' is all I get.

But he's far from fine, miles away in his own little world, refusing to let me in. I know he's struggling because his eyes are dark ringed, his complexion ashen, and his body stooped. Even if I hadn't seen him through the window, I'd have known something was up.

Shortly after we met, we went on a first date to the Jolly Arms near King's Cross. I loved that he was so at ease with the world, and comfortable in his own skin. Confident, quietly spoken, and relaxed to a fault. I constantly rack my brains to pinpoint exactly when he changed, and became edgy, crochety, and aloof.

In the early days of living together, before we were married, he'd get home from work, sneak up behind and pull me close, nudging himself hard against my body. I'd close my eyes, smell him before I heard, or saw him. We were so in love. Well, I've always assumed the passion we felt was 'love'. Now I'm no longer sure what love is, except that what we have today feels anything but.

I was swallowed up by Jed, the passion, the sex. It was all pretty steamy. Until it stopped, as if a switch had been flicked. It wasn't that long after we got married that everything started going downhill, until there didn't seem to be a way back. I couldn't put my finger on it, wondering all the time what I'd done wrong.

Even when I'm watching from the café, shaking in disbelief, I still believe he loves me. Otherwise surely he'd have left.

Sometimes while I sit there, waiting for the time to pass, I doodle in a small notebook. It's my memories log. I try to remember, over and over, exactly when, and how things changed. I make notes of dates, months, occasions when something off kilter happened. Something that didn't feel quite right.

It was about a year after we got married that Jed withdrew. I've logged the date when I first asked him what was up. It was his birthday. He simply shrugged, and said everything was fine. Then he repeated, over and over, how much he loved me.

'You'll never know how much,' he said, his voice thick with emotion.

Nothing stacked.

We made love, but it was different, not like when we were first together. We went through the motions, but the sparks had flown. Jed repeated endlessly that he was tired, and stressed from work. He wanted me to know it wasn't my fault, buying me flowers and chocolates as if every day was my birthday.

When I confided in Teagan she said all married couples go through a natural cooling off. She assured me it was quite normal.

'Wait till you have kids,' she said. 'You'll have even less energy for it then.' She laughed, but her levity didn't dispel the doubts. It felt far from normal.

Since I've been watching him with the woman and the lad, I pray over and over that he'll own up. Tell me where it all went wrong. Yet deep down, I don't think he's going to tell me. Unless I push, and ask him straight. I want to ask, but every time I'm close, the questions stick in my throat. I'm much too scared of what I'll hear. *There's always punishment for those who pry.* Dad's voice rings in my ear.

I've logged another date. It was a few days before our first anniversary, and I was fretting that Jed might forget. So I got in first.

'Shall we go out Saturday?' I asked. When he looked confused, I added, 'For our anniversary.'

'Yes. Why not?'

He'd just got home from work, and was tugging at his tie. He set his laptop down, and gave me a peck on the cheek. Like he does his mother. I felt part of an old married couple.

'The Hermitage?' I suggested.

'What?'

He wasn't even listening. That's how far away he was.

'The Hermitage. Saturday night? To celebrate.'

'Sounds like a plan. I'll book it up,' he said, walking away.

His voice trailed off as he crossed the hall, and climbed the stairs.

When Saturday came round, I got even more upset. He gave me a card, and a sad bunch of flowers with the price still attached.

I began to imagine all sorts. That he might be having an affair with his secretary; Janey with the silky hair and irritating laugh. I also mooted the possibility that he might have had a one-night stand when up the West End with colleagues.

Instead of confronting him, I tried to pretend everything was okay. I bottled up the misery, like I did as a child when I hid in my room and my parents crept about.

Despite the pretence, anger built inside me until it bubbled dangerously close to the surface. The way it did with Dad, before I exploded. The only difference is that I hated Dad, but I don't think I could ever stop loving Jed.

At least now I'm piecing together the puzzle. It's so tough watching him without speaking out, and I feel sick to the core.

I'll wait a while longer, and if he doesn't tell me soon, I'll have no choice but to make him.

15

I wander in behind Angelo, as he struts a few paces ahead and slips in behind the counter.

'Your usual, Izzy?' he asks.

'Please.'

The top half of the café opens out into an atrium of sorts. A large domed glass ceiling is festooned with artificial greenery threaded through white painted struts. It's much brighter at this end, away from my window seat. But even if I wasn't watching the scene outside, I'd still opt for the quietness of the darker corner.

'No Candy today?' I ask, looking all around. I strain my neck to see into the small, secluded alcove by the toilets. Sometimes she sits there with a wake-up hot chocolate.

'She's got the day off. The accident yesterday seems to have taken its toll.'

Like me, Angelo is reluctant to get drawn into small talk. This morning he seems to be making twice the usual noise from frothing the milk.

'Oh. I hope she's okay.'

I suspect Candy might have used events as a means of getting a day off. She surely can't be that traumatised, especially as she never actually saw the accident happen.

As I wait by the counter for my coffee, I wipe a hand across my damp forehead and round the back of my neck. The café is still cold, although I'm bathed in sweat. Angelo has turned on the overhead heaters, and the one directed towards my face isn't helping.

Angelo hands me my mug, holds up a silver shaker and asks if I'd like chocolate sprinkles. I've been coming here for three months, and although I always decline, he still asks. Perhaps he thinks I need fattening up the way Jed used to, always encouraging me to up the calories. Another thing that suddenly stopped.

I mosey back to the window, and try and settle. I'm beyond anxious, as if waiting for some dreadful news. I set the mug down, before I angle my seat into the exact same position I take up every time. Directly behind the planter. Then I check my phone for the millionth time, but still nothing.

After yesterday's accident, I cling to the faint, but bizarre hope that Jed might even turn up this morning. Just to let me know he's still alive. Yet, if by some miracle he does show, I've no idea what I'd do then. The accident has made things even more complicated.

I look up at the flat across the way, and my body stiffens when I see the red-haired lady by her window. She's looking down onto the street. Could she be expecting Jed? The thought that he might have contacted her, and not me, is too much to bear.

A few sips of coffee, and I come over nauseous. It tastes much more bitter than usual, and my stomach churns. Today might be the first time ever that I can't finish it.

I close my eyes against the sickness when someone walks by talking into a mobile. I guess it's a mobile, as they're talking so loudly I doubt it's to a person beside them. Perhaps the line's bad, but they're almost shouting.

When I open my eyes, I swivel my head round to see who it is. The guy is six foot, dressed in jeans and t-shirt. I doubt he's off to work in an office. Perhaps like me he works from home, and is treating himself to an early-morning walk and caffeine fix. Although I can only see the back of him, the broad shoulders, the dark wavy hair, there's something familiar about him.

He asks Angelo for a double shot macchiato in a takeaway container. With *just a stain* of skimmed milk. I've been a connoisseur of Italian coffee for as long as I can remember, and know all there is to know about how it should be served. Macchiato means *stained* or *marked* in Italian.

When I used to work in the library, cocooned in silence, I genned up on all things Italian. Food, coffee, wine, and Roman history. In the early days, Jed and I talked of tours of Italy, and maybe one day buying our own place in Tuscany.

It then hits me why the guy is so familiar. It's Mr Hard Hat, without the hat. His voice is smooth, deep, and velvety. The jeans and t-shirt could mean it's his day off, but perhaps he'll throw on overalls later if he's heading for a construction site.

16

I bend over my phone with fake concentration, as he heads my way. I will him to pass, praying he won't recognise me. I can't face an interrogation about Blanche and the dilapidated state of Miners' Terrace.

But no such luck. A whole empty café, and he pulls out a stool less than three feet from where I'm sitting. I assumed with a takeaway container he'd be heading straight off.

'Hi.'

Although I know I'm the only other customer, I look all around to make sure it is me he's talking to.

'Oh, hi.' I nod, and look away, my cheeks aflame.

'Do you come here often?' He lets out a puff of laughter at the well-worn pick-up line, and smiles broadly.

He's handsome in a macho, rugged sort of way. His tanned skin could be from sunbathing in the tropics, but more likely from working outdoors in all weathers. If I hadn't seen him in his hard hat, I might have assumed the former.

'Yes, I do.'

'Me too. Great coffee.'

'The best,' I say. I concentrate on my mug, trying to stomach another couple of sips, hoping he'll get the hint and leave me alone.

He sips from the miniscule paper cup, the size the yummy mummies ask for when baby wants a *babyccino*.

'I know this might sound corny, but have we met before?'

He gives me a quizzical look, as if he's just twigged.

He makes me nervous with his cheeky grin, and cocky manner, but he's not going to give up.

'I don't think so,' I lie.

While the guy is early-morning laid back, my hands come over shaky as I try to grip my still overflowing mug. All of a sudden, a load of creamy-coloured liquid spurts over the rim.

'Shit.' I look in horror as it dribbles over my legs.

'Here.' He reaches to his right, and pulls out a wad of serviettes from a holder. 'These any good?'

'Thanks, but I think I'll head to the ladies'.'

My cheeks are burning up, and heat sears up the back of my neck.

I grab my bag and phone, and scurry up past the counter, taking a left towards the toilets.

Shit. Shit. Shit. Brown patches dot my light-coloured tracksuit bottoms, and even my navy sweatshirt hasn't avoided the explosion.

I spend a good ten minutes locked in. After soaking the stains on my thighs, I contort my body to get them in the hand dryer's line of fire. By the time I re-emerge, the café is filling up, and Candy has appeared behind the counter. Obviously feeling better since yesterday's drama.

I breathe more easily when I see Mr Hard Hat up ahead making for the exit. He hovers a moment, turns back, and waves at me. He's holding up something in his hand. It looks like a business card, and he props it against my coffee mug, and smiles. Even from this distance, I know he's flirting. Jed hates his type, but doesn't believe me when I say I do too.

I hold back until he's gone, and rather than rush back to my seat, I turn to Candy. I smile at her, but she doesn't reciprocate.

'Hi. You made it. Angelo said you wouldn't be in.'

'Yes,' she says, keeping her head down as she concentrates on grinding beans. She doesn't even look at me.

She's usually really chatty, even at this early hour, and doggedly persistent when I'm reluctant to engage. But this morning she's strangely quiet, as if I've upset her in some way.

I leave her to it, and head back to my seat.

Adam M. Finch BSc's business card is no longer propped up against my half-empty mug, but lying on its side. I pick it up, and read the scrawled message on the back.

Fancy a drink sometime? Adam

I stare at the message, surprised yet flattered. Guys like Adam Finch don't chat up girls like me. When I first met Jed, he said it was my aloofness that attracted him. He found it a challenge. Only later, when he learnt my story, did he really understand my crippling shyness. Jed is the only other person besides Teagan who knows the reasons.

I glance back over my shoulder, and notice Candy staring at me. It crosses my mind her chilliness might have something to do with Adam Finch. Maybe he's a regular customer.

It's 8.30 by the time I get going. I have one last look across at the flat. It's the first time in months that I haven't been fixated on watching out for Jed. Worrying about what I might see has been replaced by worry about what has happened to him.

I shudder to think he might be seriously injured, lying alone in a hospital bed. I'm sure he's not dead as I think I'd know if he was. I'd have been contacted by now. Also, call it sixth sense, but I've a feeling that he's still alive. Although heaven knows what state he's in.

I'll sit it out today, and if I still haven't heard, I'll have no choice but to face the music.

17

As I head back to my car, praying it'll start without a battle, a new slant on affairs is buzzing round in my head. Meeting Adam Finch has set the cogs in motion. Hopefully, working on my column will keep me occupied while I wait for news on Jed.

As a norm, I generally only produce two letters a week (the magazine's minimum requirement), sometimes three if I make them short and snappy. It's an endless treadmill cashing in on people's misery. That said, readers seem glad of the chance to confide, especially anonymously.

Watching out from the café window has helped fire my imagination. As well as looking out, I listen inside to personal conversations. Especially those in hushed tones. This is where I get fodder for fake letters I compose if nothing particularly juicy from the public catches my eye.

On the way past the bakery, I pick up a warm almond croissant. I need something to soak up the caffeine, and settle my stomach. I need to regulate my eating, but it's not easy as my insides are constantly queasy.

It's only when I get home that I realise I haven't checked my messages for at least half an hour. I perch on a swivel stool in the kitchen, and boot up my laptop before pulling out my mobile. I hunch over the breakfast bar as I check the screen.

Oh my God. There are three. All from Jed, from an unknown number.

> Hi. Sorry I haven't been in touch. Had my phone stolen on the train when I fell asleep! Popping into Edinburgh later to get a new one. Will call you then. Hope all okay? J XXXX

I feel an instant relief that he's okay, but it's soon replaced by hurt and anger as the nagging doubts come flooding back.

It looks like he's not going to tell me he flew over the handlebars, and is going to carry on the pretence. I'm not sure which is greater, my relief or my fury. At least I'll have a while longer before the need for confrontation. I'm petrified of confrontation, especially as I'm petrified of what will follow. My whole life could change in an instant.

However, I am intrigued as to how he's going to explain the signs of injury. He's likely to be really badly bruised as he took an almighty hit, and I wouldn't be surprised if he's broken something.

As I reread the text, I'm wondering whose phone he's using. Maybe a nurse's or another patient's. If he really had lost his phone, wouldn't the normal thing have been to borrow someone else's, and call me before now? I'm guessing his phone got smashed in the accident, as it's usually tucked into his cycling shorts.

Jed's not shy like me in coming forward, and asking for help wouldn't bother him at all. And if he had got to the hotel without a phone, he could have called from reception. Doesn't he think I care enough to wonder?

I can't remember if he was supposed to be travelling alone or with Elisa, his new assistant with legs up to her armpits, and hair down to her waist. I've no idea why the vision of Elisa springs to mind. Likely because she's been the inspiration for a few of my columns.

I wonder what lies he might tell me if I ask whose phone he's borrowed. But I'm not up to playing the game any more than I have to.

The next message is about Blanche.

> Also could you pop in on Mum again today?
> Hope you saw her yesterday, but I'm worried as
> I can't get hold of her. I've tried several times,
> and left a message, but she won't pick up.
> Thanks. Love you XXXX

Jed is dutiful towards his mother, but recently has become oddly irritable with her. He's been asking me to help out more and more, telling me he's worried she's become so frail.

Although he says he's worried, I think his irritation trumps his concern. The fact she won't move out, accept the developers' inflated price, has been mentioned more than once. We're so short of cash that it could be the answer to our problems. The financial ones at least.

I toy with including the subject of Madison, his mother's new cleaner, in my reply. Perhaps he could ask her for updates on Blanche. The thought makes me want to hurl my phone across the room.

Rather than his messages putting my mind at rest, they've made me even edgier, and my stomach is back in revolt. Worry and anger have tied me up in knots.

His three messages were all sent within five minutes of each other, and the third one seems to have been an afterthought.

> BTW, was Mum eating okay? Was she still in
> bed? Talk later XXXX

Of course, I've a long list of questions of my own.

Why didn't you tell me about Blanche's new cleaner? Where did she come from?

Why didn't you phone me from the hotel when you got there? It wouldn't have mattered how late. Or perhaps sent a short message at least?

Is Elisa with you?

I'd probably ask them if he was telling the truth, and I believed him. But no doubt he has all sorts of convoluted answers up his sleeve.

Instead, I keep it short.

> Glad you're there safely. I was worried by the
> lack of messages! Blanche is in bed, very weak.
> I'll pop by to check on her later. X

I press send to the new number, but the message doesn't go through straightaway. Again I wonder whose phone he's using. Perhaps they're out of signal range, or perhaps the person has already taken their phone back.

Anyway, I now need to get my head around work. I open a new blank Word document and entitle it:

Cheating on a Cheater

18

Dear Bella,

I was devastated a few years ago when I discovered my husband had cheated with my best friend. He swore it would never happen again. But I'm suspicious it's happening all over again.

This time though, things are completely different. I've met another man who is giving me lots of attention and I now wonder if I should have a fling myself. Neither Bobby, my husband, nor I have ever talked about divorce and I'm not sure how the children or I would cope if it ever came to it.

Do you think it would be okay for me to go out with this new man (he's single btw) and have some fun myself? What would be the harm?

Yours,

Excited

* * *

Dear Excited,

A very good question, and a very difficult one to answer.

Logic and common sense would suggest you sit down and talk things through with your husband. Ask him straight if he is having another affair. But don't forget the old saying, 'Leopards don't change their spots'.

If he admits to seeing another woman, then you have several choices: Leave him. Agree jointly to an 'open marriage', staying together for the sake of the children. Or enjoy yourself first and make any bold decisions later.

If you're not sure whether he's telling the truth (he may lie to save his skin) there are always private detectives. If he has lied, would you really want to stay married to both an adulterer and a liar?

Also, remember, before you jump into a relationship with this other man, ask yourself how well you know him. What is he after? And what happens if you fall in love? Is he looking for a committed relationship, or a casual liaison?

I do hope I've given you food for thought. Meanwhile, don't forget to check out my Facebook page for reader responses to your letter.

Good luck with whatever path you choose.

Bella

When I make up readers' letters myself, I get fodder not just from watching and listening to people in the café, but also in the park, and even from whispers in the library. Inspiration and ideas strike at random, often from small seemingly insignificant events, or throwaway comments.

Meeting Adam Finch in the café this morning has been today's inspiration. I'm not interested in 'having fun' with him at all, although I'm certain there must be plenty of willing ladies. I'm just intrigued to see what the response will be.

It feels good putting into words what I'm going through, and maybe readers will help me work it out. I know I'll have to take my own advice soon, and confront Jed, but the thought terrifies me.

I check my phone again, and notice the message to Jed still hasn't gone through. Tempted as I am to ring the number, I decide not to. Like Excited, the reader I've just made up, I'm not sure I want to know all the answers.

I'm not ready yet to face the truth.

19

It's 4 p.m. by the time I pull up again outside Blanche's wall. I call it a wall, because her house looks one-dimensional, and I imagine nothing behind the brickwork. It's like a phony stage-set façade.

Her house is bang centre of the tumbledown terrace, and the property on one end of the row has already been reduced to a pile of rubble. There's no sign of life anywhere. When the first owners sold up, Jed couldn't hide his frustration.

'Lucky bastards. Got a great price from the developers.' Jed grumbled all weekend when he heard how much Blanche's neighbours had got.

'If Blanche would only move, she'd get a good price too,' I said.

'Possibly.' He tutted, fed up with it all.

Every time I bring up the subject, offer suggestions as to where Blanche might go, maybe even move in with us for a while, Jed goes into a tailspin.

He's been trying to persuade her to move into a home, not keen for her to live with us. He gets his worried face, telling me it's because he knows I can't stand noise. Blanche's constant chatter might be too much. Deep down I know he's the one who couldn't cope. Blanche is controlling, with an unhealthy Oedipus-like hold on her only son.

Jed insists she needs round-the-clock specialist care.

'She's frail, and getting forgetful,' he said.

Blanche won't budge, and he gets frustrated every time the subject comes up. I suspect this is why he doesn't see her much.

'She should have accepted their offer straightaway. With every new house demolished, the offer from the developer goes down, rather than up. If the council makes a compulsory purchase order, she'll get nothing like the developers' original offer.' Jed's face puckered in the telling.

But Blanche isn't going anywhere.

I'm reluctant to get out of the car. The sky overhead is rumbling, getting blacker by the second. The street is deserted, no sign of Adam Finch. I'm relieved, as he makes me feel uneasy, and using him as inspiration for my column hasn't helped.

I always get the shivers when I'm outside Blanche's house. The sight brings back the horrors of the vicarage where I grew up. It was nothing like the mid-terrace cottage, but it's the cellars. That's the similarity.

The steep stone staircase, and the flimsy single flickering electric bulb in Blanche's cellar, could have been transported straight from the rectory. When I stand at the top of Blanche's staircase, I remember, much too vividly, looking down into my father's cold, windowless wine cave. It was kitted out, floor to ceiling, with rows of cobweb-covered bottles. I hid behind them, always silent, and played peek-a-boo with imaginary friends.

I sit in the car for several more minutes, my knuckles white from gripping the steering wheel, before I make a move. As I lock the car, I look at the cottage for signs of life. As before, there's nothing. No curtain twitching, no wrinkled face peeking out from behind one of the postage-stamp-sized windows.

The heavens suddenly open, and I make a dash for the front door. I fumble with the key, and manage to duck inside just in time.

The silence is seriously creepy, even worse than usual. Normally, if Blanche isn't waiting by the front door, she yells out, 'Is that you, Izzy?' as I enter.

But as before, there's no sign of life. I poke my head into the lounge, and it's in darkness. The heavy velvet curtains are still drawn tight.

'Blanche? Blanche?' I call out from the hallway, already anxious that she might be too weak to answer.

The kitchen blinds are open, and the first thing I notice again is how tidy the place is. Not just tidy, but there's nothing lying around. Not the usual dish or cup. The place is spotless. The linoleum floor is damp, as if it's been recently mopped. It's dangerously slippery, like an ice rink.

I climb the steep staircase, gripping the banister. It's like a ghost house, each tread groaning with an eerie creak.

'Blanche. It's only me, Izzy.' I speak loudly as I don't want to frighten her with my sudden appearance, as she might not have heard me come in. Also the sound tempers the spookiness.

'In here, Izzy.' Her voice is barely audible, but it's definitely coming from the bedroom.

20

Blanche looks even worse than she did yesterday. She's lying like a cadaver, her dead eyes staring towards the ceiling. Her pile of pillows is on the floor.

'Oh, Blanche. Are you all right?'

I snatch my phone from my bag, preparing to call an ambulance. She looks as if she's already dead.

'*Don't*! I'm fine.' She springs to life at the sight of my mobile.

'You don't look fine.' I feel her forehead, which is bathed in sweat. 'Did you take your medication?'

I spot the assorted bottles of pills on her bedside table.

'Yes. Madison gave them to me. She knows how many I need to take.'

'Who?' It takes a moment to register she's talking about the new cleaner. 'When was she here?'

'Earlier today. She warmed me up more soup.'

Her chest wheezes when she talks.

I lift the pillows off the floor, and help her into a more upright position.

'Have you heard from Jed?' she asks. Her pigeon eyes are anxious.

'Yes. He's fine. He had his phone stolen, but he said he left you a message?'

'The phone is downstairs, and I couldn't get to it.'

'Okay. Anyway, he should be back in a couple of days.'

'There you are then. I'll be okay till he gets back.' Her voice fades to a whisper, and she closes her eyes.

She looks worse than I've ever seen her. I need to contact Jed, find out what I should do. Blanche is petrified that if she leaves the property for even a minute, the developers will blast the building to smithereens, and she'll lose her home forever.

I make a cup of milky, sugary tea, and take it back upstairs. I hoist her up, stuffing a pillow behind her head. She manages to dunk a ginger snap with a very shaky hand, and suck at the soggy ends.

She asks me to check in the cellar to see how many logs are left. Jed has been promising to light the log burner so she can come back downstairs.

I make my way to the steep stone staircase that leads off the utility room down to the cellar. My nightmares come flooding back. I brace myself to look down, but first I check there's no key in the door. I wouldn't want to get locked in. It's irrational, as there's no one here but Blanche, and she can barely walk. But my skin prickles.

The single electric bulb swings on a threadbare cable, and flickers on and off when I trip the switch.

I manage to reach the bottom where the cold envelops me. The floor surface is laid with black stone slabs, and ratchets up the chill. I flap my arms around my chest. There's a bad smell in the air, a rotting, damp, cesspit odour.

Off to one side is a small metal door which leads out into the yard. I pull across the heavy bolt, tug it open to let in the fresh air. I squeal when a bird flies straight at me from the outside toilet cubicle, and smashes against the door.

At least there are plenty of logs, but they're damp as hell. Jed will need to carry a load up, and dry them out.

As I scurry back up into the house, I wonder if the log burner will ever be lit. Blanche can't live in this rickety deathtrap any longer. It's like a house perched on the edge of a crumbling cliff.

Half an hour later, I say goodbye to Blanche, tell her that Jed or I'll be back tomorrow. She says that Madison has also promised to call in, so I'm not to worry.

Before I leave, I pop into the lounge to check the answerphone. The light is flashing, and I press *play*.

'Mum. It's Jed. Sorry, had my phone stolen. Back Friday. Hope Izzy is looking after you. And Madison. She's flexible with her time, and a great cook. I've told her to rustle up one of her tasty soups. You'll like her if you give her a chance. Take care.'

I press *delete*. Hairs stand up on my neck. It doesn't look as if Madison is any old random cleaner. Who the hell is she? I don't know where I thought she came from, but it looks as if Jed might know her rather well.

21

After a light supper, I'm so exhausted, I go to bed early and crash out around nine. Having heard from Jed, knowing he's alive at least, I fall asleep as soon as my head hits the pillow.

When my mobile vibrates at 6.30 a.m., I come to with a start. It takes a moment to register where I am, and what's been happening. It's a call from another random number which I don't recognise.

'Hello?'

'Izzy. It's me.'

The single word *me* tells me who's on the line, otherwise I'd have no idea. The reception is so fuzzy, and he sounds miles away. He could be in another country for all I know.

'Jed?' I croak into the handset while trying to haul myself upright, but the phone slithers to the floor before I get a proper grip.

'Shit.'

'You okay?' Jed's voice is quiet but concern seeps through.

'Yes, just dropped the phone.'

'Listen, sorry I didn't get back last night. I've only just managed to sort out the connection for my new mobile.'

At 6.30 in the morning? Is he serious? He sleeps like a log, while I'm the one fiddling with gadgets in the middle of the night. He really thinks I'll buy it, but I'm so relieved to hear his voice that I let it go.

'When are you coming back?' I ask.

'Friday. Probably late afternoon.'

There's a lengthy silence, as if he's waiting for a barrage of questions.

'Jed, Blanche isn't too well. She hasn't been out of bed for a few days, but won't let me phone the doctor.'

'She's scared if she leaves the house for five minutes, she'll never get back in.'

It's hard to hear him because he's talking so quietly, but I manage to pick up a puff of exasperation. His words get lost in the poor connection.

'Madison has been very helpful though,' I add, now wide awake, and speaking very clearly.

A couple of seconds pass, and when there's no response, I think he might have disconnected. Then I hear someone else's voice in the background, and more muffled noises.

'Listen. Must go. Glad the cleaner turned up,' he says. 'Bye. Love you.'

The line goes dead, before I have a chance to say, 'I love you too.'

I can guess where he's calling from. Most likely a hospital bed, but it's all such a convoluted game of deceit. If I'd asked, he'd likely have said he was up early, and the background noises were from guests milling round reception. Or chatter from the dining room, as he breakfasts early when he's away.

Why is he doing this? All the lies? Wouldn't it be easier for him to just leave me? Or does he think I'm such a basket case that I wouldn't cope?

The thought that he feels sorry for me, and that's why he hangs around, makes the tears flow. They pour down my cheeks and I sob silently. I'm not sure, if he did leave, I could feel any worse.

My head throbs, and my tongue tastes of sawdust. I fall back down, pull the duvet round me, but the damage is done. I'll never be able to get back to sleep.

I'm so sad that I'm almost tempted to pack my bags and run away. But I know I won't, not until I've unravelled the mystery that is Jed and me.

If he doesn't come clean soon, I'll ask him straight, and own up to what I've seen through the café window. If only I could get Dad out of my head.

Don't ask questions. The devil is on the lookout for nosy people. Hell awaits.

I take a tissue, honk away the tears, and decide to get up.

Jed will be home soon. Until then I need to keep myself busy.

22

I shower, get dressed and decide not to go to the café straightaway.

I know Jed won't be visiting the woman, as I'm assuming he's likely still in hospital. So there's no rush today, but nonetheless I'm still intrigued as to what she might get up to.

She walks away from her flat every morning, but I'm curious as to what she does the rest of the time. Perhaps she works. Goes to the gym. She looks fit, proud of her appearance, but who knows? Maybe she stays in and watches daytime TV. Finding out more about her seems important, as if it might give me clues as to what's going on.

I'm hoping that having a break from the early masochistic ritual of waiting for Jed to turn up, and delaying my trip to the café, might help calm me down.

I set to work on my column, a double espresso kick-starting new ideas, and manage to concentrate for a couple of hours.

It's eleven o'clock exactly when I close down my laptop, and set off for town. Rather than take the car, I decide to walk. The air is crisp, but soon whips colour into my cheeks, and by the time I'm near the café, I feel more positive. More able to cope.

I pause outside the jewellers', a few doors down from Angelo's, and look in the window. Jed used to buy me random pieces of gold and silver: earrings, a love-heart necklace, a diamond-studded bracelet. I blink away a tear, trying to remember when the gifts dried up. Six months? A year? Maybe longer? He still plops an occasional bunch of flowers from the petrol station my way, with a soft appreciative kiss on the cheek.

Suddenly, I nearly jump out of my skin when a face appears reflected in the glass behind me.

'Boo.'

Holy shit. 'Don't do that.'

It takes a couple of seconds to work out who it is.

I swivel round, taking a couple of steps to the side.

'You scared me to death.'

'Sorry. Too tempting. What are you looking at?' He nods at the display.

It's Mr Hard Hat, minus the hat again, and grinning from ear to ear.

Although Adam Finch's face crept into my dreams last night, he's the last person I'm expecting to see. My first thought is that he's stalking me, but I've no idea why I think this. My nightmares have been so vivid, spine-chilling, and his face keeps appearing.

'Just window shopping,' I tell him.

I glance back at my own reflection in the glass. My fine hair is awry, and my fringe is drooping over my eyes. Behind me, Adam is hovering. He's not unlike Jed in height, and colouring, but he's more muscled, and sun-tanned. His appearance matters to him, whereas Jed and I don't worry about how we look. We've got each other.

Whereas Jed makes me feel at ease, Adam makes me nervous. He's too cocky by half, and overly flirtatious.

'I wondered if I'd bump into you again.' He points a waggling finger at me.

I edge round him, and we walk the few yards together to Angelo's. The place is heaving, and the sight makes me panic. I no longer want to go inside. The chock-a-block sight sets my pulse racing, and Adam's proximity isn't helping.

'Jeez. It's busy. I think I'll give it a miss,' I say, not looking directly at Adam. I scan the street as if deciding what to do, and where to go next.

'I know somewhere quieter if you fancy it. There's a great little place up Tilehurst Street. It's small, but the coffee's great, and we won't have to queue.'

He dares to touch my arm, and smiles.

Over my shoulder, I notice Candy near the door. Next to the window, where I usually sit. She's looking out. I smile at her, but she doesn't reciprocate.

I stiffen, look from her to Adam and back again. It's hard to say whether her menacing stare is aimed at me or at Adam.

23

I don't think I can face going home yet, so I give in and go with Adam. A change of scene might provide a momentary distraction.

We set off, and Adam runs ahead as if late for a train. He's a man on a mission, and I have to jog to keep up. Only when we reach Waterstones does he slow down.

'Are you always this slow?' He's grinning like a Cheshire Cat, hands on hips.

'I'm not in a particular hurry. Don't let me hold you back.'

I sound churlish, but he makes me so uncomfortable with his over-the-top charm offensive.

Jed has likely met him, though I can't remember his name ever being mentioned. It was possibly Adam who made Blanche the sizeable offer to move out of her home.

Adam makes a play of holding his stride in check, and I giggle when he takes two steps forward, then one back, so that we stay in line.

'A couple more streets and we'll be there. A right turn by the piano shop, and it's a few yards up on the left.'

We walk on in silence. I feel like a child being led to a sweetie shop. I'm so out of my comfort zone. It's not only that I feel shy in Adam's company, but I'm more at home in familiar places. Jed and I never venture up this end of town.

As we draw closer to the café, the aroma of fresh coffee wafts out on to the street. Despite the chill in the air, the door is slightly ajar.

'Don't you love the smell of coffee?' Adam says, reading my thoughts.

'It's my favourite smell in the world.'

'Hmm.' He sniffs like a gundog with his nose in the air. 'Here we are.'

He pulls the door wide, and motions me to go ahead.

The coffee bar is very snug, so snug that there's hardly room to move. Adam stands close and my heart beats a little faster. There's an air of danger about him, and my anxiety mingles with a flutter of something else.

'Let's sit by the window,' he suggests. 'Watch the world go by. It's one of my favourite pastimes.'

He seems to know I'm a people watcher too.

Funny, I think of Jed. He's so different and hates lingering anywhere without intent. He jiggles his feet when I sit too long, joking that I need to find a new hobby.

'What's your fix?' Adam asks.

'Macchiato, please.' I'm scared to ask for a cappuccino, remembering the spillage last time Adam was near. A camomile tea might be better for me – herbal teas are easier to stomach, and I know I need to cut back on the caffeine – but the smell of coffee is too tempting.

'Good choice. Make that two,' he tells the girl behind the counter. She's not unlike Candy. Young, pretty, eager to please. I can see why they're both eager to please Adam. He directs his full-on charisma at all the girls like it's another favourite pastime.

We settle on black swivel stools by the window. My elbows rest on top of the wooden bar that faces out on to the street, while Adam spins round and round.

'Okay. Now we're on a date, why don't you tell me your name?'

My cheeks burn up. I must look horrified because he laughs. 'Okay, it's not a date, but we are sharing drinks.'

He fixes his dark eyes on my mouth.

'Izzy. I don't need to ask yours,' I say, gripping the miniature cup with shaky hands.

'Go on then. What's my name?'

'Adam. You left me your card, remember?'

'That's my first name but my friends call me Marco. It's my middle name. Italian ancestors.'

'Oh.'

Marco does suit him better, with its more exotic connotations. I feel horribly tongue-tied. He's so at ease, and I'm so edgy.

'You know what I do for a living, now what about you?'

His deep chocolate-coloured eyes, dangerous in their depths, watch me. My insides somersault.

'I'm an agony aunt, Adam.'

I deliberately call him Adam, rather than Marco, to let him know I'm avoiding familiarity. He smiles, picking up my intent.

'An agony aunt? I'm intrigued.' He raises a single eyebrow, and starts to swivel his stool round and round even faster. I giggle when he loses his balance and tilts to the side.

'You're making me dizzy.'

It's the first time I've laughed in ages. Properly, that is. Jed and I used to laugh all the time, always at the same things. We'd watch reruns of our favourite sitcoms, over and over. *Only Fools and Horses. Friends. Keeping Up Appearances.* We'd cuddle up, and I'd never felt so safe, warm, or loved. Jed was my happy ending after so much heartache. He was my Mr Right.

'Tell me then. What is an agony aunt?' Adam stills his stool, and his eyes rest on my lips.

He's a good listener. I'm not sure if he's really interested, or if he's humouring me, but as he relaxes, I find it easier to talk. Jed no longer asks how my work is going, his mind elsewhere, and I can't remember when he last read my column.

Twenty minutes pass quickly.

'I really need to get back to work,' Adam says, adding, 'It's been fun.'

'Back to Miners' Terrace?'

'Yep. You've got it in one.'

I pick up my bag, and stumble awkwardly off the stool. He puts out a hand and catches me as I fall towards him.

'Oops. Thanks.'

'Anytime.'

Even though I googled Adam Finch, and found no mention of a wife, I find myself checking for a wedding band. His fourth finger is bare, and again I wonder why. He must be well into his thirties. Maybe he prefers being a bachelor, playing the field.

I pull my coat back on, and follow him out into the crisp November air. We shiver at the same time, and chuckle in unison.

'That was fun,' he says again. 'Looking forward to reading your column.'

He stands with his hands in his pockets, and I'm unsure what to expect. Will he lean in for a cheek-to-cheek kiss?

I needn't have worried, as he doesn't linger.

'I must be off. You've already taken up far too much of my time. Bye, Izzy.'

'Bye, Adam. And thanks for the coffee,' I call after him.

But I'm talking into the wind, as he's already racing back the way we came.

I stare after him, and before he turns the corner into Sun Street he slows, and waves over his shoulder without looking.

I feel a flutter inside. Is this how cheating starts? With an innocent cup of coffee?

As I saunter back, butterflies in my stomach hint at excitement over something other than having gained fodder for my column.

24

It's Friday, and Jed is finally on his way home.

He texted earlier, about three hours ago, saying he was on the train back from Edinburgh and should be here around 5.30.

I can't focus on anything, and have been hopping from one thing to another all day. I've tried to come up with new ideas for my column, doodling in a notebook, but with the concentration of a gnat. There's a mountain of real letters to plough through, but I'm becoming obsessed with using content that relates to me. It's like talking to a therapist when I get it down in print.

But my head is so fuzzy that I finally give up and start preparing supper. I need to act as normal as possible when Jed gets here, although I've no idea how I'll cope. And no idea what tales he's going to spin.

I freeze when I hear a key in the lock. It must get stuck, because through the door I pick up the sound of swearing. He then rings the bell, stab after stab, assuming I've snibbed it from inside. I don't move, instead count down the seconds, until he finally gets it open.

'Hello. I'm home,' he yells more loudly than usual.

'In here.' I aim for quiet, but sing-song.

I hear the thud of a bag being dumped in the hall, and I wander out, spotting the scruffy navy rucksack by the stairs. Not his expensive Gucci black leather overnighter which he usually takes away on business. Perhaps he meant to come home and pick it up before his trip. I recognise the rucksack from the morning of the accident.

'Hi. Problem with the key?' I nod towards the front door.

'Yes, bloody thing keeps sticking. Come here.' He steps towards me.

I'm watching him, checking for signs of injury. His face is unmarked, but he's walking awkwardly. Stooped and leaning heavily on one side.

He opens his arms wide, and I hear a creak. But there's no mistaking his relief at being home. It could be the pain, but I could swear he's crying. There's definitely moisture in his eyes. It's as if he's back from war.

His body might be broken, but his smile is so wide, and genuine. He's thrilled to see me. It couldn't be an act, as all I can see is my old Jed.

'Did you miss me?' he asks, as he tries to wrap his arms round me. He has trouble stifling a groan, as his body goes rigid, and he winces.

'You okay?' I pull back, aghast at his strained features. He's in agony.

'Fine,' he wheezes, closing his eyes. Rather than giving me an explanation, he asks again, 'Did you miss me?'

I wonder if he's got answers planned as to what he'll tell me if I push. Did he really think I wouldn't?

But I don't ask. I carry on the charade.

'Of course I missed you. Silly question,' I say. 'Now, more importantly, are you hungry?'

I slither from his loosened grip, and nudge his arms aside.

He doesn't answer straightaway, but looks at me intently. As if trying to gauge if he's got away with the latest round of lies.

Yet his relief and joy at being home is not a lie. It's written all over his face.

'Izzy, I can't tell you how much I've missed you. Really missed you,' he says. His intensity is frightening.

'Listen, enough of that. Now are you hungry?' I emphasise the words.

'Silly question.' He laughs, but not without a sharp intake of breath and agonising grimace. 'What's for supper anyway? Smells good.'

I turn away, unable to look at him.

'Roast chicken, roast potatoes, brussels with chestnuts and pancetta, and onion and parsley stuffing.'

'Wow. You're spoiling me. Sounds amazing.' He smacks his lips.

It sounds like Christmas dinner, his favourite meal of the year. That's why I've cooked it. I've even baked a home-made apple crumble. The way to a man's heart, and all that. I might be overdoing the wifey bit, but I need his guard down. I don't want to give a hint of suspicion, as I want him to talk. He talks when he's relaxed, but never when he's pushed.

'How long will it be? Have I time for a quick shower?'

He tries to stretch out his neck, side to side, but there's an almighty crick.

'You look tired,' is all I say.

'A bit tired. It's been a long day. But I'm fine,' he repeats for the umpteenth time.

I've no idea how he's upright, let alone walking. His whole frame is distorted.

Jed isn't a complainer by nature. He's from the old school of stiff upper lips. Blanche reminds me of this whenever I dare mention I'm tired or have a runny nose.

When I met Jed, his stoicism was one of the things I most admired. He doesn't whinge, and *silent suffering* is his mantra.

But this is different. He's not aiming for stoic, he's trying to act normal, to cover up what's happened. Cover up the lies.

I suspect he's doped up on painkillers, otherwise I doubt he'd be here at all.

'You grab a shower, and food will be ready in ten minutes,' I say.

Despite everything, I can't bear to see him in such pain. It breaks my heart.

25

Our kitchen lies directly below the bathroom. Through the ceiling I can hear the shower crank up. I'm tempted to sneak upstairs and peer through the frosted glass.

I wonder if he's tried to cover up all the bruises, perhaps with make-up. But that's not Jed. He's not vain, but then this is different. He won't want me to see the marks. I bet his body is covered in bruises of all colours. Black, purple, blue, and yellow. Like a devil's rainbow.

At least he's alive, without visible signs of broken bones. Or worse still, a broken back. This has been my second-worst nightmare, other than death.

I take out the chicken, transfer it to a separate dish, and put it back in the oven as I prepare the gravy in the roasting tray. My mind wanders.

It feels like a lifetime ago since I started watching Jed through the café window. Watching as he parked his bike up, and ambled across the road towards the flat. Yet it's only been a few months.

Jed still thinks I go to Starbucks on the edge of town for my morning caffeine fix before I start work. I keep reminding him of this, repeating over and over that Starbucks is my all-time favourite haunt. I emphasise the name, so that he'll never imagine I'd go anywhere else. When he calls me from the train to ask what I'm doing, I get the name in somehow.

'I'm off to Starbucks.'

'You're an addict,' he tuts, but doesn't doubt that's where I'm going.

I've been tempted to say that I've heard Angelo's do great coffee, and might give it a try. I'd love to watch his reaction, but I can't risk blowing my cover. Not yet anyway.

He really is none the wiser. He's so wrapped up in his own world that he's no idea Starbucks had a refurb. It's never crossed his mind that I might be going somewhere else. If I hadn't seen him that first morning visiting the lady across the road, I'd likely have told him about Angelo's. But now it's much too late.

'Can I smell burning?'

Jed suddenly appears in the doorway, and shocks me back to the present.

'Shit.' I smack my leg against the oven. I was miles away. 'You scared me to death. Don't do that,' I snap. I don't mean to snap, but I'm so on edge.

'Sorry. I didn't mean to scare you.'

He comes up behind me, encircles my waist, and asks, 'Is that the gravy?'

I look down at the roasting pan.

'Shit. Shit. Shit.'

I've been stirring the wooden spoon round and round, and didn't even notice that all the liquid has evaporated.

I stare at the charred remains of the chicken fat. Black smoke rises, and an acrid smell of burning envelops me.

26

We sit through the charade of supper, making all manner of small talk and skirting round the trivia of our everyday lives. I'm not sure which of us is the better actor.

He tells me Edinburgh was fine, that the client seems happy going forward. I don't push for details, as I can't stomach more deceit.

Instead, I suggest, as it's the weekend, we give work a break.

After we've eaten, we head into the lounge with our coffee. The idea is to snuggle up and find a good movie or series to watch.

Little does Jed know that I've already chosen the series. It's all about a cheating husband, and a wife who knows but doesn't tell. It could be our life on the big screen.

I take charge of the remote.

'How about this one? *Wilderness*. It stars Jenna Coleman. You like her, don't you?'

'Yes. She's good. What's it about?' he asks, collapsing onto the sofa.

His eyes are black-ringed and heavy. He's so exhausted, but

doesn't want to go to bed. Watching movies together is one of his favourite things.

I know exactly what *Wilderness* is about. I watched it while he was away, and it is so not his sort of series. It's a dark, domestic noir thriller. Wronged wife. Affairs. And murder. Jed recoils at anything to do with lying and cheating. I now get why, but tonight I'll make him watch it.

'Jenna Coleman plays a wronged wife. She knows what her husband is up to, but doesn't let on. She takes him on a trip to a sprawling National Park, and plans revenge.'

'And? It sounds ridiculous.' With an effort, Jed tries to haul himself up out of snuggle position.

'Let me put it on, and we can watch together. I've already seen it, so can fill you in. It's really good.'

'Whatever. Not sure I'll stay awake though.'

But he stays awake. Wide awake. He's soon getting up and down, despite his creaky bones, making all sorts of excuses not to watch. Going to the toilet, trying to call his mother, checking his emails. Anything but watch. Yet his eyes are drawn back to the screen. If he is stiff from the accident, his body is now rigid.

As the series is so long, I fast forward to make sure he sees the scenes I want him to. I skip over the filler, concentrating on the main plot, as this is likely the only chance I'll get to make him watch.

'Can you sit still. Please.' I'm snappy, but tactile. I keep pulling him back down, tutting every time he moves.

As Jenna Coleman pushes her cheating husband to his death – or at least who she thinks is her cheating husband – Jed yawns loudly. And carries on yawning with a cavernous gaping mouth. He's not bored, he's petrified. He keeps snatching looks at me, and I can feel his eyes, but I keep mine firmly on the screen.

Jenna Coleman never tells her husband she knows he's

cheating. She plays along. Even after meeting the other woman, she plans silent revenge. Like me, she was hoping he might own up. Before it's too late.

My mind ricochets back and forth between anger, doubt, and fear. If I thought it was as simple as Jed cheating, I might be tempted to push him over a cliff. But I'm not convinced. I feel there's something more. There's part of the story missing.

'What a load of nonsense,' Jed blurts out as the credits roll.

'Didn't you enjoy it? I thought it was great.'

Jed is struggling up.

'Really?' He looks at me strangely, as if he can't believe I asked such a stupid question. 'Not my sort of thing,' he says. 'But as long as you enjoyed it, that's what matters.'

I switch off the telly, looking anywhere but at him.

Without further comment, Jed wanders out of the lounge. Watching *Wilderness* has hit a nerve, no doubt, but if he still won't open up, he must at least suspect I know more than I'm letting on.

27

When we finally crawl into bed, Jed is asleep within minutes. I'm not sure how many painkillers it took to knock him out, but as he swallowed the last capsule, he owned up to having a really sore back.

'I didn't want to worry you,' he said, wincing with the effort of lying on his side.

'You can rest up tomorrow. Let's have a lazy weekend,' I whispered.

I spoon up close, sucking in his bodily warmth, kissing the back of his head as his snores begin to rumble, but I can't stop shivering.

Jed groans in his sleep, and is soon bathed in a wet slimy layer of sweat. I toss and turn, my thoughts in turmoil.

When daylight creeps through the curtains, I slide out of bed. Jed is still fast asleep, his hair as wet as the rest of him, as if he's showered. I tiptoe from the room, along the landing and down the stairs.

The sun is bright in the sky, and heat is already nudging through the long expanse of glass doors that lead into our back garden. Even so, I'm still shivering, chilled to the bone, and my feet are like blocks of ice.

I switch on the coffee machine, and take out a capsule. I'll need several of these to get through the day. I pause when I hear movement upstairs. Jed is out of bed, and through the ceiling I hear his feet clump around. Even from down below I can pick up how slow he's moving.

I make my way quietly back up the stairs. Last night Jed got dressed in the bathroom and came to bed wearing a full set of pyjamas. I can't believe he thinks his bruises (there must be plenty, surely) will clear up before I notice anything.

He never closes the bathroom door tight, so I'm able to see through the crack as he's about to step into the shower. The bruises on his arms and upper body are horrific. As I suspected, they're black, blue, purple, and yellow. Multi-coloured agony. Strangely, his legs have escaped relatively unmarked.

I gasp, a hand shooting over my mouth. I can't bear to look. I stay quiet until the shower jets are on full before I head back to the kitchen.

I take my coffee to the table, ease into a chair. Part of me wants to yell at him, explode in fury and ask him what the hell is going on. But I'm too scared to face the music. I need to know everything first, and finding out the answers for myself is preferable to having to stomach a load more lies that he might have already prepared. I feel sick to the core.

'You're up,' I say, when he finally hobbles into the kitchen. 'You were fast asleep when I left you.'

'You know I can't sleep when you're not there.' He blushes, like a young lover.

He's dressed in shorts and a long-sleeve polo-shirt, the bruises well hidden.

'Tea?' I ask.

'Please.' He nods, and sits down. Even falling into a chair takes a Herculean effort.

I put the kettle on. Jed likes the smell of coffee, it's the taste he can't stomach. I make him a strong builder's tea, milk and two sugars, and hand across his drink of choice.

I rest my hands on the sink surround, with my back to Jed, and look out the window. I can see his reflection in the glass. I close my eyes, breathe deeply, before offering up my suggestion. Firstly, I ask him how his back is this morning.

'A bit stiff, but much better, thanks,' he says, rubbing a hand over his coccyx.

'If you're up to it, why don't we go cycling? When your back's been stiff before, you always say cycling is the one exercise you can do.'

I can hear his ragged breathing, and imagine his mind in overdrive. He wasn't expecting the suggestion, that's clear. When he doesn't say anything, I turn to face him.

'The weather's perfect. We could go round the Greenway, stay off the roads,' I suggest.

His bike hasn't been mentioned since he got home. He has no idea that I know he used it the morning he planned to go to Edinburgh. Although he often cycles before work, he rarely does before he travels.

It's mean for me to push when he feels so rough, but I want to know what excuse he'll make. *The bike's in the shed with a puncture. I forgot my bike, left it on the train, or it's at the station. I've lost my helmet.* Perhaps he'll simply say he's not feeling up to it, or ratchet up the severity of his tweaky back. There's a long list of possibilities.

I watch him, with a hopeful smile in place.

'Izzy. I wasn't going to tell you, but...'

Even the effort of speaking makes him grimace.

'Tell me what?'

'I took the bike out before I left for Edinburgh, and...'

There's a lot of pausing for thought. I wonder if he's been planning his speech, or if he's adlibbing now I've brought up the cycling subject. He'll have assumed that I thought the bike was locked away in the shed.

'And?' I watch him like a hawk.

'I had an accident. I didn't want to worry you but I fell off my bike. I came a cropper.' He swallows hard.

'That's why all the bruising.' I roll my eyes. 'I guessed something had happened. You should have told me.'

'You noticed?' He looks sheepish.

'Come off it. Of course I noticed. I wondered when you were going to tell me what happened.'

He blushes, rubs fingers along his early-morning stubble.

I sit down beside him, tempted to take his hands and hold them tight. I'm torn. This would be the natural thing to do, not to arouse suspicion that I might already know about the accident. He'll assume that if I'd already heard, I'd have brought it up before. I bet he's relieved that I don't seem to know anything about it.

'Where?' I ask. One more question can't hurt. I do the sign of the cross, just in case.

'Where what?'

'Where did you come off?'

'Near the train station.'

This is three miles from where we live, and in the completely opposite direction from Angelo's and the town centre.

'Oh. That's awful.'

I'm curious now how much more he'll tell me.

'I ended up in hospital.' He grits his teeth, rolls his eyes. 'That's why I didn't get back to you sooner. I didn't get the train until much later in the evening. But no bones broken, thank God. But...'

'But?' My eyes are wide in their sockets.

'My bike's a complete write-off.'

I laugh. It breaks the tension.

'Well, better the bike than you,' I say.

28

I remember the first time we met. Fate threw us together.

Jed was so thirsty after an early-morning cycle ride that he dared venture into Starbucks. It wasn't far from where he was living with his mother at the time.

He nudged open the door with his shoulder, gripping his helmet in one hand, and cycling gloves in the other. I didn't look up properly, not until the door swung back and smacked him on the arm. He winced, but I was the only one looking.

It was really hot that day. I remember the heat, and the sickly stench of all things sweet. I was in a corner, another café corner facing outwards. Starbucks has the best location in town for people watching, and I liked to stare out and soak up the bustling activity on the market square when I wasn't trying to work. On that particular day I was having trouble concentrating, and my gaze wandered more than usual.

I started to feel uneasy when I became aware of the cyclist staring at me. He carried on staring, and wouldn't look away. I grew even hotter and more uncomfortable. When I accidently caught his eye, he smiled. A warm, gentle tilt of his lips.

Jed isn't hot, as in hunky handsome hot, but he's cute. We're pretty similar with our less than dynamic appearances, but the similarities don't end there. We've both got deep-rooted issues. He's insecure, and I'm unbalanced, on the cusp of crazy.

He queued patiently for a drink, and was soon standing by my table. He jiggled a scalding container of tea from one hand to the other. As luck would have it (for him, he later said) the table next to mine was empty.

'Mind if I sit here?'

No idea why he asked, as he wasn't sharing my table. I couldn't very well say I'd prefer it if he moved farther away. He could have been a weirdo for all I knew, as random men don't chat me up.

'Sure,' I mumbled, and looked back at my screen.

'Thank goodness it's stopped raining,' he said, with a nod towards outside.

Jed is determined, never one to give up if he wants something. His proximity made me nervous, as he scraped his chair closer and closer.

He flipped off the plastic lid of his drink, and stirred vigorously with a wooden stick.

I looked round when he spoke, not instantly twigging his words were aimed at me. He still wouldn't stop staring. Firstly at my face, then at my hands, and back to my nose, and ears. Later, he told me I reminded him of a young Audrey Hepburn. It was the nicest compliment I'd ever had.

'Sorry?'

'The rain. Thank goodness it's stopped,' he repeated.

'Yes,' I said, turning my head to look through the window.

In situations like these, I never know what to say. My shyness is crippling, but Jed didn't take it as a slight. He carried on regardless.

'At least it's nice and warm in here.'

Warm was an understatement. I was boiling, and sweat was pouring off Jed who was swaddled in thermal cycling gear. His top and bottoms clung to his skinny taut body. Perspiration dripped from his brow, and his thick fringe flopped into his eyes.

'It is,' I answered, blushing under my own fringe.

Much later, he told me he thought I was cool, aloof, playing hard to get. He'd no idea then how shy I was.

'It's like a sauna,' he said, flapping a hand up and down in front of his face.

I closed down my laptop, and began to pack it away.

'You're brave cycling. The traffic's dreadful.'

I was proud of myself later that I did engage. Our lives can change in a moment, *turn on a sixpence* as Mum would say. It was that day in Starbucks that my life changed forever. It didn't take Jed long to tell me that, for him, it really had been love at first sight. It took me a while longer. I had no idea what real love was, despite being twenty-eight. Netflix romcoms were the extent of my knowledge.

'I cycle every morning before work. It wakes me up, prepares me for the day ahead.'

He blew, and blew into the hot tea, which made me laugh. He was like one of the three little pigs. He huffed and puffed with such intent, while gripping the container with bloodless fingers.

Jed has a lovely smile, and a great set of teeth. Naturally white and straight, sparkling like a tooth advert. I remember that day thinking how perfect they were. Mine are small, terrier like. But they do their job.

'You like your coffee, I see,' he said, pointing at my two empty mugs.

'I need them to wake up.'

'Like I need cycling.'

We laughed together. The first laugh of many. Jed woke me up, as if I'd been asleep for a thousand years.

The day we met, I had a busy day planned. I was never late for work, and needed to get going. I had also promised the library that I'd stay late that evening, and do some overtime. I was so conscientious back then, refusing to take days off, even when I felt rough, hungover, or full of cold. For the first time, on the morning I met Jed, I was tempted to hang around, and perhaps play hooky.

We chatted, until I knew I had to go. He had made me feel so at ease, that I dared to say, 'I come here every morning.'

When he didn't respond straightaway, I blushed, embarrassed that I might have misread the situation.

I stood up, pulled out a scarf from my rain jacket and wound it round my throat.

He stayed sitting, but looked up at me. Up and up. He told me later that he wasn't expecting me to be so tall.

I'd almost given up, when he suggested, his eyes mushy like a puppy's, that perhaps we'd meet again.

'I really hope so,' he said.

'Maybe we will.' I kept it simple, unwilling to jump in deeper.

I zipped my laptop into my rucksack, but my Carstairs Library keyring, which was attached to the zip, got stuck, and I had to tug and tug to get it loose.

'Yes, maybe we will indeed,' he smiled, intent on my every move.

'Bye,' I said, nudging past his outstretched legs.

'See you later,' he called after me.

Only when I was outside did I breathe more easily.

29

When Jed turned up at the Carstairs Library, the small private library where I worked at the back of King's Cross, I recognised him. Well, I knew his face, but couldn't for the life of me remember how. It had been two weeks since we'd met in Starbucks.

'Hi.' He smiled like a long-lost cousin.

'May I help you?'

'You don't recognise me, do you?'

You could have knocked me down with a feather. It suddenly twigged when he offered up his boyish grin. Starbucks in the centre of town.

'Erm. Of course I do,' I mumbled, tongue-tied, and shocked by his sudden appearance. When he spoke in a normal speaking voice, I pointed at the *hush* sign on the pillar, and held a forefinger to my lips.

'Sorry,' he whispered.

It was then he took out a small notepad, and I began to freak. He scrawled something on a piece of paper, folded it in two and handed it across. I thought I might pass out, I came over so dizzy and nauseous.

I could have been looking at my father. That's how freaked I was. In that one moment, all the memories came flooding back. The nightmare of silence, and written notes flashed before my eyes.

Jed noticed something was up, he looked so concerned. He tapped my shoulder and asked if I was okay.

If he'd used his phone, texted me instead, I'd have been fine. But, of course, he didn't have my number. How could he possibly have known what a basket case I was, tormented by the past?

I sat down on a chair while he stood over me. The thousands of books lining the walls were no longer comforting, as the cases seemed to teeter.

My fingers shook as I unfolded the note. At least it was only folded in two, not with the eight origami creases I was used to.

Fancy a drink after work? The name's Jed, by the way *smiley face emoji*
And what's your name btw?

I borrowed his pen and with shaky fingers wrote two words in reply.

Okay. Izzy.

And that was it. The start of something magical. It was only a month before our wedding that I told him everything. Every gruesome detail about my past, including my phobia for notes. It was a risk, as I'd have likely run a mile if he'd shared such a story. But unless I could trust him, what was the point in *us*?

Jed didn't run. If anything he held me tighter, and we forged ahead as one, and got married.

It's only now that I'm obsessed by dates, going over and over them in my head. Jed's stag do had been two months before our wedding. In Ibiza. When he got home from the revelry he seemed somehow quieter. Less ebullient, and not so excited about the wedding.

I was so scared that he was having second thoughts, deciding I had too sinister a past.

As I walked down the aisle on Teagan's arm, my heart beat like crazy. She had to calm me down, convince me pre-wedding nerves were all too common. She giggled and told me Jed was beyond jittery, and was even more nervous than I was.

I trusted Teagan, but she had no idea why he was such a wreck.

And back then I didn't either.

30

It's Monday morning. Jed is already acting as if everything is back to normal, and the accident hasn't been mentioned again. He's passing it off as a minor tumble, despite his bike being a write-off.

I've hardly slept since he got back, as the lies gnaw away at me. He's still pretending that he went to Edinburgh, when I'm guessing he came directly home from the hospital. I don't know how much longer I can hold out without coming clean, telling him what I know, and demanding he fill in the gaps. I'm trying to be patient a while longer, but it's tough.

Somehow, he's made it into the office, despite the fact that he's walking with such a stoop. He messaged when he got there, adding an overeffusive set of love hearts. A second message has just arrived.

First at my desk! XXXX

I reply with a single thumbs up.

I'm pretty confident he's telling the truth, and that he is at work. He stressed over the weekend about how much he had to catch up on. And without a bike he couldn't have got to the apartment, and then on to the train station, without leaving the house a lot earlier than he did.

I opt not to go the café first thing again. I also have to work, and a trip later will give me a break. I quite enjoy saving my treat till mid-morning, and the thought that I might bump into Adam Finch makes me nervous, and excited. I shouldn't be thinking about him, but it's not that easy. If things do work out with Jed though, I'll have nothing more to do with Adam.

Once my column hits the shelves on a Saturday, the comments on my Facebook page mount up quickly. It's a first that I haven't checked in yet. By midday on a Saturday they're already piling up, the number depending on the level of contentiousness in the letters, along with my response.

Usually by Monday morning, I've cleared away a lot of the dross, leaving short succinct responses to most messages. Simple *likes*, *loves* or *laugh* emojis are often all that are needed. But since the accident, I haven't been able to concentrate.

Grayson warned me when I first started the job that I needed to be thorough in checking messages. *Delete*, *delete*, *delete* anything unsavoury straightaway. By Wednesday the barrage of comments has generally dried to a trickle, and by then I'm usually well into composing the next edition's column.

Sometimes I take my laptop to the café, and if there's nothing much to see outside, I get to work.

I like not trekking up to London, and although I miss the graveyard library silence, working from home is the next best thing. Grayson is none the wiser if I work from my study, or from the café. I could probably work from anywhere in the world without him knowing.

Life is so much easier when I don't have to make small talk.

It's a skill I've never mastered, and Jed likes that I'm shy. It means I'm all his.

I finally open up my Facebook column page and start reading the responses to the two letters printed in the weekend copy. I'm more eager, and twitchy, than usual, as the letters were pretty personal to my situation. I'm intrigued to see what others might think.

There are already 324 responses to the first letter. The one where a lady has just discovered her husband has another family.

I reread the first letter, along with my response before I run through the comments. I told the woman who wrote in, if I were in her shoes, I'd pack her husband's bags, but strongly advised against 'killing the bastard'. (I had to edit her letter, changing *killing the bastard* to *doing harm to her husband*.)

Okay, I'm in her shoes, and haven't packed Jed's bags. I wonder if I might when I have the full story. I'm so angry at the moment that I can't think about what's to come. Maybe once I have all the details, I'll feel like killing Jed. Every day that goes by, every new lie is pushing me closer to the edge. But he's my husband, and I still love him.

But I need to rein in the anger, and be patient a while longer. Patience is my virtue.

So far the responses are pretty standard. What I'd expect.

> Pack his bags.

> Good riddance. You can do much better

> Go and front up Cassandra and tell her she can have him... and tell her there'll be no money left when you take him to the cleaners.

Then a particular response makes me sit up straighter. My heart thumps. It's from someone going by the moniker Hawkeye1234.

> Maybe he's got his reasons for not telling you. Do you really need to know the sordid details? He's still with you. Doesn't that tell you something? Leave the guy alone.

31

I look round at the door of the study, expecting Jed or someone to suddenly appear and boo at me. I've a weird feeling that I'm being watched, crazy considering I'm in the house alone. Aren't I? I hop up from my desk and peer through the window, looking left then right. There's not a soul in sight.

I've no idea why the response has set me off. It feels personally targeted, rather than meant for the fictitious writer of the letter. I'm definitely suffering from paranoia, and need to get a grip.

I'm now so hot and clammy that my fingers slither across the keyboard. I take a screenshot of the message from Hawkeye1234 on my phone. Messages from the main Facebook response page get deleted automatically at the end of each week.

It's a struggle to work through all the other responses to the first letter, but I work methodically, deleting swear words, and threatening content.

I go into the kitchen, boil the kettle, and make a camomile tea. Although it's supposed to calm me down, I can hardly grip the mug. My hands have serious tremors. It's almost 11 a.m., and I desperately want to get out of the house. But first I need to skim through the feedback on my second letter before I leave.

All the lies and deceit are definitely getting to me. The message from Hawkeye is likely a random response, probably from another guy up to no good. But why aren't I convinced?

Rain starts to batter against the windows, until I can no longer see out into the lane. I keep my eyes glued to the screen and start scrolling again through more responses. There are 489 messages relating to the question: *Do you think it would be okay to sleep with a new man when I know my husband is cheating?*

I'm quite stunned by the number of unhappy ladies out there. Can they all really have cheating husbands they're willing to stay with? A lot of the content doesn't surprise me though, as I could have predicted much of it.

> Leave him. Start a new life. You deserve it. He's a scumbag.

> Have it out with him, and then pack his bags.

> Take him to the cleaners. Divorce him.

> Even if kids are involved, they'll be fine eventually. We divorced years ago when my husband cheated, and we share custody of our two boys. Don't stay with a cheater. It never ends well.

Then my stomach flips again, and I feel sick and weak for a second time. I have to stand up, and walk around again. No. This can't be a coincidence. I slump back down and reread the new comment from Hawkeye1234.

> You want to be unfaithful? I'd be careful, as the husband might take it out on the other guy. Men have murdered for less. If you don't want a divorce, and your husband is still with you, what is your problem? Be grateful for what you have.

I smash my finger on the delete key to get rid of the word *murdered*. Grayson will be after my guts. But I don't care about Grayson at this moment.

I can hardly breathe, even more convinced that Hawkeye is targeting me personally with their messages.

It's not the advice that's freaking me out, rather the thought that someone is watching me, and might even have picked up on my situation. Could it be someone close to home?

I know Jed read my column over the weekend (I snooped on his browsing history when he was asleep), and perhaps knowing this is making me even more paranoid. If I'm wondering what he's up to, maybe he's trying to find out what's on my mind.

32

Ten minutes later I'm scrabbling my things together. I slam shut the study door, and pick up my house keys from the hall table. I'm desperate to get outside.

At least the rain has stopped, although I have to sidestep the puddles as I head into town. I walk briskly, and twenty minutes later I'm outside Angelo's. The place is heaving, which sets me off again, but I'm in luck. The only vacant seat in the whole place is mine. The one by the window.

A quick scan of the customers, and at least there's no sign of Adam. I'm so spooked from my letter responses, especially the one that mentioned jealous murdering husbands, that he's the last person I need to see. The fear that someone is watching me might be illogical, but I can't shake the feeling. Teagan always tells me to trust my instincts.

Despite the noise, and the coven of yummy mummies with screaming kids, I don't turn tail.

Candy is fussing about, her hair more flyaway than usual, and she looks completely flustered. At first I think she's too busy to talk, which suits me fine, but maybe I'm being overly sensitive, as she seems to be avoiding eye contact. There's a definite lack of trademark pleasantries.

'Cappuccino, please,' I say. 'My usual. Minus the chocolate.'

Without comment she froths up the milk, and plonks my drink in front of me. She doesn't apologise when liquid splashes over the top, and is soon on to her next order. I lift a serviette and sop up the mess, and at the same time Angelo appears from the kitchen. He apologises on Candy's behalf and gives her a warning look.

I try and settle in the corner, and drown out the noise by concentrating my gaze through the window. The sun has broken through, and the grey clouds have dispersed. It's cold and crisp outside, whereas the café, as always, is boiling. I take off my coat and bobble hat before letting my eyes wander up and down the street.

I'm over-the-top edgy, and keep looking towards the first-floor flat across the way. It's such a habit, even though I'm not expecting any action. Jed's at work, so he'll not appear, but I can't help wondering about the lady. What she might be doing.

The scene is completely different to that of the early morning. For a start the traffic barrier is pulled across to stop vehicles getting through, and unloading their wares. Pedestrians are milling from side to side. I'm suspicious of everyone, my mind is so alert. If anyone so much as glances at me, my stony stare makes them look away.

When my phone pings, I jump. It's a message from Jed.

> Hi. How's things? What say we eat out tonight?
> Your choice. My treat. XX

It's the third message of the morning. Why do I feel he's trying too hard? We never eat out during the week unless it's a special occasion. If I didn't know he was already guilty of so much deceit, I'd be seriously questioning his suggestion. I'd be half-expecting a bunch of red roses as a guilt offering.

Maybe he's twigged I'm suspicious about his bike story. His bruises are such a giveaway. It hurts that he thinks I'm so naïve to believe he went up to Edinburgh after a quick scan in A&E. I phoned the hotel, and they confirmed he never made it.

I'm about to reply when another text pings through from a number I don't recognise.

> Think carefully about what you do next. Maybe staying with your husband is the wisest move.

Attached to the end of the message is a warning sign emoji. A yellow triangle with an exclamation mark in the centre. WTF! Who the hell has sent the message? I look round the café which is buzzing with noise and activity. But no one is looking at me.

I'm so wound up that I have to get away. I don't even finish my coffee, which is a first, before putting my coat back on and scurrying outside. Despite the bright blue sky, and glaring sun, the air is biting.

I've only been out of the house for less than an hour, and can't face going home. I decide after the walk back that I'll pick up the car, and head earlier than usual to check on Blanche. Anything but reading through more messages.

* * *

By the time I get to Miners' Terrace it's almost one o'clock. I don't get out of the car immediately, and watch in horror as builders work on demolishing two more houses at either end of the terrace. They're actually removing single bricks, one by one, from the façade. I count the remaining properties. There are only eight homes still standing, although Blanche's is the only one still occupied.

Suddenly Adam Finch appears from around the back of one end of the terrace. I duck down behind the steering wheel. He's covered in dust, and the hard hat is back in place, but it's definitely him. Shit. Shit. Shit. I toy with driving off when he starts heading in my direction, waving a glove in the air which he's just tugged off.

A quick glance in the mirror and I frantically straighten out my hair. But before he gets anywhere near the car he stops right outside Blanche's house. The front door has opened. A woman strolls out, yells something back over her shoulder, and slams the door after her. It must be Madison, Blanche's new cleaner.

While I watch her step out onto the street, I realise it's her Adam is waving at, not me. The woman looks familiar, but out of context it takes a minute to register who she is.

I stare out the window for what seems like an eternity, although it's actually only a few minutes.

Adam is waving at the woman I've been watching from the café window. The woman with the young son, and the very same person Jed has been visiting for the past few months.

The hall clock has just chimed six o'clock.

I'm in the kitchen, still agitated. I hear the front door open, and close. Then there's a deathly hush. I imagine Jed with his eyes tight shut, slumped up against the door. His body must be racked in pain, but he'll be preparing his brave and chirpy face. The way his mother taught him.

Even when I can't see him, I sense his worry. He'll be wondering why I've ignored his texts. The last one was telling me when he'd be home, with ten kisses attached.

I know when I tell him I've been too busy to text, he'll sense a cop-out. My phone is always by my side. Yet despite his mountain of lies, he'd never suspect me of subterfuge. After all, I opened my darkest soul to him. What more could I have to hide? Playing private detective, and keeping tabs on him, is not deceit. It's survival.

Jed used to call us soulmates, professing he could read my inner thoughts.

'You can't fool me. I know exactly what you're thinking,' he would say.

We were once so in tune. Until I started watching him, seeing things I wasn't meant to see. I believed we were solid, yin and yang, dependent on each other. Everything seemed so perfect. Even when he started acting strange, deep down I still believed in *us*.

When I owned up to my gruesome past, just a couple of weeks before our wedding, he soaked it up. As I howled, he held me close, and told me he'd never let me go.

I've done nothing since getting back from Blanche's. Nothing except stress and wander round the house. I've been too scared to check for new column messages, and have kept my laptop closed.

When I realised who Madison was, I drove off pretty quickly, leaving her deep in conversation with Adam. I watched them from a side street across the road. No more than five minutes elapsed before they wandered off, but the image of Adam's hand resting on her shoulder has thrown me. I can't smother the recollection. They're close, intimate.

Once the coast was clear, I sneaked into Blanche's, no idea what I expected to find. A sense of dread followed me. I needn't have worried because the place was spotless, with a wafting scent of vanilla. And Blanche had even managed to get downstairs, with the help of her new cleaner apparently.

Tonight, Blanche's future is on the agenda. And the subject of Madison. How much will Jed tell me about her? Where he found her. Why she's the cleaner. And why he didn't let me know.

I'm not ready for a full confrontation, but perhaps tonight he'll start the ball rolling, and begin to open up. My stomach is in knots thinking about it. Deep down, I don't think he will, but if he doesn't start talking soon, I'll have no choice but to force him. The thought terrifies me.

'Jed?' I call out. It seems ages since the front door closed.

'Coming.' I hear him shuffle along the hall. When he appears at the kitchen door, I stiffen. He looks like a stranger. Bent, and broken. His skin is mottled, his lips cracked, and he looks seriously ill.

'I wasn't sure if I heard the door,' I lie.

'Sorry. I did call out. Are you okay?'

'Yes, I'm fine, thanks. But you look exhausted,' I say. I can't tear my eyes away. If he told me he was dying, I'd believe him. That's how bad he looks.

He simply nods, and even that makes him wince.

I busy myself with emptying the dishwasher.

'You didn't get back to me today. I was worried,' he says.

He still looks worried, although it could be the pain puckering his features.

'I've been busy. Sorry.' I know he'll not believe me, but he's in no fit state to battle.

My heart breaks at the sight of him. I go and plant a kiss on his cheek. He shrinks from the lightest touch, the agony written all over his face. He seems even worse than he did yesterday.

My angry mood mellows. He looks so vulnerable, like a little boy lost. How has it come to this? For a brief moment, I can almost forget my soulmate has a lover. And most likely a son.

'Supper's nearly ready,' I say.

'Oh. You don't want to eat out?' His face lights up. It's hard not to miss the relief on his face. He's so glad not to have to go out again.

'No. I've got a casserole in the oven. And...'

'And?' He uses a hand to steady himself against the door frame. He hitches a single eyebrow.

'We need to talk.'

His Adam's apple bobs up and down as he swallows. Even the involuntary movement seems such an effort.

'Sounds serious.'

'Why not get changed, and we can talk over supper.'

'Should I be worried?' Blood drains from his already ashen face.

He should, of course, be worried. But I don't want him forewarned.

'Not really. It's about Blanche.'

'Oh. Okay. Won't be long.'

He hobbles off. His shoulders visibly slump as he reaches the stairs, and I watch through the open door as he grips the banister with both hands to help him up.

34

Fifteen minutes later, he reappears in a loose-fitting navy sweatshirt, and jogging bottoms. He slumps into a chair with as much ease as he can muster.

If I think watching through the café window is like a soap opera, this takes the biscuit. We playact like a normal married couple. Jed takes stoic to a whole new level.

He is soon drinking wine much faster than usual. When I comment, he says he needs to relax, and it helps dull the pain. He's on his second glass before he asks why I'm not drinking.

'Don't you want a glass?' he asks. His lips are already plum coloured from the tannins.

'I'm trying to cut back. Remember?'

'Sorry, I forgot. Hope you don't mind me drinking though. I haven't got your willpower,' he says.

'You go ahead.'

He's more picky with his food though, nudging the beef cubes around his plate. I'm eating even less than he is, each mouthful a Herculean effort.

I'm procrastinating. A big part of me wants to forget I have questions to ask. Pretend a while longer. I'm so petrified of what might come out. I now understand all the women who write in to Bella saying that they've turned a blind eye to their husband's cheating. Especially women like me. Women who can't see any other choices, and are shit-scared of being left on their own. And some simply love their partners too much.

Jed looks so contented, and happy to be home. Funny, when we're together like this, just the two of us, I can pretend all is good. His deceit somehow seems less threatening, and the horror becomes diluted. If only I hadn't seen what I had. Mum used to say *ignorance is bliss*.

I toy with letting it go, for another night. But I don't, and out of the blue the question tumbles out.

'Who is Madison?'

'Sorry?' He coughs, then takes a large slug of wine as if to dislodge a piece of food.

'Ma-di-son.' I widen my eyes, pronouncing each syllable as if to a child.

'Madison? Yes. She's Mum's new cleaner. Is she doing okay?'

Nothing to hide here is the tack he's going to take.

'Great with a mop and bucket.' I expel a sarcastic puff of air. 'Jed, what I want to know is, where did you find her? And why didn't you tell me?'

'It must have slipped my mind. But I did say I'd find someone to help out, didn't I?'

His hands are shaky as he sets his glass down.

'Where did you find her?'

I'm worried now I've started asking questions that I'll not be able to stop.

'Ouch.' Jed grimaces as he moves in his chair, and tries to reel in his skinny legs. I'm not sure if it's a delaying tactic, or genuine pain.

'Go on,' I hiss.

He looks shocked by my tone. Or shocked by the turn of the conversation.

'Through a work colleague.'

His feet are now jittering up and down on the floor.

'Who at work?' It's another question, and sets my heart racing.

'I've forgotten his name. The guy working on the terrace demolition. Fitch? Lynch? Something like that.' He tries to sit up straighter, but slouches back down.

'You mean Adam Finch. He's not exactly a work colleague, is he?'

I put a hand on the table to stop the room from spinning.

'Finch. That's it. How do you know Adam Finch?'

He's not going to respond to my question, more concerned that I already know him.

His eyes narrow, and for a split second I see it. The doubt. Or is it mistrust? Perhaps he's on to me. Could he know I had a coffee with Adam? The Facebook warning springs to mind.

'I met him outside Blanche's talking to Madison. He's the developer, I presume, who's trying to move Blanche out?'

'Yes. That's him.'

35

The revelation that Adam is the person who introduced Madison to Jed has thrown me.

I don't know why, but I assumed Jed asked Madison himself to do the cleaning. Perhaps he did, as he sees her often enough. But why tell me Adam recommended her? Madison and Adam did look on familiar terms when I saw them, but I feel I'm missing something.

When I asked Jed how he found Madison, a very small part of me thought he might come clean, and admit to knowing her well. A big ask that he might own up to visiting her in the early morning for months, but even a small admission would have been a start.

Although it's twisted reasoning, a bigger part of me is glad that he didn't say any more. Unless he tells me the whole story, I can't stomach more fabrications.

Give him his due, he was quick off the mark to involve Adam. The thought that he's been planning for this moment, and how much to tell me, makes me so upset. My already high blood pressure won't let up.

I clear away the plates, clattering more than usual. I load up the dishwasher, before I take the cut-up fruit platter from the fridge, and set it on the table. He sniffs, getting the whiff of cherry liqueur on top.

'Hmm. Just what the doctor ordered,' he says, staring at the fruit. He's avoiding eye contact, and desperate to steer the conversation in a different direction.

Yep, he's actually going to carry on as if everything is okay. That he's not in the slightest perturbed by the talk of Madison. He must know I'm edgy by all the clattering, but edgy doesn't come close. Inside I'm screaming, and know I must calm down.

I count to ten before I start up again.

'Jed.'

'Yes?' He drops a piece of pineapple onto the floor, and it shoots under the table.

'Leave it. I'll get it later.'

'What did you want to say?'

He looks at me, his eyes thick with worry.

'Blanche is really poorly. She needs to get proper care.'

His puckered brow gets ironed out when Madison's name isn't mentioned again.

'Is she that bad?'

He leans back, relieved but concerned.

'Yes. That bad. She can hardly get out of bed.'

I don't mention that with Madison's help, she managed earlier to struggle downstairs. It's better he thinks she's bedridden.

Jed puffs out air in frustration.

'I've tried to get her to move out, you know that. But she won't listen.'

It's one more thing he can't deal with.

'The houses are coming down all around her and soon she'll have no choice. Where's she going to go then?' I ask.

'She's so bloody stubborn. The longer it's gone on, the more the offer from the developers has gone down. Soon we'll get next to nothing.'

He hangs his head in his hands. I know he's overloaded with worry, but my sympathy has its limits.

'Madison has been helping with her medication. Do you think this is a wise idea? How well do you know her? Can you trust her?'

It's torture waiting for his response. I hum quietly, bracing for what's next.

He takes a moment.

'She's okay. I trust her.'

'How? How can you trust someone you hardly know?'

'I told you. Adam recommended her.'

'How well do you know Adam?'

'Well enough. He's an established contractor, and I just trust him. Okay?'

He snaps. He's had enough of this conversation.

'But how can you trust her?'

Go on, Jed. Give me something.

'Adam and Madison are brother and sister. That's good enough for me. Satisfied?'

36

I don't know why I'm so shocked to learn that Adam and Madison are brother and sister. It seems a huge bit of the puzzle, but I've no idea why.

We don't talk much after this. Jed becomes detached, distances himself from further conversation. He pours a medicinal whisky nightcap, lots of ice, and suggests we turn in early.

'I'm sorry, but I'm so tired,' he mumbles.

He sits on at the table while I wipe down the surfaces. He usually offers to help, but not tonight.

I'm exhausted too, although my mind is racing. I have one more thing to ask while his guard is down, now the subject of Madison has been dropped.

'Have you read my column recently?' I ask.

'Sorry?'

He's miles away, but tries to hoist himself up. His eyes are barely open as he fights the urge to fall asleep in situ.

'My column. I seem to have hit a nerve with my latest one, getting loads of heated responses.'

'Oh. Why's that? What's it about?'

I thought so. He's not going to own up to reading it, despite his browsing history. I shouldn't have snooped, but it's a very minor sin in our coupledom of sins.

'It's to do with cheating, and people having secret families.'

His eyes lose their glaze, and the whisky tumbler slips from his grasp. The icy contents land on his sweatpants. He's wide awake now.

'Shit.' He uses a paper serviette to blot the mess.

'Don't worry. Give them here, and I'll put them in the machine.'

I hold out my hand, and with a monumental effort he somehow gets his sweatpants off.

For the first time I notice an enormous black bruise at the very top of his thigh. He also looks as if he's seeing it for the first time, and rubs a finger across it.

He hovers in his boxer shorts, one hand on the back of a chair for support.

'I don't have a copy of your magazine,' he offers in a very quiet voice.

'It's not important,' I lie. It's very important, but I've dug enough for tonight.

His reaction tells me I've definitely hit a nerve. It could be the mention of second families, cheating, or the fact I'm getting loaded responses.

Could Jed be Hawkeye1234? Warning me not to leave him, or else...

* * *

Jed goes upstairs first. By the time I get to the bedroom, he's already under the covers, but despite all the drink, painkillers and exhaustion, he's still awake. As always, he's waiting for me before he gives in to sleep.

'Hurry up,' he mumbles.

I go round his side of the bed, and kiss him on the forehead.

'Jed, I'm going to sleep in the spare room tonight. You need your rest, and I'm still wide awake.'

'Don't be silly.' His eyes widen, and he looks horrified as if I've suggested divorce.

'We both need our sleep, and when I drift off, you'll be awake again, tossing and turning. I know you're in pain.'

'Just tonight though,' he says, no energy left for argument.

He looks so broken that part of me wants to comfort him. Hold him tight, and tell him he'll feel better soon. But I can't.

His breathing finally slows, and when I know he's asleep, I close the door and tiptoe along the landing and back downstairs. Hard not to be jealous that he can sleep. I'd need a whole strip of sleeping pills to knock me out. It's past eleven, and I'm hyper-alert. My mind is skittering all over the place.

I remember my phone is on charge. When I unplug it, I see a new message from Adam Finch. It's the last thing I need. It feels covert, secretive, as if I'm the one doing something wrong. All we did was share a coffee, but the way things are, it feels like a cardinal sin. As if I'm the guilty party.

> Hi. Wondered if you fancied a drink one night.
> Might be more fun than a coffee. Adam Finch

I manage a wry smile at the fact he's used his full name. He could be aiming for not-too-personal, but more likely he's worried I mightn't remember him.

Now I know that he's the developer waiting to get to work on Miners' Terrace, as well as Madison's brother, I'm much more wary of him. He could be using me to get to Blanche. Or even to

Jed. He's likely as fed up waiting for Blanche to move out as we are.

I delete the message, and switch the phone off. I slide my laptop across the kitchen counter, and boot it up.

My mind is awash with thoughts for my next column. Grayson is already pestering me to get a move on. I'm full of inspiration using the next bit of my own story as content, and am desperate to get the ideas down.

I've so many issues in my own life now that I could fill several months' worth of copy. I could carry on with themes of infidelity. Secret families. Even stalking one's spouse. But this week, I want to try and draw out the poison. Find out who might be on to me. It may be a dangerous game, but I'm running out of options to find out what Jed is up to. And who is Hawkeye, if not Jed? The feeling that someone is watching me is seriously freaky. I doubt I'd be as worried about the column responses if I hadn't had the threatening phone text as well.

I'm so on edge, anxious all the time. Sometimes I fear I'll explode, like I did once before. On the day my father died. The nightmare that I killed him never goes away.

I put a match to a couple of tealights, and let the scent of vanilla tickle my nostrils. The blinds on the windows are still open, and I revel in the comforting envelope of the outside darkness. A half-moon is nestled among a group of stars. In the silence I try to muffle the tears, but they trickle silently down my cheeks. This is not how I imagined our marriage would turn out. Not so quickly. Where did it all go wrong? And when?

My fingers hover over the keys, as my mind roams with ideas and themes. Affairs. *Ménages à trois*. Revenge. But it's pointless. I've already decided where I'm going. I've something much more important I need to get out there.

The tealights flicker as if a ghost is hovering. Then I type with furious fingers.

Is it wrong to try and force someone to move out of a property in order to get your hands on a large sum of money? Even if they are family. An obscene amount of money when you can hardly make ends meet.

These are the bare bones of my first letter. I'll beef it out, but I'm desperate to hear how far people might go if they were in such a situation. It'll be like talking to a therapist.

The second idea has been festering now for weeks, not just a few days. Not only do I want to draw out a potential stalker, but I'm genuinely floundering about what I should do with the next bit of my own story. The bit of my story that is the main reason I won't confront Jed.

Should being pregnant make you think twice about leaving a cheating spouse?

37

Jed gives me the merest peck on the cheek when he appears this morning. It feels like a punishment, letting me know that he wasn't at all happy sleeping on his own. When I ask how he slept, he admits like a log.

'I'm feeling much more like my old self,' he says.

'I thought you must be feeling better because you're leaving really early again.' I point at my watch, and give him a quizzical look.

'Hm, yes. I've still some serious catching up to do.'

I bet he does. He's already got his jacket on, and scalds his tongue on a too-hot tea.

'Let me know when you get to the office. I worry, you know.'

'I'm fine, but I'll give the early bike rides a miss for a while,' he says with a wan smile.

I bite back the sarcasm of saying it might be tough without a bike.

He leans in for another kiss. The familiar scent of woodland pine clings to his freshly shaven chin, and he laughs when I cough.

'It's that bloody aftershave,' I say, covering my mouth, and flapping the other hand in the air.

He lifts his rucksack, hesitates a second, and adds, 'I might be a bit late this evening.'

'Oh.' I don't ask why. 'No worries, I'll be here.'

I see him out the front door and watch him stroll down the path, and out into the street. It's exactly 7 a.m. On foot it would take him at least half an hour to get to the flat across from Angelo's. The state his body's in, it would likely take him a lot longer. But by car, I can get into town, and be at the café well before 7.30.

I grab my phone, bag and laptop, and set off. The bloody car hiccups through half a dozen splutters, and sends my pulse skyrocketing.

I need to calm down. Now I'm pregnant, I don't need my blood pressure going any higher. It's one thing risking my life in a bashed-up rust-bucket of a car, but I won't risk the baby's. Jed, no matter what happens, will be buying me a new car. Come hell or high water. Solid and roomy, with space for the baby and me, and perhaps a dog one day.

At least parking in town should be easy, as rush hour hasn't kicked in yet. If I'm quick I can reach the café before opening.

I leave the car up by the market, and hurry down the back lanes. There's a small alleyway next to the café where the refuse bins are kept, and as it's only 7.20, there's as yet no sign of life. I push myself up against the wall, try to steady my breathing and begin counting down the minutes. Then, on the dot of 7.29, I hear Candy's voice.

I sidle out from behind the bins, inch onto the street, and with a quick glance left and right, I scurry inside the café. I didn't know I was holding my breath, but exhale like a puffer fish when I'm in off the street.

I hover by the window, and take a quick look outside. There's no sign of Jed, although there's still time for him to appear. But I'll not relax until at least eight. If he's not here by then, I doubt he'll be coming.

I wonder if he's already contacted Madison to warn her that I might be on to them. Perhaps he's waiting to talk to her face to face. Either way, it's torture trying to guess.

I unravel my thick layers of clothing, and fling them on the chair before heading for the counter.

'My usual, please, Candy.'

She lifts down a mug, starts grinding beans and frothing milk, without so much as a pleasantry.

'Are you okay?'

She looks nearly as run-down as Jed, but with a pouty surly expression. She's definitely out of sorts.

'Yes. Why wouldn't I be?' she snaps. Once again, she bangs the mug aggressively onto the counter, and rather than apologise, turns away.

My hand is so shaky I'm scared I'll spill more by the time I get back to my seat. Candy hasn't helped the butterflies with her sullen mood, but I haven't energy to worry about her as well as everything else.

I hunch down behind the glass, which today is seriously murky. It's hard to get a clear vision on to the pavement, let alone across the road. I freeze when a guy appears in my line of vision with a bucket and squeegee. He nods, and with a wicked grin, blurs my vision completely as he smears the pane with a soapy mixture.

It's at least ten minutes later when he manages to clear the glass and I'm able to see again. Not much has changed, except for a couple of vehicles unloading outside Boots. Then I see a cyclist. His helmet looks the same as Jed's.

No. No. No. The guy gets off his bike by the health food shop, the one where Jed padlocks his bike. I think I'm hallucinating, because as he secures the chain to the post, he looks my way. Shit. Shit. Shit. He's seen me.

It's only as he strides past the café, shoulders upright, no limping movement, I realise it's not Jed. The guy glances through the café, and smiles at me. He looks nothing like my husband.

I need to get out of here, as the paranoia is gripping. It's past eight, and I'm confident that Jed won't turn up now. I finish my coffee, and wrap up again.

As I'm about to step out onto the street, I jump back inside. Across the road, Madison has appeared. She's dressed as if she's off to clean. Her hair is swept up, and she's wearing a coloured overall. It's the first time I've seen her in work clothes.

Holy shit. She's waving at me. My mind goes into overdrive. How does she know who I am? Perhaps Jed has shown her photographs. Maybe he has contacted her since our conversation last night. She's frantically trying to catch my attention.

Oh my God. What am I going to do? I can't acknowledge her. My whole life flashes before me. I have no idea what to do, as this wasn't in my script.

Then I hear someone come up behind me, and I nearly jump out of my skin. It's Candy. But she's not looking at me. She's waving, and walks on past.

Soon she's kissing Madison, cheek to cheek.

38

I'm not sure why I'm so shocked at seeing Candy and Madison together. Madison might pop into the café at times when I'm not here, but I'm not convinced she's a regular punter.

They look like good friends. Friends who don't see each other that often, but warmly familiar. I can't imagine Candy rushing up to me on the street and throwing her arms around me.

My café viewing has all been about Jed. Madison. And the boy. Their relationship. I assume the lad is Jed's, as I've seen them all in plain-sight togetherness. Candy has never figured in anything before. A tingling down my spine hints that there's yet another thing I'm missing, and Candy's recent aloofness isn't helping the worry.

Then the little boy suddenly appears alongside his mother. Candy lifts him up, swings him round as he tugs her hair, and squeals.

Watching them makes me crack inside. I barely manage to contain the tears, and swipe a hand across my cheeks. Being pregnant is making everything seem much worse. I've dreamt all my life of a proper family. When I hid in cupboards, under beds, and in the slimy dankness of the cellar, I promised one day I'd build my own family. It would be full of love, happiness, and light. When Jed appeared, I believed I'd found my happy-ever-after. Now everyone else seems to have got there first.

I tug up the top of my black hoodie and stuff my hair inside, before I slink away. I keep my eyes to the ground, and creep back through the alleyway, past the bins, and on towards the car. I'm acting like a wanted criminal, even though my husband is the guilty party.

When I reach the car park, the heavens open, but I relish the deluge, turning my face upwards to take the full force. It mingles with the tears, and tries to wash them away.

I sit in the car for nearly an hour trying to unwind. I hold both hands over my stomach, in a ritual of comfort for the baby. The urge to protect, fight for its survival, is overwhelming. As the downpour abates, my eyes start to dry.

Rather than go home, I turn the car in the opposite direction, and head north out of town. Towards Blanche's. I promised Jed I'd do a quick check in on her, and now is as good a time as any.

The car skids on the wet roads, and the wipers barely manage to sweep away a persistent drizzle. My driving is worse than usual, and I have a couple of near misses. The early rush-hour traffic is relentless, and when a van overtakes on a bend, I smash my horn over and over. When the driver slows down, glowering in his mirror, I'm terrified he's going to get out and kill me. I need to calm down.

When I finally pull into Blanche's street, there's a dearth of activity. Even the small area of grass opposite, which is usually dotted with dogwalkers, is deserted.

As yet, there's no sign of Adam or the builders. Everything is strangely quiet. There are only two cars parked along the full length of the road, and they're at the far end.

I squeeze out of the car, swearing when the door doesn't open the full way. When I yank harder, it bangs against my leg.

'Shit. Shit. Shit.' I yelp in pain.

A black cat whizzes past, scoots under the car, and out the other side. It won't need one of its nine lives here, as it's like a ghost town.

The gate to Blanche's is open. Jed tells me to always make sure it's closed when I leave. I gingerly step over the cracked slabs, and dig out my door key.

Inside, the silence is even creepier than on the street.

'Blanche? Blanche?' I yell from the hallway. 'It's only me. Izzy.'

She's likely still in bed, asleep. But there's something else, I can feel it. My skin prickles. Something is off kilter. Hairs bristle on the back of my neck, as I grip the newel post, and yell louder.

'Blanche?' I yell again. But there's no response.

I look into the lounge, where the air is thick with toxic fumes of furniture polish and air freshener. The curtains, as always, are slightly cracked, but the usual soft comfort from dimmed side lamps is missing.

Something is definitely off.

I tiptoe up the stairs, each footstep ratcheting up the dread. My insides gurgle, and I'm scared I might throw up. Each creak from the uneven treads makes it worse.

'Hello? Yoo-hoo?' My voice trembles.

Gingerly I nudge open the bedroom door.

The bed is made up. The pillows have been plumped, and the duvet is straight. Blanche's nightclothes, her long white nightie and blue dressing gown are neatly laid out on the bed, the way she leaves them once she's got dressed. She's like her son, obsessive in habits, and meticulous in the details. But where is she if she's dressed, and the bed is made up?

For some reason, I look in the wardrobe. As if checking for clues. But I'm only playing for time. Everything is as it should be. Six pairs of shoes are arranged side by side, and Blanche's uniforms of tweed skirts and button-up blouses are neatly hung.

Suddenly I freeze. There's a loud noise coming from outside, amplified by the quiet inside. It sounds like the grind and groan of heavy machinery. I move to the window, and down below I see Adam, hard hat in place, directing a bulldozer and a troop of builders in frantic activity.

The racket outside somehow feels connected to the lack of movement inside. As I stare out at the scene below, my head throbs. But there's only one thing now on my mind.

Where the hell is Blanche?

39

I check the bathroom. The attic room. The downstairs cloakroom. The kitchen.

There are only two rooms left to check. The utility room, and on through the door by the washing machine... down to the cellar. I've deliberately left these till last. I'm so scared to look that my legs have turned to jelly.

Before I enter the utility room, I start to have flashbacks. Images and memories come hurtling back, and I have to put my hands over my ears to muffle the screams. I'm not sure if the screams are memories, or if I've actually let rip.

It all comes flooding back. It was my birthday, I was fifteen. Friday the 13th. I was done with skulking under the bed, in dark corners, and worst of all, not being allowed to talk.

There was a storm raging outside. Thunderclaps and streaks of lightning were company in the gloom. Mum pulled me back inside when I tried to go for a walk.

She gave me a note. It was my birthday. Couldn't she just open her bloody mouth and talk for once?

Dad was on his way to the cellar, 'for a celebratory bottle of wine,' he told us. He hadn't bought me a present, or even a card, so I had no idea what he was celebrating. Certainly not my birthday. He'd already downed a whole bottle, so was very drunk. And aggressive. He had swiped at Mum a couple of times, swearing at me to disappear.

He staggered towards the cellar, but didn't know I was behind him. He wobbled on the top step, as he tried to lean across for the light switch. He was so unbalanced he couldn't quite get there. He kept swearing, cursing under his breath.

I crept up so close that I could almost hear his heartbeat.

And suddenly I let rip. I started to yell, and couldn't stop. I even covered my own ears against the onslaught of noise. Dad was never going to get back his balance. He tried to turn, and I remember his face was puce with rage. But I kept screaming.

Then he lost his grip on the handrail, then his footing. His lardy body tumbled like a cheese barrel down a hill.

Even as urine dribbled down my legs my lungs kept going. Only when I vomited did the noise stop. The silence was the worst noise I'd ever heard.

Then Mum appeared. I've no idea how much she'd seen, or how long she'd been behind me, but without a word, she careered down the stone steps.

I stared down into the black hole. Mum hunkered beside Dad, felt for a pulse, and then looked back up at me. All she did was shake her head, but I knew he was already dead. My actions had killed him.

I didn't speak for months after Dad died. I couldn't. I'm not sure if Mum thought I'd pushed him, but she never said. Instead she told police she'd seen him fall. He was so drunk that he lost his balance.

Afterwards we never talked about what happened to Dad. But to this day I wonder if Mum killed herself because she believed her daughter was a murderer.

In my heart, I blame myself for both their deaths.

40

I manage, inch by inch, to make it into the utility room. My head spins, and I feel I'm going to pass out. The door to the cellar is ajar, but I can't bear to look down. My hand nestles protectively on my stomach.

It seems to take forever to cover the short distance to the cellar door. Each step is such an effort, I could be climbing Everest.

Down below is in darkness, as the light bulb isn't on. But I can feel the cold. An icy chill envelops me, and I can smell a rotting stench rising up. Somehow I make it to the iron railing, and hold on tightly until my breathing steadies. Although it's pitch black, I know what I'm going to find. As I flick the light switch, the bulb on its frayed cable blinks on and off.

I close my eyes, swallow back the bile, until I finally force myself to look. Blanche's body is lying distorted at the bottom of the stairs. It is twisted, and there's no sign of movement. One leg is splayed off to the side at an obtuse angle. I think of Teagan's old Barbie doll whose limbs I tried to snap. And an arm is contorted behind the head.

Strange, my first sense is one of relief that I won't need to check for a pulse. No one could have survived such a fall, could they? Even from this far up, there's no mistaking the pool of blood haloing around the head.

Slowly, carefully, I edge backwards, but can't tear my eyes away until I can no longer see the body. I'm shaking from head to toe. Even though I've seen death before, it's still a shock.

Somehow I manage the short distance to the front door where I struggle with the key. It's almost impossible to turn, as my hands are damp and trembling.

When I get outside, I gulp greedily at the fresh air. It's so cold I cough until pain sears across my chest. Although the sun is trying to break through, everywhere is wet. The front path is like an ice rink, and I'm so unsteady on my feet, it takes forever to reach the road.

Then I see Adam only a few feet away. Thank God. He's talking to a couple of builders, but with his back to me. I keep tight to the property fencing, and try to quell the panic.

He turns, and smiles as I approach.

'Adam.' My voice is hoarse, and his smile turns to a look of concern.

'Izzy. What's up?'

'It's Blanche.'

'What? What's up with Blanche?'

He's curious, nothing more.

'She's... she's...' I can't form the words.

'She's what?' He touches my arm, and his voice speeds up.

'I think she's dead.'

'Dead?'

He doesn't gasp, or look horrified. His lack of urgency sets me more on edge. I need him to believe me.

'Here, let me come with you.'

He puts a comforting hand on my arm, and helps me make the journey back. Strange, but a rogue thought crosses my mind. It's fleeting, but why do I get the feeling that he might already know what's happened?

Otherwise, how can he be so calm?

* * *

We go back into the house together, me a few paces behind Adam. He tells me he'll check on Blanche if I'd rather wait, and strides purposefully down the stone staircase. As if in a trance, I follow a few seconds later.

Adam kneels down to check for a pulse, and I linger, several feet away by the damp rotting log pile.

'I'm sorry,' he says, as if somehow it's his fault. He looks at me, his fingers still straddling her neck. 'There's nothing. I can't find a pulse.'

I'm too shocked to cry. This can't be happening. All over again.

'Thanks,' I say.

'What for?'

Adam gets up, and puts a comforting hand this time on my shoulder. His eyes rest on mine, and he pushes a strand of flyaway fringe from my eyes.

'For being here.' What else can I thank him for?

'We need to call an ambulance. There's no signal down here, so I'll have to go up.'

'Okay,' I say, unable yet to move.

Adam pulls out his phone, and begins tapping on the screen as he heads back towards the utility room. When he reaches the top, he seems to get a signal.

He calls the ambulance, mentions the words death, accident,

witnesses, and speaking very clearly, gives the address, postcode, and full name of the victim. How did he know Blanche's middle name was Enid? I've never heard anyone other than Jed use it before.

I take a moment to look around the cellar. Then I see it. A small circular piece of metal. It's only inches from Blanche's body, between the bottom step and her foot which dangles from the misshapen leg.

I bend and pick up what looks like a broken-off piece of a keyring. It's a small metal clothes peg of tarnished silver attached to a snapped-off chain.

I slip it in my pocket, and then struggle upwards into the light.

41

I don't get home much before Jed. As soon as the police finished asking questions on site, I went down to the station and gave a statement. I then walked round and round the park, working up the courage to call Jed.

My voice sounded like an automated message when I told him his mother had died. My shock smothered any emotion. I held on the line for ages, repeating several times what had happened.

When he finally found his voice, all he said was, 'I'm leaving now.'

I'm now sitting in the hall on the bottom stair, waiting. When I hear Jed's footsteps I jump up.

If I was in a bad way when I found the body, Jed looks as if he needs a blood transfusion. He's like a ghost, and I've never seen him so distraught. His body has shrunk in on itself, and he looks like a completely different person to a few hours ago.

'Izzy. Izzy.' He collapses into my arms, and I smooth down his hair as if he's a child and I'm his mother. 'What am I going to do?'

I wonder what he means. Do about what? It's a strange first question. He wasn't dependent on Blanche for anything, and he hasn't seen her much lately.

His arms envelop me so tightly that I can hardly breathe. Over his shoulder, I notice two policemen keeping a respectful distance. They're watching intently as I try to coax Jed inside. He finally cracks, and starts howling like a baby.

I knew he'd be upset. Blanche was his mother, after all. But the sight of his uncontrollable grief is hard to bear. He was close to his mum, despite leaving the daily care to me. And Madison, of course. This random thought makes me stiffen, diluting the sympathy.

I'm having serious difficulty keeping him upright, until a policeman steps forward.

'Let me help,' he says. The guy is young, tanned, and clean-shaven, and could be a male model. But he looks strong.

'Thanks. Come in.'

When the guy tries to support Jed's body, Jed snaps at him.

'I'm fine.' He gives the young man daggers.

With an almighty effort, he pushes us both away, and heads for the kitchen. The policemen, caps tucked under elbows, follow behind.

Jed collapses onto a chair, and hangs his head. The sobbing continues, with intermittent bouts of coughing, until he manages to quieten down.

When Mum died, I cried alone for weeks. I can't share grief nor happiness, except with Jed. My heart aches watching him, although I'm shocked by his hysterical display in front of the officers. No sign of his usual stoicism.

The policemen watch on like mourners at a funeral. I'm embarrassed, and wish Jed could pull himself together, at least until they've gone.

'I'll put the kettle on. Please, have a seat.' I indicate the two chairs on the opposite side of the table from Jed.

I fill the kettle, lift out some mugs, and close my eyes. Nausea is clawing at my insides, and a determined headache is thumping. I presume it's normal procedure for police to turn up after an old person's death. Blanche was frail, likely stumbled and lost her footing. That's what it looks like. Are they just following protocol?

The kettle takes forever to boil, and I'm so dizzy I'm scared I'll pass out. Perhaps she didn't fall, stumble, or lose her footing. What if she was pushed? That could be their agenda.

'We need to ask you a few questions, sir.' The young male-model lookalike speaks quietly. He's trying to catch Jed's eye, which is difficult as my husband's head is nestled on his arms on top of the table.

'Pardon?' Jed splutters a phlegmy cough, and hauls himself up. He swipes a sleeve across dripping nostrils.

'A few questions, sir. We know you've had an awful shock, but we need to know where you've been all day. And yesterday.'

42

I don't know why I'm so taken aback by the turn of the conversation. Of course the police will want to establish the cause of death, but I'm not prepared. And Jed certainly isn't.

'Why, for God's sake? My mother has just died, and you're asking me where I've been? She fell down the stairs, broke her bloody neck. Why the hell do you want to know where I've been?' He spits out the words.

My eyes widen in shock at the outburst. His red puffy eyes no longer look like my Jed's.

I give him an encouraging smile, with a warning look to calm down.

'I'm really sorry, Mr Hardcastle. But we have to ask.'

'Why? Why do you have to ask me?' Jed's tears dry up as he gets angrier, but his whole body is quaking.

'We're trying to establish the exact cause of your mother's death. We have to be certain that there was no third party involved.'

'You think someone else was involved? That someone might

have pushed her down the stairs?' He laughs, and his features contort.

His face is now crimson, the pallor of shock having given way to that of anger, and frustration. His blood pressure will have rocketed, and a vein protrudes in his neck. I've never seen him this furious. He has to calm down. I need to tell him it'll all be okay. We're a team, for now at least, and I can't bear to see him so upset.

I land the mugs down with some force.

'Could we not do this tomorrow? It's been a dreadful shock,' I ask, suddenly the calmest person in the room. 'My husband has just lost his mother.'

'If Mr Hardcastle can tell us his movements yesterday and today, then we'll be on our way. We're really sorry we have to ask.' The more senior officer speaks this time, from a very upright sitting position. He fiddles with his cap, swirling it gently with stubby fingers.

Jed glowers at him.

'I was at work yesterday. Got home around six.' He looks at me. 'That's right, isn't it?'

I nod.

'Then I had an early night, as I wasn't feeling so good.'

I wonder if he's going to mention coming off his bicycle, and being in agony ever since. I doubt it, as he'll not want to embellish the accident details in front of me.

'Did you leave the house anytime during the night?'

'No,' Jed snaps. 'Now if you'll excuse me, I'd like to be on my own.'

'Last question. Where have you been today?'

'At work. I have at least twenty colleagues who'll vouch for me.'

With that Jed struts out of the room, and heads for the

lounge. He slams the door behind him, and a deathly silence follows.

The police officers stand up, knock back their drinks, and a few seconds later I'm walking them down the hall.

'Thanks for the tea, Mrs Hardcastle.'

'My pleasure.'

I pause by the front door.

'Do you think someone else could have been involved?' I look directly at the senior officer.

'I can't say anything more, except that we have to ask the questions. Mrs Hardcastle was elderly, and quite frail from what we understand, but this is pretty routine.'

'Oh. I see.'

'We will need Mr Hardcastle to make a statement. Perhaps he can pop by the station tomorrow? Or the day after?'

'I'll tell him. Thanks.'

'We'll be in touch.'

They put their hats on, and make their way back to their car.

I linger as they drive off, and watch their vehicle disappear round the bend. I lock the door, and pull the chain across. A trickle of tears dribbles down my own cheeks.

I should have shown them the silver clothes peg I found by the body. I know that. But it might make everything worse. It could be an innocent find, and for now I'll keep it to myself. Deep down it bothers me though. I would have seen it on the floor before now, surely? Although I can't remember when I was last in the cellar.

Someone may have pushed Blanche. I know it doesn't make sense, but I have a queasy feeling that her death is somehow connected to things going on in my life. And it would have been easy for someone to push her.

A few minutes pass before I'm able to face Jed again. I've so much I want to say. We need to talk, and I think I've held back long enough.

As I open the door into the lounge, Jed's red eyes look up.

'Did the police ask where you were today and yesterday?'

'Of course. I've already given my statement.'

I see a moment of doubt in his eyes. Does he really think I might have pushed his mother?

43

A year before I met Jed, I moved out from living with Teagan and my aunt. I'd been with them since Mum died, but knew I had to stand on my own two feet.

Ever since, Teagan has kept in touch. She texts regularly, and we meet up at least once a month. She's the only real friend I've ever had.

I check my phone shortly after the police leave, and there's almost like a sixth-sense message from her.

> All okay? Haven't heard this week. Fancy a
> catch-up tomorrow? T xxx

Teagan is like a big sister and mother all rolled into one. Ten years older than me, she hauled me back from the brink of madness after everything that happened.

> Tomorrow sounds good. I've so much to tell
> you. Blanche has just died. XX

I add a horror face alongside a sobbing emoji.

I watch the screen, and soon she's typing. Her phone is glued to her hand.

> OMG. How dreadful! How's Jed? Come to me at 11? XX

I type:

> Will do. Thanks XX

Jed isn't a fan of Teagan's. He feels threatened by how close we are. But apart from Jed, she's the only person in my life who knows my story. I don't think I've ever needed her as much as I do now.

* * *

Jed and I manage only fitful sleep, but we're both still up early. Jed is subdued, uncommunicative, and when I tell him I'm off to see Teagan, he doesn't protest. He's too wrapped up in what's happened, and is staying at home for a few days.

'I need to phone round,' he says, ticking names off a list. 'When will you be back?' he asks without looking up.

'Not sure. I'll text.'

'Okay.'

I pop a kiss on top of his head.

He takes my hand, grips it so tightly that I'm the one to grimace.

'Ouch.'

'Don't ever leave me, Izzy. Promise me.'

'Why do you say that?'

'You're all I've got now.'

He manages to hold the tears in check.

I kiss him again, this time on the cheek. I don't say anything else. What more can I say?

44

Teagan lives at the opposite end of town, in a small semi-detached maisonette. It's five minutes by car, twenty on foot. I opt to walk and clear my head.

Teagan's own mum died about a year after Jed and I got married. She likes living on her own, and I doubt she'll ever marry.

'Three cats and two dogs are all I need,' she says.

Teagan, like me and Jed, isn't too worried about appearance. Yet when she opens the door I'm shocked. Devoid of make-up, her straggly hair unbrushed, and dressed in baggy trousers and tatty yellow t-shirt, she looks like a down-and-out. But I've never been more pleased to see anyone.

Before we speak, I collapse against her.

'Oh, Izzy,' she says, soothing down my hair.

After a lingering hug, we head for the kitchen where the mugs are out, and the kettle on the boil.

'Tea? Coffee?'

'Either.'

'Something stronger? I've got wine opened.'

She lifts a bottle from the fridge, shakes it in front of me. Her smile is like a warm blanket. I'd almost forgotten her wicked grin.

'Why not? A small glass though.'

I'm trying not to drink, but I need help to unwind. I'm coiled tight as a spring. A small glass must be better than rocketing blood pressure.

I've decided not to tell Teagan that I'm twelve weeks pregnant. It's still early days, and I don't want to jinx it. Also, I don't want it to affect her responses to Jed's infidelity. I've enough to tell her.

'I'll pour, and you tell me all about it.'

She knows I'm struggling, can read me like a book.

Five minutes later, a platter of nibbles in front of us, we settle at the breakfast bar.

'To Blanche,' she says, clinking our glasses.

'To Blanche.'

It feels odd, as if we're celebrating. Shouldn't we be sad?

'Right, Izzy. What's been going on?'

'It's Jed. He's got another woman.'

Her glass nearly slips to the floor, and she catches it just in time.

'Nooooo. You're not serious.' Her eyes are agog.

'I've been watching him. Yes, he has another woman. And...'

'Go on.' Her happy face evaporates.

'A son, I think.'

It all comes tumbling out. I never thought I'd be able to share, but it feels so good. And once I start, I can't stop. I tell her everything. Well, almost everything.

Teagan doesn't take long to respond.

'You need to confront him, Izzy.'

'I can't. I'm too scared.'

'Of what?'

'That he'll leave me.'

'He might leave you anyway. You need to ask.'

She gets up, puts an arm round my shoulder.

'I know you don't like asking questions, but this is different. It's Jed. He's not your dad.'

I tell her about watching from the café. About Jed's accident. The lies. All the lies. Finally, I tell her about how Blanche died.

'You don't think Jed had anything to do with his mother's death?'

She puts a hand over her mouth.

'I don't know what to think any more. I think the police are treating it as an accident, as there's no evidence to the contrary. It's not like when I murdered Dad.'

'You did not murder your father!'

She's told me this hundreds of times, but I know I'm to blame. What is murder? I didn't even own up to manslaughter.

'He wouldn't have died if I hadn't screamed. I wanted him to die, and he did. I carried on yelling, and prayed he'd tumble backwards.'

'That doesn't make you guilty of murder. We've been through this. How many times?'

'Maybe Jed knew how easy it was to get away with murder. Pushing someone down stone stairs is pretty foolproof.' I give a wry smile, a light puff of laughter. 'I've gone over a thousand times with Jed how Dad died.'

'I think your imagination is running riot. You need to worry about what Jed is up to. With this other woman. I wouldn't even think about how Blanche died. Leave that to the police. She was elderly, wobbly on her feet.'

Teagan gets up, wanders round the kitchen, and lifts the

wine bottle out from the fridge again. I put a hand on top of my half-drunk glass, while she tops herself up.

I don't mention the keyring, as I've said enough. She might make me go to the police, hand it in, but it's all too much. Would I really want to know if Jed killed Blanche? How would it help anything? I killed my own father, so I'd be a hypocrite to land Jed in it. Even if he didn't do anything, it would mean more questioning, more upset.

'Right. When are you going to confront him? You know if you don't, you're as sneaky as he is.'

She laughs, trying to tone down the harshness. But she's right. I need to get a move on.

I don't own up to trying to dig out information through my column, as it makes things even more complicated. And I don't want Teagan thinking I'm any crazier than she already does.

'I will. Promise.'

And I mean it. I need to pick my moment, but it can't wait much longer.

I'll have decisions to make once he talks. He'll either come clean, or tell me more lies, but I'm terrified of what the future might hold.

Meanwhile, I'm drawing up a plan to find out as much as I can beforehand. If I know everything, then I'll be better prepared.

Teagan has convinced me I need to act.

45

Jed stays at home the next couple of days, phoning relatives and friends of Blanche. He can't plan the funeral until the body is released, but it looks as if the death will be logged as an accident.

We don't talk much, and whenever I try to comfort him, he nudges me aside. Saying he'll need time to come to terms with what's happened.

'At least the police have backed off. Can you believe they think I might have killed my own mother?' He repeats this on a loop, disbelief etched on his wrinkled brow.

'They have to do their job. They need to consider the possibility that someone might have killed her. It is possible.'

'Whatever. There's nothing we can do now.'

'Aren't you curious?'

'No, not really. It'll not bring her back.'

He doesn't want to talk about it. He says he'll go into work tomorrow, as he needs to get back to some sort of normality.

I haven't managed to get any work done, and Grayson is chasing me for column copy. His sympathy doesn't run deep when I tell him what happened. *It wasn't your mother* is his angle.

But I don't want to risk him bringing someone in to cover for me, not at the moment when I'm using my column to weed out personal answers.

Blanche's death has given me an idea for my next column. I keep going over the two messages from Hawkeye. The repetition of 'he's still with you' feels as if it was meant for me. I'm likely paranoid, but I can't discard the responses. I'm certain Hawkeye is using the column to communicate with me.

If Hawkeye is someone who knows me, someone involved in my life, then running a piece on Blanche's death might weed them out. The thought terrifies me. Why? Because I'm not convinced her death was an accident. The broken keyring could have been lying on the cellar floor for weeks, and maybe my mind is just in overdrive. But deep down, her death feels too random. Too convenient.

With Blanche dead, there are a few people who might benefit. Adam Finch for one. He's been inside the building, as has Madison. Adam will have as much to gain from her death as Jed. If not more.

Last night, I had the most dreadful nightmares. I was standing at the top of the cellar stairs, and felt someone creep up behind. I was too scared to turn, but knew I was going to fall. The fear has stuck, even though I'm wide awake.

With Jed mooching around today, I decide to work from the library in town. There's no way I could concentrate in Angelo's, as I'm not ready to face Adam or Candy, or to see Madison through the window. I need quiet to piece my thoughts together.

* * *

I pick up a rare mug of Starbucks coffee on the way, cringing at the bitterness, so unlike the smooth Italian blend that I've grown used to. I think pregnancy might be altering my tastebuds, and telling me that I need to cut back on the caffeine. It's going to be tough.

When I reach the library, the upstairs space where I like to work is already busy. But it's quiet, that's all that matters. There's one cubicle free at the far end, and no one looks when I slip in, and take out my laptop.

My fingers don't linger for long, as I've been toying with the words in my mind since Blanche's fall. I can't mention murder, but maybe someone reading my words might. Someone with an agenda.

46

Dear Bella,

My aunt, my mother's only sister, lives on her own and is no longer able to cope. She's got trouble moving around, and no longer eats properly. But she refuses to move into care.

She screams and yells whenever the subject comes up. She also doesn't want to leave her own home, which she has lived in for forty years. It's a long time!

Mum says she can't have her move in with her, as Mum worries my aunt might also be losing her marbles. Problem is, Auntie is increasingly suspicious that Mum might have ulterior motives... that she might be after her own sister's money. This is making her more determined than ever not to even consider moving.

What do you suggest? Moving her into decent assisted-living accommodation is really expensive and would eat into all her hard-earned capital. Actually, it would eat it all up. Mum can't help with the expenses as she is really strapped herself, and I certainly don't have any spare cash.

It's a tricky one. What do you suggest?

Best regards,
Confused (and worried)

* * *

Hi Confused,

It's a difficult one when elderly relatives whom we love can no longer look after themselves. And I'm sorry to say that it will likely only get worse.

Perhaps take her to look at a few retirement properties where there are full-time wardens. If she can afford it, some even have spa centres with swimming pools and on-site restaurants. Maybe when she actually visits these places, sees what's on offer for herself, she might decide this is the way forward. Until she does, she'll likely be reluctant to leave the safety and familiarity of her own home.

As for suspicions about reasons for wanting her to move, and sell up, these are sadly all too familiar between families. At least your aunt has caring relatives who want the best for her. This is, unfortunately, not always the case, and money can become quite an issue.

Thanks for sharing, and I hope this has been of some help.

Bella

My fingers hover over the keys, as I reread what I've come up with. Grayson won't be too impressed with the deviation from unfaithful spouses, and domestic noir. The content won't make him drool, but if I spice up the second piece, it might keep him happy. An idea is already swirling round in my thoughts. Should I, or shouldn't I?

I glance round the library. The six computer cubicles are

occupied, and other than the click of keyboards there is total silence. Yet once again I have the strangest feeling I'm being watched. The idea of a stalker is likely all in my mind, but the notion won't go away.

I get up to stretch my legs, and head for the toilet. My stomach is gurgling, the morning sickness getting worse, and I'm constantly swallowing back the nausea. I peer in the grainy mirror, and can't believe how pale I look. My eyes are dark ringed like a panda's, and my lips dry and cracked. I look even worse than Jed.

Suddenly, I feel a blip. Nothing earth-shattering, but a definite blip. I look down at my stomach. My growing companion is talking to me, reminding me to be careful.

'I will be careful, you can depend on it,' I whisper. 'I'll think carefully about what I do next.' I caress my mini bump with gentle fingers.

Once back at my laptop, I go through what I've written. It's certainly to the point, with its aim to draw out Hawkeye again. I've no proof, just gut instinct, that they're someone I know. If so, they might have had a connection to Blanche's death. It's a slim hope they'll respond, but it's worth a try.

If nothing comes back, then I'll accept that my hormones must be playing havoc with reality.

47

I fire off the draft of my letter to Grayson, and set to packing away my things. It's then I notice two new messages on my phone.

The first is from Jed.

> When will you be back? I'm starving. What's for lunch? Missing you XX

His loss of appetite certainly hasn't lasted too long.

I'm tempted to tell him to check the fridge, or remind him that Tesco is a fifteen-minute walk away, and Uber Eats is pretty quick. Instead I play fair with my reply.

> Still working. I'll cook something nice for supper. Hope you can make do till then. XX

It's uncomfortable adding kisses, but he's still my Jed. I haven't given up on him yet.

However, I do get the feeling he's suspicious about something. Whenever I don't reply immediately to his texts, or reply in a way he's not expecting, he becomes inquisitive. Almost obsessive, wondering why I'm not around. Since Blanche's death, he's texting twice as often. They say cheaters are extra vigilant with their partners, and this could be making Jed more wary.

The second message is from Adam Finch.

> If you're in town do you fancy a coffee? Hoping all okay after what happened. Adam.

(He's attached a sad emoji face followed by a hug emoji.)

As soon as I've read the message, I spin round, half-expecting to see him lurking behind the shelves. Does he know I'm in town? The quiet comfort has been replaced by an unsettling silence. Even the rhythmic click of keyboards has dried up.

How does Adam know I'm about? Maybe he doesn't and is just hoping. Maybe he wants to pick my brains about what is going to happen to Blanche's house, and when he'll be able to demolish the terrace.

I'm certainly more suspicious of Adam, now that I know he's Madison's brother. Does he know what Madison and Jed are up to? And does he know how close they are? Maybe Madison is involved in the terrace development with her brother.

> Okay. Meet in Angelo's in 15 minutes? Could do with a coffee

I reread several times before I press send.

A thumbs-up emoji instantly bounces back.

I must be crazy, but I'm certain there's more to Adam than meets the eye. Because no way could he be interested in me.

48

When I reach the café, I don't immediately see Adam.

He's settled in the alcove at the far end where it's dark, and dimly lit. His eyes are fixed on his mobile, and he only looks up when I get close.

'Izzy. Hi.' He stands, and opens his arms.

For an awful second I think he's going to zoom in for a hug. I'd forgotten how tall and muscular he is. My cheeks redden.

'Hi.'

'What'll you have to drink? A macchiato?'

I'm oddly chuffed that he's remembered, but I can't stomach more caffeine.

'A peppermint tea, please.'

'Oh. You must have had a couple of coffees already?'

'Yep. In one.'

He walks with confidence towards the counter. Candy's eyes light up. She toys with her hair, runs her tongue over newly glossed pink lips.

I wonder what they're saying. Their body language is familiar. Adam has got his flirtatious hat on, and Candy's laugh is loud. Out of the blue, the baby squirms. It's like a reminder that Candy's and Adam's familiarity is nothing to do with me. I've no idea why watching them makes me feel unsettled.

Adam chatters away as Candy froths the milk. Usually a waitress brings the drinks to the table, but Adam's happy to wait. Candy glances my way with an icy stare. She must be jealous because why else is she so frosty? Reading between the lines, I suspect she has a crush on Adam. Could they have gone out? But Adam must be in his early thirties, and Candy only in her late teens.

'Here you are. One peppermint tea, madam.' Adam sets it down with a flourish.

'Thanks.'

His long legs have trouble getting under the snug-to-the-wall table. He stretches them out to the side, so close that I could touch them. A tingle goes down my spine.

'Well, what have you been up to? Hope you're okay after what happened, and how's Jed coping?'

His eyes crinkle with concern.

'I'm doing much better than Jed. He's really struggling.'

'Well, it was his mum.'

'He's still at home. I had to get out of the house for a bit, so have been working from the library.'

'On your column? I read it last week. Hot topics.' His eyes widen, and he laughs.

'Hot topics sell. Affairs and cheating top of the list.' I roll my eyes.

'I can imagine,' he says.

I bet he can.

Anyway, we chat about work, the weather, and even touch on Christmas. When he asks about my family, siblings, or lack of them, I keep it simple. I tell him I'm an only child, both parents dead.

'Oh.' He looks serious. 'I'm sorry.'

'Thanks. But I'm fine.'

I take a deep breath and take my chance.

'What about you? Brothers or sisters?'

I find it hard to look at him, as I know he has a sister, but I'm willing him to talk.

He pulls himself up, recoils his legs.

'One sister.'

'Older? Younger?'

'Older. Just a couple of years. She's thirty-four.'

'Is she married?' I bite down on my bottom lip.

'No.'

He goes quiet, as if swallowing back information.

I'm struggling with how I'm going to ask if she has any children, as it would be an odd follow-on question, considering she's not married. I needn't have worried because, as if reading my thoughts, he tells me.

'She's got a kid, though. Great wee lad.'

'Oh. That's nice.'

The corner spot where we're sitting is like a sauna, an overhead heater pointing directly onto our table. I must look like a beetroot, and keep worrying a hand round my damp neck.

'How old is he? Is she with the father?'

It sounds like an interrogation, but then I suppose it is.

To give Adam his due, he doesn't hesitate.

'Benjamin is two, and no. She's not with the father. The lad was the result of a one-night stand.' He tuts. 'That's my sister for you.'

49

I want to ask if his sister still sees the father, or if the man is involved with the boy. Does he come to see them? Does he pay maintenance?

Although I know most of the answers now, it's tempting to carry on. Adam is a good listener, relaxed, and easy company. At least the words *one-night stand* should give me mild comfort. If he'd used the word *affair*, I don't know how I'd have reacted.

Rather than carry on talking about Madison, Benjamin, and his father, I switch tack and tell Adam about Jed. How we met, about his work, things we do together. I'm careful not to give Adam the wrong idea. He doesn't tell me much about himself, other than he's keen to get started on the development at Miners' Terrace. His eyes light up in the telling.

'Blanche's death should speed up the start date,' he says. 'Sorry, that sounds unfeeling.'

'It's okay. I understand.'

He looks genuinely sorry, but he can't take the words back. He has a lot to gain from her death, and the thought sets my teeth on edge.

I check my watch, and am shocked a full hour has passed.

'I need to get back to work,' I say.

'Snap.'

We pull on our layers, and I stroll slightly ahead of Adam as we head for the exit. Candy is busy with a customer, but still manages to yell after us.

'See you later.'

Although she says this to all the regulars, she doesn't usually scream. Especially when the customers are halfway out the door.

Adam turns, and gives the briefest of waves. Did he wink at her? Jeez, I need to get out into the fresh air, and breathe. I'm so strung up.

He asks if I'd like to go for a drink one evening, saying he'll leave it up to me.

'You've got my number. Right?' he asks.

'Yep.'

I'd like to meet him again, but not with romance in mind. I'm married to Jed, and would never be disloyal. I made my vows, and with a baby on the way, I need to be extra careful. Yet I'm desperate to pick his brains more about Madison. And to talk about Miners' Terrace. The thought that Blanche was killed won't go away. Adam could have let himself in, assuming he has a key, and pushed her down the stairs.

He's certainly more upbeat than I've seen him, his mood likely helped by what's happened. Jed told me that Adam Finch and his development company will make serious money once the building works are complete. Luxury townhouses with a capital L. Jed also owned up that we'll also make a healthy profit if we sell up quickly.

I head back to the library, picking up a sandwich on the way. I'm far from hungry, but know I have to eat. Another hour tops, and I should be done. First, I'm desperate to get the words down for my second letter while the thoughts are buzzing.

The library is even quieter than it was earlier. This time round there are three empty cubicles, but again I pick the one nearest the toilet. In case I have to make a dash for it.

As I start to type, I know I'm baiting Hawkeye. Whoever they are. I must be crazy. If it really is someone I know, I dread to think what their response to the letter about the aunt living on her own will be. My heart races when I imagine they might have a link to Blanche's death. I've always trusted my sixth sense, it's how I've always got by. Now it's taking me down the road of suspicion.

Soon I have the second letter typed up in draft form, ready to send.

If Jed reads my next column, he'll likely put two and two together.

50

Dear Bella,

I've never had an affair before, but this guy from work is so persistent and so bloody gorgeous that I'm sorely tempted.

My husband strayed, okay, it was only the once, but I've never really been able to forgive him. It's always there, in the back of my mind, even though it was a few years ago. He promised he'd never do it again, insisting it was only a drunken one-night stand.

Anyway, Travis (this isn't the guy's real name, of course) bought me love-heart chocolates the other day and told me he's never been so in love before.

What should I do? There's only one stumbling block about going in headlong. I'm pregnant. And no one else knows yet. Not even my husband. Help! What should I do?

In Two Minds

* * *

Dear In Two Minds,

Thanks for sharing your quandary. It's a difficult one, that's for sure. It must be very hard living with a man who has cheated on you. Even if it was only the once. And as I keep repeating, leopards don't change their spots.

That said, only you know if your husband really means that he'll not stray again. Being pregnant makes the situation doubly difficult, as I am presuming the baby is your husband's?

Does Travis know you're pregnant? This is very important, and I'm sorry to say that he might not be as interested in a pregnant woman. He may only be looking for some excitement with a married woman. Even a future together. But a baby certainly complicates things.

My suggestion, although it won't be easy, is to come clean. To both your husband about being pregnant (he deserves to know) and Travis as well. If Travis really does love you, he might surprise you.

Until you know each man's reaction to the news, then you'll not be able to make a clear decision on the way forward. I don't like to be the voice of doom here, but I think it's more likely your husband will be thrilled, and Travis might run a mile.

I wish you the best of luck with everything. Especially with the baby. Keep me posted on what you decide to do.

Best,

Bella

It's like writing in a diary, therapeutic getting my own thoughts and worries down on paper.

While I'm desperate to tell Jed about the baby, and will do

soon, I've no intention of having an affair with Adam. It's all a fantasy, and spicy content for my column.

Waiting for the weekend responses will be torture. It's so masochistic, but I'm desperate to find out if someone is watching me, the way I do Jed. Hawkeye's answers have certainly hit a nerve.

There's a link between everything that's going on. Jed and Madison. Blanche's death. The little boy. Adam. Even Candy is in the story somewhere.

Meanwhile Teagan is on my back, telling me I need to confront Jed. *Now*. She's even threatened to talk to him herself if I don't. Yet old habits die hard. When you've spent most of your childhood communicating through notes, it's not so easy to ask straight out. I'm still praying for answers without the need for questions.

The magazine, as always, will hit the racks early Saturday morning. This Saturday I've decided to leave home first thing. I'll tell Jed I'm going for a jog, but instead I'll head for the library. I need somewhere quiet to go through the responses on my own.

I won't want Jed anywhere near me.

51

Jed has been lounging on the sofa since supper. He's skimming through a magazine, with the TV running in the background. It's the most relaxed I've seen him since Blanche died. This would be the ideal time to confront him, get it all out in the open. I could tell him what I know, what I've seen. And ask him what the hell is going on.

I only look away when a text pings onto my phone.

Have you spoken to Jed yet? YOU MUST! T xxx

It's the third text from Teagan today. She's not going to back off. She means well, but she's pushing too hard. I glance at Jed, lost in his own world, and delete the message.

Despite Teagan's pestering, I'm not there yet. Instead, I've come up with a plan, a new angle to glean more information. Only once I have the full deck will I confront him. That will be the end game.

'Jed.'

'Hmm?' He doesn't look up.

'Saturday. I'm thinking of asking Jordan, Giselle, Marty and Taylor over for supper.'

He sets the magazine down, slides his glasses up onto his head.

'Why?'

'I thought you'd enjoy seeing your old friends. It might help take your mind off things.'

'I'm fine. You don't need to worry. It'd be a lot of hard work for you.'

'I don't mind. Really.'

'But you can't stand Jordan. And Marty for that matter.'

He mutes the telly, cursing when the remote slips from his hand.

'Shit.'

'I thought it might cheer you up.'

'Honestly, I'm fine.' He forces a smile. 'Stop worrying about me.'

'Giselle messaged when she heard about Blanche, and said it would be nice to get together.'

'You didn't tell me?'

'It didn't seem important. We've had so many messages. Anyway, I suggested a get-together might lift your spirits.'

I like Giselle. We might have become good friends, if it wasn't for her obnoxious husband, Jordan.

'Perhaps another time. I'm not sure I'm up to entertaining yet.'

I grit my teeth, breathe in, then hit him with it.

'Thing is. They're all free this Saturday.'

The silence seems to go on forever. I can almost hear his brain working.

'You mean you've already asked them?' The accusatory tone is mild, but it's there.

'Yep.' I give him puppy-dog eyes. 'You're not mad, are you?'

His shoulders slump, and he rubs his neck, twisting it from side to side. A crack sounds like the snap of a wishbone.

'I'm not mad, but wish you'd told me first.'

'Sorry. I will do next time.'

I go and pop a kiss on his cheek. His hands shoot out and grab mine.

'Come here, Izzy Hardcastle. If it makes you happy, then it's okay by me.'

He pouts his lips for a full-on kiss, and I giggle.

'Love you,' he says.

'I know.' It's a lie, as I've no idea how he feels about me any more. With another woman and a son in the background, how can I know?

Yet when he holds me tight, kisses me long and lovingly, it's hard to doubt his feelings. If Madison was just a one-night stand, perhaps he really has regrets. Perhaps all he wants is to save me hurt, but I doubt a confession could hurt more than all the lies.

The last thing I want is to have Jordan and Marty to dinner. But it's the only way I could think of to move things on. Jordan has a big mouth, and I shouldn't have too much trouble getting him to talk about Ibiza, and Jed's stag do. That is the most likely place Jed met Madison, and the most likely time that she got pregnant.

Planning the dinner party will keep me busy. What with that and reading my column responses, Saturday is going to be a long day.

52

Once Jed has calmed down, having apparently put the dinner party conversation to bed, I decide to bite the bullet and ask one more thing. I leave him browsing a *Top Gear* magazine when I pop back through to the kitchen.

I open a bottle of Merlot, and pour out two glasses. A large one for him, and a thimbleful for me.

'Fancy watching another movie?' he suggests when I reappear.

I nod, and snuggle up alongside him on the sofa. He wraps me in his strong arms, fiddles with my hair, and curls the ends round his fingers. It feels like old times, and it's tough to spoil the moment.

'Can I ask you something first?'

'Go on. Hit me.'

'I was wondering...' I swallow hard.

'What were you wondering?'

'It's about Madison. Blanche's cleaner.'

'Madison?' He unwinds his fingers sharpish. 'What about Madison?'

'I was thinking, now she's out of a job, that she might help me round the house.'

His arms fall away, and he groans.

'I'm not that heavy, am I?' I giggle nervously.

'It's my ribs. They're still really sore.'

He rubs a hand across his chest.

'She could help me clear out all the cupboards, and spring clean the house.'

I've started, and need to push him.

'Why can't you do it?'

He furrows his brow, and nudges me along the sofa.

'Grayson has offered me the chance to interview B-list celebrities online for the magazine. It would be on top of my column work, but the money's good. I'd be extra busy.'

This isn't a complete lie. Grayson has been mulling the idea, although there's nothing concrete yet. I don't feel guilty embellishing the truth, as it's the only excuse I could come up with that Jed might believe without arousing suspicions.

'Oh. You didn't say.'

He looks offended that I haven't told him before. His mouth droops.

'And you tell me everything?' My eyes widen.

He takes a couple of sips of wine, swivelling the glass by the stem.

'I don't think Madison is looking for more work, to be honest.'

'You told me she was hard up, and cleaning paid the bills.'

'I can ask if you insist.'

I doubt he'll ever ask, but I'll remind him later that he said he would.

'Thanks. Where's she from, by the way?'

I'm on a roll, and can't stop.

'She lives in town, I think.'

'No, silly. I mean, where are she and Adam from originally? He sounds as if he's from Yorkshire.'

'No idea, to be honest. Now can we get back to wine and telly?'

He starts flicking from channel to channel.

'Does she have a family?'

Jed flicks more intently, tutting when the signal comes and goes.

'What?'

'A family. Does Madison have a family?' I regret snapping, but I'm like a dog with a bone.

'I think Adam mentioned once that their parents are both dead.'

'Children?'

'Not sure, to be honest. Listen, can we get back to watching a movie?'

By not telling me about the boy, he's digging his hole deeper. I struggle off the sofa, coming over hot and nauseous for the umpteenth time today, and am about to make a dash for the cloakroom when he throws out a piece of the puzzle without prompting.

'She did work in Ibiza for a while. Bar work, or something like that.'

My stomach lurches.

'Sorry, I feel really queasy.'

Ten times worse than a moment ago.

I put a hand over my mouth, and dash from the room. I bolt the toilet door, and collapse onto the floor.

Jed has at least mentioned Ibiza. It's a small step towards the truth.

He didn't mention meeting her there, but I'm now almost certain it's where they slept together. Either as a one-night stand, or for the first time.

53

It's Friday morning, 7 a.m., and Jed has left for work.

I take a few minutes and scribble a shopping list for Saturday's dinner party, as the aim is to shop today. Tomorrow, I'll be too busy dealing with all the column responses. I'm not sure whether the dinner party or checking responses fills me with more dread.

The police haven't been back since we gave our statements. It's looking more and more likely that Blanche's death will be logged as a tragic accident.

Jed is desperate to get on with the funeral arrangements, and to get probate sorted as soon as possible. He's the only beneficiary in the will, so it shouldn't be too difficult. He's not ready though to sort through her stuff, so I've promised to help and to make a start in a few days' time.

Today, before I head for the library, I decide to visit the café first. The thought that Jed might restart his visits to Madison fills me horror, but I need to know.

He hasn't got a new bike yet, and rather than walk to the station this morning, he took his car. He said his body was particularly achy. He left early enough that if he does go into town first, he should easily find a parking space.

I keep checking my watch, knowing that I need to get a move on. Ten minutes after Jed has left, I lock up and head for the market-square car park. Jed never uses it, so I'm confident I wouldn't bang into him even if he hasn't gone straight to the station.

I park up, and jog the short distance to Angelo's to try and loosen the tension, but my body is so tightly coiled that every step is an effort.

Candy is opening up when I appear through the alleyway. It's now exactly 7.30. She hauls back the heavy door, pins it back, and with a faint nod, marches back towards the counter.

She seems to have given up talking to me altogether, and thrusts my coffee across without comment, before busying herself with the pastry display.

It's as if she's had a character transplant. Not only is she acting on the rude side of churlish, but she's binned the pink theme. Dressing head to toe in black, as if in mourning, seems to be the new look. She's rebelling against something, or someone, but I've no spare energy to worry.

Instead I head straight to my seat and start the countdown. It's 7.38.

The café windows are coated with an early-winter fog, and I have to rub a sleeve against the pane to clear a circle.

The coffee tastes extra bitter today, and leaves a sour coating on my tongue. The acid reflux from my stomach isn't helping.

I start counting down the seconds, petrified that Jed might still turn up. I'm praying he's gone straight to work.

All at once, a young, good-looking guy catches my eye as he ambles past. He glances through the window, but only for a second. He then looks right, left, and right again, before crossing over.

I'm suddenly bolt upright when I see where he's headed. I set my mug down, as my hands tremble. He's ringing the doorbell of the flat across the road, the same bell that Jed has been ringing for the past few months. It's 7.45 a.m. exactly.

A couple of minutes later, Madison appears. I might be shocked by seeing a strange handsome young man enter her apartment, but I'm even more shocked by what she's wearing.

Even through the frosted window glaze, you can't miss the red silk nightdress barely covered up by a matching gown. I gawp at her generous breasts. When Jed calls on her, if she's not already dressed, she's usually wrapped up in a button-up fleecy dressing gown, and sometimes in a flowing winceyette night-dress. Certainly not in anything sexy.

But today, she's dressed up for more than coffee and pleas-antries, and there's no sign of the little lad clinging to her ankles.

54

I sit for ages staring out the window, unable to tear my eyes away.

I'm so wound up, I'm scared I'll have a full-blown panic attack. I practise my breathing exercises, but they don't help. My mind is in freefall. The sight of the stranger visiting Madison has thrown me off course. Could she be a prostitute? Has Jed been visiting a prostitute all along? Or is this guy the dad, visiting his son? Possible scenarios swirl around in my head, and I think I might pass out. The sour taste from the coffee isn't helping.

I try and pull myself together, remembering that Madison usually dresses in mumsy nightwear when Jed visits. The young guy could be a boyfriend, even though I haven't seen him before. I wonder if Jed was going to visit today, and maybe Madison cancelled.

Teagan is right. I need to put a stop to it all. I've had enough. One more week, and that's it. At least I'm coming up with a plan to bring the whole sorry mess to an end once I've carried out a last bit of detective work.

I get out my phone, and send a reply to Teagan's latest round of texts.

> Please don't worry. One more week only. I
> promise. Love you too. XXXX

Somehow I make it to the library, where I let the silence massage my tangled thoughts. Instead of working on my column, I make notes about how I'm going to end it all. I fill several pages of a small pad, outlining the plan in detail.

Two hours later, I'm done.

* * *

Jed and I don't communicate much this evening as we're both so exhausted. I sense he doesn't want to talk about tomorrow's dinner party, and it's only mentioned as an afterthought when we crawl into bed.

'All okay for tomorrow?' he mumbles, pulling the duvet round his ears.

'Yes. Shopping done.'

Before I say any more, he's whistling in his sleep.

I manage to doze off and on, but it doesn't stop me waking every half hour or so, and checking the time. My mind is on full throttle.

There are the responses to my column. The dinner party. And added to the mix is the nature of Jed and Madison's relationship. Could she really be a prostitute?

At 6 a.m., bathed in sweat, I give in and get up. Jed stirs when he hears movement.

'Izzy? Where are you going? What time is it?' His voice is thick with sleep.

'It's early. You go back to sleep. I feel a bit nauseous, but I'll be fine.'

'If you're sure.'

It's strange that he's not concerned by my nausea. He used to fuss if I had so much as a sore finger. Pregnancy will be the last thing on his mind, especially as sex has dwindled to, at most, once a month.

He still tells me he can't wait to have children, but adds there's no hurry. We've got time on our side. When it's meant to be and all that. Little does he know I'm being eaten away knowing he already has a son.

I get dressed, as quietly as I can, willing him to go back to sleep.

'Will you be okay for tonight? The dinner party. We can always cancel,' he says. The hopeful tone is hard to miss, as he turns onto his back.

Thinking about the dinner party fills me with dread, but there's no way I'll cancel. It'll be a last chance to do some digging, and finding out about Ibiza is key.

'I'll be okay, stop worrying. I'm off for a walk to get some fresh air, then I'm popping by the library.'

'You're not going to work, are you?'

'Just to check out replies to my column. You know they start coming in Saturday morning.'

He lets out a deep sigh, and I think he's about to say something else, but instead rolls back onto his side.

'Whatever. Don't be too long though.'

'I'll be back at lunchtime. Now enjoy your lie-in. And...'

'Yes?'

'Maybe you'd set the table for tonight. That would really help.'

'Will do.'

I land a kiss on his forehead, and close the door gently after me.

55

I have a peppermint tea, and a piece of toast to line my stomach before I leave the house.

Everywhere is quiet. There's little traffic, and the pavements are empty. I jog lightly, and soon fall into a soothing rhythm.

I opt to avoid Angelo's this morning, and instead pick up a coffee-to-go from the sandwich shop. Afterwards I head for the newsagents and linger outside until it opens.

Jed doesn't get why I buy a hard copy of the magazine when I can get it online. I tell him it's not the same. It's much nicer reading a thick glossy copy, and it's still a thrill to see my name in print.

When the doors open, eight o'clock on the dot, I hurtle towards the magazine rack. I scour the shelves, panicking when I can't see the magazine. A few minutes pass until I spot a single copy of *Echoes of London* on a top shelf.

Once I've paid, I stuff the magazine in my rucksack, and head the long way round to the library. It won't be open for another half hour, but it's good to be outside. The morning sickness is getting worse, not helped by the nerves, and I'm so dizzy I'm scared I'll pass out.

I take a detour past the small herb garden at the back of the library grounds, and sit down on a bench. I could sit here all day. I want to forget everything that is going on, and wind the clock back a couple of years. When life seemed so full of promise, and Jed and I were so in love. I'm about to let the tears roll when the baby squirms. It's too early for kicks and bumps, but it's enough to make me smile.

'Don't worry. We'll be okay. We've got each other,' I bend my head and whisper.

56

As soon as the library doors open, I scuttle through, and head straight up the stairs to the first floor. I decamp to my usual cubicle, open my laptop at my column's Facebook page, and smooth out the magazine alongside.

With shaky hands, I turn to the page at the back of the magazine. I scan the two phony letters I composed. What to do with sick relatives living on their own, and is it okay for a pregnant woman to have some fun?

There's a large round clock on the front wall, and the second hand is like a hypnotist's pendulum. The minutes drag, and it's 8.52 when the first response lands. At 9.10 the second, 9.20 the third, and by ten o'clock I have already nine responses. Slowly, tentatively, I read each one as they come through.

We had to move Mum out when she nearly set fire to her kitchen! We had her sectioned before she blew up the whole street. But it was the best thing we could have done. Mum is now very comfortable in assisted-living accommodation. It's really expensive, and eating up all her savings. But it's our mum, and she deserves the best.

Care homes are a rip off. Families should take care of their own!

Relatives wait for the elderly to die. Desperate for an early inheritance. My dad abused me, so I wouldn't care if he wasn't here. And I could do with his money.

I delete the third response. Abuse is on the list of content that can't get through. Even the word *abuse* breaches Grayson's rules.

Once I get to work, and nothing sinister catches my eye, my heart calms down. I get up to stretch my legs, and grab a beaker of water from the dispenser in the corner. An old lady reading a book by the window smiles at me, and I think of my own mum. She loved to read, and encouraged me in the silence to keep my head in a book. She was right, reading transported me to magical worlds. Worlds of make-believe. I blink back the tears.

Before I get back to the screen, I check my phone messages. There's already one from Jed.

Laid the table. Going into town to check out the bike shop. What time are you back? XX

I wonder why he's texting, as I told him I'd be back around lunchtime. I keep my reply brief.

> Not sure yet. Thanks for doing table. XX

Mention of the bike shop winds me up. I'll blow a gasket if he spends what little savings we have on a new bike before a car for me. But one thing at a time. I need to switch my phone off.

I settle back into work mode, and scroll through three more responses. Nothing nasty. Until I see it. Oh my God. It stands out. Loud and clear. A message from Hawkeye1234.

> The kindest thing of all is death. Everyone is out of their misery then. Right? More money for waiting relatives, and the end to suffering. If she had a nasty accident, I'd be inclined to turn a blind eye. Wouldn't you?

My vision blurs, and I've trouble focusing. This message must be meant for me. Like the other Hawkeye messages, it's warning me not to upset the status quo, and this time, to turn a blind eye to any fatal accidents. It's ambiguous at best, but it's loaded, standing out above the other measured replies. It's as if the respondent knows there's already been an accident. It can't be a coincidence. Could Hawkeye be in some way linked to Blanche's death? I might have a broken-off piece of keyring, but on its own it proves nothing.

My heart batters in my chest, and rather than risk passing out on the library floor, I grab my phone, and bag, and stagger down the stairs. I leave my laptop in the cubicle, for when I dare to come back.

First, I need fresh air. I need to breathe.

The sky overhead is black, rain threatening to explode from the heavens. But I don't care. I pull my hood up, and start walking. Walking. Walking. Walking.

If I was brave enough, I'd walk to the ends of the earth, and never come back.

57

An hour later, and I've calmed down just enough to face the library one last time.

I'd love to collect my stuff, and go straight home, but I can't. Hawkeye would win if I gave up. One thing I do know is that I'm not a quitter.

I've more responses to get through, and while I'm on a roll, I need to keep going. I brace myself again for what's to come, allowing myself one more hour, tops.

All the distress of the past few months makes me realise how much I miss working in a library. In the silent world of books rather than people. Even communicating through my column has become a challenge. People are the problem, not the work. I'd work 24/7 if I didn't have to deal with individuals.

The small cubicle wraps around me, and the enclosure gives a momentary illusion of safety. I take a sip of water from my plastic cup, and hunker down.

The responses to the second letter, the one from the fictional person asking if it would be okay to have an affair when pregnant, are starting to come in.

So far they're much as I would expect.

Leave your cheating husband.

Have some fun.

An open marriage perhaps?

I take a short break from looking at the screen, my eyes dry and scratchy, and open the hard copy magazine. Flicking through the pages, scanning a few articles, gives me momentary relief from checking my Facebook feed.

When I dare get back to it, replies to both letters are piling in. It's not even midday, and there are over another 100 messages.

Then I see it. A new one from Hawkeye.

If you go out with this Travis, then you're worse than your husband. You're lucky to have him. And are you serious? You'd go out with another guy when you're pregnant? Aren't you scared what might happen to you or the other guy when your husband finds out? Or someone else for that matter?

I make a grab for the plastic water cup, but knock it sideways. Water splashes over my jeans which are already sodden from the rain.

I've had enough.

58

I trudge home, no idea how I'll face Jed. Or the dinner party. I'd love to crawl under the duvet and sleep forever.

I must have been mad, baring all in my column. The aim was to get some answers, opinions, ideas about what to do. It seems crazy the more I think about it. Teagan is right, it's time to talk to Jed, and stop hiding behind my own excuses, and the dread at what he might reveal.

Each step forward is an effort, as Hawkeye's messages play on a loop. Could Jed be replying to my column? Warning me off from having an affair with some fictitious man? If it is Jed, and he suspects the letters relate to me, wouldn't he likely have brought up the topic of pregnancy during the week? Perhaps in a roundabout way at least. Does he know I've shared a coffee with Adam Finch? Perhaps he does, and is jealous.

The thing that strikes me about the Hawkeye messages is the subtle warnings. *Not to rock the boat. Leave things as they are. Be grateful for your husband.* The last message has a red alert as to what might happen if I did stray.

But it surely can't be Jed. He'd talk to me directly, wouldn't he? No idea why I think this, as he's got a whole other secret life going on. But my Jed would never hurt anyone. *Gentle as a lamb? Or a wolf in sheep's clothing?* My mind is all over the place. I think I've already gone mad.

I try and conjure up other people who might be Hawkeye. I'm 99 per cent certain it's not some random reader.

Candy's face pops into my head. She's been really off lately, likely because of Adam. Perhaps she's really jealous that he seems interested in me. She knows I write the column, so maybe she's warning me off him. But why would she be interested in killing an old person? She's never even met Blanche, as far as I know. Perhaps she'd kill for Adam, as love can make you do crazy things.

Then there's Madison. Reasons for her trying to get at me are complicated. I can see why she might be happy Blanche is dead, as it will give Jed more money to help continue to support her and Benjamin. Then Adam is her brother. With Blanche out of the way, he stands to make a lot of money from the development. Maybe they're doing a two-pronged attack to make me leave well alone.

By the time I reach the front door, I'm so drained from everything. I'd love to run away, and find a safe haven miles from anywhere, for me and the baby. Perhaps we really could cope without Jed.

I slip the key in the lock. It used to feel so good coming home, knowing Jed was waiting for me. He's still waiting, still saying he loves me, but everything has changed. My whole life feels as if it's built on a lie.

'Hi, I'm home.' No sooner have I called out than Jed appears in the hall.

'Izzy.' He kisses me on the lips, as if I've been gone for months.

For a brief second, I want to blurt it all out.

But when his phone pings with a message, the moment passes.

59

It's almost time for the guests. I head up for a shower, and Jed tells me not to be long. He seems even more nervous than I am.

I linger under the warm jets and think back to childhood, and what made me the way I am. I remember a fixation with jigsaws.

I'd crawl under the bed, lay out the pieces by torchlight, and quietly build the picture. I'd start with the four corners, then work along the edges. Patience, concentration, determination, and I'd get there in the end.

That's what I'm now doing. Building a personal jigsaw, the pieces floating around in my head. The fear I'll lose a piece, and not complete the task, battles with anticipation of seeing the final picture. Tonight, I'll be working on the picture. Adding colour and depth to what I know. I feel more positive having a plan.

Jed is toying with the table settings when I appear. He's realigning the cutlery for the umpteenth time, and glances up when I walk in.

'You look nice,' he says.

'Thanks.'

I know I'll look dowdy in my navy trousers and button-up blouse, in comparison to Giselle and Taylor. They're ridiculously glamorous.

'Come here,' he says, just as there's a loud knock on the front door.

'I'll go,' I say, bypassing his outstretched arms.

I open the front door, and cringe at the sight of our dinner guests on the front step, along with their boisterous greetings. Jordan and Marty are soon marching off to find Jed, followed by Taylor.

Giselle holds back.

'Izzy, it's lovely to see you. Are you okay?'

She puts a hand on my shoulder. I know I look pale, washed out, and the last thing I want is to entertain, but she seems genuinely concerned.

'I'm fine, thanks. You look great,' I enthuse, redirecting her concerns.

We join the others, and after ten minutes of pleasantries, we sit down round the table. Jed fills the wine glasses, and there's a second's hesitation when he comes to mine.

'Just a little,' I say. Does he look at me strangely? He knows I'm trying to cut back, but has he guessed I'm pregnant?

I feel detached from the guests. More detached than usual. Jed has put on soft background music, and lit a few candles, but it feels more séance-themed than romantic.

As I serve up the main course, my stomach is in knots preparing to somehow steer the conversation around to Jed's stag do. I'm after the detail of what happened.

I'm certain it'll give me a vital piece of the jigsaw.

60

Jordan is my trump card. He's drunk, and loose tongued. I haven't seen him since our wedding, but he's still loud mouthed and arrogant.

In the half-light he looks like an ageing hippy. Balding on top, he's trying to compensate by keeping the length. Wispy strands straggle round his crimson-coloured neck.

When there's a brief lull in the conversation I take my chance.

'Doesn't the wedding seem so long ago?' I ask.

Everyone looks round, wondering who has spoken.

'It does indeed. A lifetime. Glad you guys are still going strong though,' Jordan laughs, raising his glass. 'To Jed and Izzy.'

Six glasses clink in the middle.

'It's over two years ago, you know,' Jed adds. 'But I couldn't be happier.'

I blush when he looks at me, and winks. He sounds so sincere. Like Jed of old.

'Remember the fun we had in Ibiza,' Marty pipes up. He's not as cocky as Jordan, but acts as one of the lads when they're together. He's like the sidekick to the class bully.

'Great fun.' Jordan empties his glass, and coughs.

He lifts the wine bottle, swills the contents, and helps himself.

'Izzy? Top-up?'

I'm the only other person with an empty glass.

I put my hand over the top.

'Aren't you drinking?'

'I'm on a detox.'

'Detox? Jeez. I didn't know people still did that.'

'Izzy has been a bit under par,' Jed says, letting me know he's got my back.

He must surely guess I'm pregnant because I usually drink in company. Never copious amounts, but enough to relax and be sociable. And if he has read my column, goodness knows what he's thinking.

'Good for you, Izzy. It's not easy cutting back,' Giselle says, glowering at Jordan.

'Where were we?' Jordan starts up again. 'Ibiza. You never did tell us where you got to on your stag night, Jed.'

I should get up, clear the plates away, set out the cheese and biscuits. Make the coffee. Change the music. Better still, change the subject. But I'm glued to the spot, holding my breath.

Jed is drumming his fingers on the table, looking down at his feet. He nudges his wine glass to one side.

'Maybe Izzy doesn't want to hear any more.' Giselle looks from Jordan to me, and rolls her eyes.

'Don't worry. I'm okay. It might be fun to hear what happened.' I try to sound relaxed, but it's such an effort. I'm dreading what's to come.

Jordan's on a roll. He tells us about how they all ended up in a lap-dancing club near the beach.

Jed looks as if he might throw up, his cheeks quivering. I could put an end to it, saying I don't want to hear any more, but I do want to hear. I need to hear. Jed could tell Jordan to shut up, but that might make things worse, and spur Jordan on even more.

'La Trinidad,' Marty pipes up. We all look at him. 'The name of the lap-dancing club.'

'How did you remember that?' Jordan asks. 'Nothing wrong with your memory, old chap. Anyway, Jed. Are you going to tell us what happened?'

Jed looks defeated. Even in the candlelight I clock his distress, and despite everything, my heart aches for him.

'I've no idea what happened next.' He throws his hands in the air, looking at me.

'We'd been having a wild time. Drinking, dancing, ogling the lap dancers. You know how it is.' Jordan carries on. No one bothers telling him that he's dribbled red wine onto his white shirt. I doubt doing so would shut him up. 'Then suddenly Jed disappeared. To the toilets, we thought. But he never came back.'

'That's enough, Jordan. Give Izzy a break. She doesn't need to hear this. Also, I'm not keen, and Taylor looks bored to death.' Giselle tries to make light of it, but gives her husband daggers.

'Okay. But there was quite a time gap between you going to the toilet, mate, and when we found you the next morning. Out cold and naked in that cheap hotel room.'

'That's enough,' Giselle screams at Jordan, smacks her hands on the table. 'I'm so sorry. He's dreadful after a few drinks.'

'No worries. Jed told me himself what did actually happen, but I'll not be letting on.'

I tap a forefinger against the side of my nose. Everyone laughs. Everyone except Jordan, whose limelight I've stolen.

And Jed, of course.

61

By the time the guests leave, I'm beyond exhausted and strung up.

Jed and I don't say much once they've gone, and sidle round each other as we tidy up. He's so drunk that I'm not sure how much he's taken in. Or how much he'll remember in the morning.

Jordan has told us enough of what happened in Ibiza for me to piece together what seems to have taken place. Jed likely met Madison in the bar, and ended up going back with her. The lurid images play on a loop.

The one thing Jed does say, as he staggers upstairs to bed behind me, is that he loves me. Over and over.

'You know that, don't you, Izzy?' he slurs.

Even though I don't answer, he keeps saying it, again and again, the way he has been for the past few weeks. Tonight, it's the last thing he says before collapsing onto the bed.

While he snores, loud guttural snorts bouncing off the walls, I toss and turn. At least tonight has been the beginning of the end. The end of all the lies and deceit. It'll soon all be over.

Before I confront Jed, I have a couple more things to do. One last column to write, and someone to see. As a plan starts to take shape, I can't stop tears drenching my pillow.

And also, it's time to own up to being pregnant.

* * *

This morning I'm first up again. Jed is still out for the count.

In the quiet of the kitchen, sipping a warm lemon tea, I go over in my mind what I'm going to do. All the frustration, hurt, and anger leave me no choice. I scribble more notes in my pad as the minutes tick by.

Before he wakes, I'm going to get out of the house.

I leave a note on the worktop, before slipping some stale bread for the ducks into my bag. I'll feed them when I reach the park.

Gone for a run. Might grab a coffee, so catch up later. Hope hangover's not too bad X

It's still early, and the café won't be open for a couple of hours. But I'm in no hurry. The park is in the opposite direction to town, and I when I get there, I settle on a bench by the lake and dig out the stale bread from my rucksack. The ducks quack round my ankles, and snap as I toss the crumbs. I could sit here forever.

I get out my phone, and see there's another message from Teagan. She's like my conscience, but she's the only friend I've got. When Jed came into my life, I sort of let her go. He became lover, husband, and best friend. She could have given up on me, but she never did.

All okay? T x

Before Mum died, I never had any real friends. Dad didn't allow people, other than members of his flock, to come to the house. The girls at school soon gave up on me. I was too shy, and getting to know me was too much of an effort.

Fine, thanks. Catch up soon X

If the worst happens, and I'm left on my own, at least I'll have Teagan. I blink back the tears, the memories. She's told me what I have to do, and she's right. But I'll do it *my way*, in my own time.

I should check my Facebook page, but have lost the heart. After yesterday's trauma, and the Hawkeye messages, I can't face it. Whatever happens, once the baby comes, I'll be handing in my notice. I've no idea if Jed and I'll still be together, as it depends on what happens next. I'm so scared to think that far ahead.

If I have to work, I might go back to the beginning, and get a part-time job in the library. It's where I'm happiest. One thing for sure though is that my next column will be the last one I use to put my personal story into print.

It has been a crazy idea.

62

I scrunch up the empty bread bag, and realise an hour has passed. Angelo's should be open soon, and at a fast walk, I can be there in twenty minutes.

I approach from a different end of the street than usual, and see Candy outside gripping the chalked-up menu board. She spots me, plonks the board on the pavement, and scuttles back inside. When I enter the café, I go to pull the door closed as it's so cold. It feels even chillier than it was in the park.

Candy yells the length of the café.

'Leave it open. Angelo's instructions.'

I look round but there's no sign of the boss. As I strip off my bobble hat and gloves, Candy wanders down, and plonks a cappuccino on my table by the window.

'I need to pay you.'

'Whenever,' she mumbles, without looking at me.

She moves to the side, and hovers by the entrance.

'Does Adam Finch come to the café on a Sunday?' I ask.

He's the only likely reason I can think of why Candy has it in for me.

'Who?' Candy eyeballs me, as if I've just accused her of some heinous crime.

'The tall, dark-haired guy I spoke to the other day. He's a builder, I think.'

She shakes her head.

'Sometimes carries a hard hat.'

'No idea,' she says, and turns on her heels.

I bring the warm mug to my lips, about to take a sip, when I sit up straighter.

Across the road, the door to Madison's flat opens. I never see her when I come here on the weekends. But it's not her appearance that freaks me out, it's Adam Finch, stepping out of her front door.

Seeing them together throws me. I've never seen him at her apartment before, and it takes a second to remember they're brother and sister. His hair is tousled, early-morning unkempt, and he's buttoning up a jacket as he steps out onto the street.

Madison is shouting at him. Her face has the set of a snarly bulldog, and she's wagging an angry finger. Adam doesn't respond, but continues tugging at his collar. She's wearing her trademark zipped-up fleecy dressing gown, and is still screaming after him as he strolls away.

It's only as he rounds the corner by the NatWest bank that she goes back inside. I'm sure I hear the door slam after her.

The random sight churns my insides, as if it's somehow linked to me. I can't face more coffee, as it's now or never. I need to stick to the plan.

I gather my things together, don't look back towards Candy, and hurry outside. I can pay next time, as I can't delay any longer in case I chicken out of what I'm going to do.

The few yards across the street could be a mile, but in less than five seconds I'm outside Madison's apartment. My finger hovers over the bell.

A deep breath, and I begin to stab.

63

I jab the button. Over and over.

When there's no response, I step back onto the pavement and look up at her window. Then I push my ear up against the door frame, and listen for sounds. Feet. Shuffling. Anything. I know she's in there, but perhaps she's looked down. If she knows who I am, she'll likely never come out.

Then suddenly, I see the curtain on the first floor being inched aside. I wave my arms wildly in the air. When the curtain slides back into place, I panic all over again that she mightn't appear.

A couple of minutes pass, and I'm about to start the stabbing again, when a key grates in the lock.

I'm thrown by her appearance, as she looks completely different than she did a few minutes ago with Adam. Her fleecy dressing gown has been replaced by a pair of black leggings, and a figure-hugging white t-shirt festooned with love hearts.

'Hi,' she says. 'Can I help you?'

She smiles politely, her tone more intrigued than worried. If she's seen me in the café window, she must wonder why I'm here. Perhaps she's spotted me coming and going from Blanche's. Jed has never tried to stop me going round there when our paths might cross.

Even if she does know my connection to Jed, she must be curious as to why I'm here.

'Hi. My name is Izzy, do you mind if I come in?' I take a determined step closer.

She gives me a quizzical look, glances up and down the street, but doesn't hesitate for long. It seems she doesn't know who I am.

'Sure. What's it about? I'm Madison, by the way.'

I don't say I know in case she asks how.

She opens the door wider, but doesn't budge until I respond.

I don't mention Jed, or the fact I'm his wife. I keep it simple so she's more likely to let me in.

'There's something I'd like to ask you. It won't take long.'

'Okay. Come in.'

I'm soon following her up a rickety uncarpeted staircase.

Her first-floor flat lies above Boots, the chemist. It's got a great location, right in the centre of town, but the rent must be really steep. The building is likely listed, as it's so old with a musty smell of damp and age.

I assume she rents, not daring to think that she might own the place, with Jed helping to fund her lifestyle.

She leads me into the lounge. Like Blanche's cottage, the ceilings are low and oppressive, blocking out the meagre natural light.

'Coffee? Or tea perhaps? I was just putting the kettle on.'

'No, I'm fine, thanks. I've already had too much coffee.'

She doesn't mention seeing me in Angelo's, although she might have done.

I move to the window. The frame is rotting, riddled with

woodworm holes. I look out, but quickly jump aside when I spot Candy on the street looking up.

The room is in a right mess. Toys are strewn everywhere, over the floor, and on every visible surface. There are a couple of dirty mugs and plates on the coffee table.

'Excuse the mess,' she says, guessing my thoughts. 'It's tough being a single mum, and impossible to keep the place tidy. Why not sit down?'

She motions to the sofa, but as I'm here on business I opt for a hardbacked chair.

'Thanks. You're probably wondering why I'm here.'

After nudging a couple of stuffed animals to one side, she lounges on the sofa. She tucks her long legs under her, and gives me a curious look.

'Hit me.'

'I understand you cleaned for Blanche Hardcastle?'

She hums, as if taking a moment to register what I've said. Possibly trying to work out my angle.

'Yes. It's really sad what happened.' She looks serious.

'I was wondering, now you're out of a job, if you'd come and clean for me? If you're looking for more work that is.'

She uncoils her legs, sets her shapely bare feet on the tatty carpet.

'I could do with the money, that's for sure. It's hard with a kid.'

My stomach churns at the mention of the boy again.

'I bet. We don't have kids, but I know they can be a drain.'

'How often would you want me?' Her right foot jiggles up and down, and she scoops a thick red fringe back behind an ear. She ignores the word 'we'. She's more interested in the job than who I am.

'A couple of mornings a week perhaps? See how it goes.'

I brace myself to carry on.

'Jed, my husband, is always moaning about the mess, wondering what I do all day. It'll be a nice surprise for him.'

Her face is a picture when I say Jed's name.

She's been too wrapped up in wondering why I'm here, rather than who I am.

64

'Blanche Hardcastle was my mother-in-law.' I drop the bombshell, and watch her like a hawk.

'Oh, I see,' she says. 'I'm sorry, I'd no idea.'

She shakes her head, looking genuinely upset on my behalf. She could be a really good actress, but she seems sincere. I've been on tenterhooks wondering how she'd react when I told her who I was.

'How could you?' I ask.

I wonder, whatever she decides about the cleaning, if she'll want to speak to Jed first. I know Jed. If she does ask him, he'll tell her *never in a million years* to accept my offer. He won't want his secrets coming out in this way. Anyway, it's no longer up to him. He's had far too long to tell me everything himself.

Madison seems completely unfazed by what I've just told her. Maybe she'd like me to find out about their affair. Bring it to a head. Does she want Jed to herself? Or is it all about support for Benjamin? My thoughts are chaotic, but I mustn't crack. Not yet.

When she does respond, I'm surprised, as I've been antici-
pating a myriad of excuses.

'Why not? I could do with the money,' she announces.

'Great.' What else can I say? It's what I was hoping for, but
nonetheless, I'm thrown. I've been expecting some sort of cop-
out.

'When could you start?'

'Tomorrow any good?' She lets out a nervous laugh.

She tells me she can be with me by nine, after dropping
Benjamin off at nursery. She has to pick him up again at midday.

It's now too late to backtrack, or change my mind. This is it.
The first step of my final plan, and I'm petrified. I lock my fingers
together, and bang my thumbnails against my lower set of teeth.

She breaks into my thoughts. 'I assume you live nearby?'

Surely she knows where Jed lives. She must do, but she's not
going to let on.

'Not far. Let me have your number, and I'll text the address.'

'Will do.' She scribbles on a scrap of paper, and hands it over.

With that I get up, feeling woozy, light-headed, and wobbly,
and tell her I must get going.

'I can see myself out. Till tomorrow,' I say, as brightly as I can.

'No worries. Slam the door after you, as it sticks.'

I'm already on the landing, gripping the wooden banister of
the rickety staircase. It takes an almighty effort to reach the
bottom.

My hand settles over my baby bump, and it takes a moment
to compose myself before I head out onto the street.

It's then I notice the magazine on the hall table. It's the latest
copy of *Echoes of London*. It's dogeared, as if it's been read cover to
cover.

I fumble with the door clasp, no idea why seeing the magazine with my column in is such a shock. It looks as if Madison

might be an avid reader. Of all the magazines she could read, why this one?

I look back up the staircase. Could Madison have anything to do with the Hawkeye messages?

Seriously, what have I just done?

65

I decide not to tell Jed straightaway about Madison. His hangover will be horrendous, and he'll be dreading repercussions from the dinner party revelations.

I'm reeling from Jordan's stories, even though there was little I wasn't expecting. I guessed Jed met Madison in Ibiza, after he told me she'd worked there. But hearing, rather than surmising, the sordid details was much worse.

By now, Jed will probably have come up with some explanation for what Jordan said. Something plausible. For the moment I'll not give him any more chances to lie. I want an end to the whole sorry saga. But it'll end my way, all the lies out in the open with no dark corners left to hide in.

He'll guess I'm upset, angry, or both, but I'll stay quiet. Convince him I'm okay, as I need his guard down for what's to come. I don't want him prepared for Madison's arrival, and then trying to warn her off. I'm hoping she won't tell him, as seeing his kneejerk reaction to the news will tell me more than his words ever could.

First though, I need to get home. The morning sickness is

crippling, getting worse by the minute, and talking to Madison has aggravated it even more.

As I wend my way home, I talk through things in my head, justifying my actions, and reminding myself of motive. Having Madison into our house is a last-ditch attempt to force the issue. If Jed still doesn't talk, and avoids Madison, then I'll make them both come clean. They'll face the firing line together.

My legs are leaden, drained of energy. An icy chill has seeped through to my bones, and even with thick woolly gloves, my fingers are numb. Pins and needles are my only feeling.

Grim memories keep me company. Although I've got Teagan, I miss my mum. I wish she'd never killed herself.

A rogue thought hits. Perhaps Blanche felt the same as Mum, and saw no way out. She wasn't well, and the future was bleak. She'd run out of options, and finally killed herself. Perhaps it was as simple as that.

I trudge on, and up the hill towards home. I think of Jed, and how hard he works.

'It's all for us,' he used to say.

Until he stopped.

He once got so excited signing up new clients. Long-term investments, endowment schemes, pension policies. These were his bread and butter, bringing in lucrative commissions. He would rush home with expensive champagne, pound signs in his eyes, and love in his heart. It was all for us.

Until he changed.

Rain mingles with my tears as I pass the large houses in The Avenue. Huge, gnarled trees line the route. Jed and I love this street. He used to tell me that one day we'd move here. A few more sales, and he'd choose the house we'd buy.

'It'll not be long,' he said. So confident. So certain.

I believed him.

He was never mean, or controlling. If he was deceitful back then, I never picked it up. He was nice about people, and life seemed so good.

I thought it would last forever.

I can't remember when he started to criticise people. His boss, his colleagues. Everyone who seemed to have more money than he did. He stopped talking up millions, or moving house.

Overnight, his dreams dried up.

As I round the bend, and head up the final incline towards our semi, a random conversation springs to mind.

We'd been talking about infidelity. I said I'd never stray, that he was the only man for me. He was so happy. I don't think I've ever seen a happier face.

But then he asked me what I'd do if he ever had an affair. It was theoretical, a bit of lovers' fun.

Only now does my reply hit a nerve.

'I'd pack my bags and leave.'

'No second chances?'

He just wanted to hear me say how much I loved him. Over and over. That was where we were.

'You must be joking. I'm soft when it comes to a lot of things, but not that. I'd be out the door like a bullet. No second chances for you, Jed Hardcastle. And that's a promise I'll never break.'

Did I mean it at the time? I doubt I'll ever know.

66

It's Monday morning, and Madison is due at nine. I'm desperate to get Jed out of the house, and although he's dressed for the office, he's lingering.

For an awful moment, I think he might insist on working from home. He's not feeling so good, his body still racked with pain. He won't own up that he's struggling, but it's written all over him.

But there's no way he can work from home. Not today.

'Oh. Are you feeling that bad?' My horror face gets his attention when he suggests it.

'Not terrible, but bloody stiff.' He grimaces and rubs his lower back.

'A couple of Ibuprofen might help?'

He hates taking medicine, even paracetamol, for anything. Yet I need to get him out of the way.

'No, you're okay. Working from home might be best, and I've no face-to-face meetings planned.'

I don't say anything, but turn away. He'll guess there's something up.

'Is there a problem? I won't get in your way. Promise.'

'Okay, I'll own up. I've arranged a special surprise for you tonight, and was hoping for the house to myself to get it ready.' I grit my teeth and say a quick prayer.

He smiles, a Jed-of-old smile.

'Oh. Sounds intriguing.' He expels a resigned puff of air. 'If that's the case then, I'll soldier on.'

'You'll be fine once you get going. Here, take these with you.' I stretch up into a high cupboard, and pull down the painkillers, and hand them over.

'It had better be a good surprise.'

He kisses me on the cheek, tucks his mobile away, and lifts his house keys from the bowl.

'Till later then. Love you.'

'Love you too.'

And with that he is gone.

67

I have one hour tops to kill before Madison gets here.

In a frenzy I start to tidy up. It's crazy, as that's what she's coming to do. I frantically scrub hard at surfaces, pull out plates and pans from the cupboards, until the kitchen is cleaner than I remember it.

As the minutes tick by, I get more and more panicky. What am I thinking? Having Madison here could be the catalyst that finally brings things to a head. Likely the thing that ends my marriage. Perhaps I should message her, tell her I've changed my mind.

But if I don't act now, then what? Carry on in limbo.

Also, although the police have Blanche's death down as an accident, I can't help the niggling doubt that she was pushed. There are several people who have gained from her death, including Madison. Jed's inheritance means he has no excuse to not keep on supporting her. And her brother, Adam, has already started on the new development. Perhaps he's cut her in.

Madison had both opportunity and motive to kill Blanche.

As I watch nervously out the window, I'm tempted to draw

the curtains and hide. But then I see her. At two minutes to nine, she appears on our drive. My heart thumps, as I sidle out of view. I almost hit the roof when there's a rap on the door.

I count to ten, then slowly open up.

'Hi, Madison. You found us okay?'

I look up and down the street. At least there are no neighbours about.

'I was hoping this was the right house,' she says, as I motion her inside.

I'm struggling to believe that she hasn't been curious before now to see where her lover lives. Father of her child at least. If I was in her shoes, I'd have been up and down the road a million times.

'Good timing. It's exactly nine o'clock.'

She smiles, clutches her cleaning basket tighter. It's a metal contraption that looks like an old milk crate, jammed with bottles of spray, and cleaning agents.

'Would you like a coffee or tea before you start?' I ask.

I wonder if she's picking up how edgy I am. My voice is hoarse.

Up close, she's a lot taller than she looks from the café window. She's taller than me, the extra inches making her more imposing.

'No, thanks. I'd better get started, as I have to pick Benjamin up at twelve,' she reminds me.

Hearing his name again stokes the pain.

She follows me into the kitchen, which looks like an untidy charity shop. At least visible surfaces are spotless, but they're few and far between. I've emptied all the cupboards, and left the contents strewn all over the place.

'If you'd clean the cupboards, the oven and hobs, and put the crockery back that would be great.'

Her eyes sweep round, and I suspect she might be trying to work out how long it'll take her. It's a mess, but there's enough to keep her busy.

'If you've time, perhaps you'd also tackle the bathroom, and toilets.'

'Sure. No problem.'

Jed will freak when he hears I've hired a cleaner. I suspect he's put our conversation to the back of his mind, assuming I've decided against it, as the subject hasn't been mentioned again. Hiring Madison behind his back will come as a complete shock, as her name hasn't come up again either.

I leave her to it, and decamp to the study. I need to get on with my next column. I leave the door ajar, and can soon hear busy movement from the kitchen.

I wait for the computer to boot up. It'll be the last time I make up a letter which relates to me. Maybe my last letter, period. I've been toying with the content, the wording, and now I need to get it down. I'll keep it vague, but if someone is tracking my column, and my life, they'll not miss the message.

It'll be the last piece of bait to try and weed out Hawkeye. Maybe a response will give me one more piece of my puzzle. I'm nearing the end of my detective work before I face the music. Teagan has given me one more week, or else.

As I begin to type, a rogue thought hits. What if Jed and Madison were in cahoots, and somehow were jointly responsible for Blanche's murder?

68

Dear Bella,

My husband won't tell me about an affair he's been having. I know he's been cheating. I have lots of proof, and have given him plenty of chances to come clean.

I even know the name, and lots of things about his so-called 'secret' mistress. I know where she lives. What she does for a living. Actually she's an old girlfriend of one of his university friends. I met her a few times years ago, and would you believe it? I bumped into her the other day. She's married herself now, and I asked if she and her husband would like to come to dinner. She didn't flinch, and would you believe it, they are coming this Saturday?

I've told Freddie we have surprise guests to supper, and he will just have to wait and see who they are. It's been really hard for me to hold my tongue for so long, especially when I have concrete proof that Freddie has been cheating with this woman.

Do you think I'm doing the right thing, having his mistress

over to the house? I'm starting to freak that maybe it's a bad idea, but I'm so flipping angry and want to get my own back. It's revenge with a twist, don't you think?

Best wishes,

Betrayed

* * *

Dear Betrayed,

How awful for you. It is so distressing when you discover your partner has cheated. You have all my sympathy.

I understand you are really angry, you want to get your own back in a novel way. It'll certainly be uncomfortable for him, and for her. I assume she knows that she will be coming to dinner with her secret lover, and wonder why she might be prepared to put herself in such a situation.

Only she knows the answer to these questions. You ask if I think you're doing the right thing. Personally, I think it would be much better to talk to your husband, to confront him with what you've found out, and see what he has to say. But then we all have our reasons for approaching things in different ways. I don't know enough about your personal situation, so it's hard to judge.

If you decide to talk it over with your husband, then you'll have decisions to make. Whether to forgive him or not. There are always at least two sides to every story. You will need to be brave, whichever path you decide to take.

That said, I'll be interested to see what our readers think about your plan.

Good luck with the dinner party, and hope things work out for you in the end.

Regards,
Bella

Although it's not mirroring my own position exactly, nor my plans, there's enough in there to catch Hawkeye's eye. Provided they read every word, it shouldn't be too hard to work out where I'm coming from.

By the time my column is in print, Jed might not be the only other person who knows Madison is cleaning for me. She'll likely mention it to Adam, to Candy, and goodness knows who else. It's a long shot, but it's a last roll of the dice to get my story out there. Having Madison in our home, albeit as a cleaner, isn't that far removed from having a husband's mistress to dinner. As well as baiting Hawkeye, I'm intrigued as to what other readers might think.

I reread what I've written several times. Suddenly a pain shoots up my arm, and hairs prickle on the back of my neck. Someone is standing behind me, looking over my shoulder, and possibly reading the letter.

Madison must have crept up, tiptoed really quietly, as I didn't hear her approach. I snap shut the laptop and swivel round.

'Jeez. Don't creep up like that. You scared me half to death.'

'Sorry. I didn't want to disturb you. You were so deep in concentration.'

I stand up, feeling suffocated by her height.

'I just wanted to say I've finished, and need to get off.'

She whips her cleaning basket to one side, and lets me past.

The kitchen is spotless, although the stench of cleaning agents catches in my throat. I'll open the windows once she's gone, as Jed's asthma will be in the firing line.

'Looks great,' I say, without making eye contact. I open a drawer by the fridge, and pull out £45 in fresh unused notes.

'Thanks.' She blushes, and slips them into her coat pocket. 'I've done the bathroom and toilets as well.'

'That's great. I'll see you the day after tomorrow? Same time?'

'It's in the diary.'

Two minutes later, she's gone.

69

I go back to my desk, at last breathing more easily, and fire off the letter.

There's been a new email from Grayson telling me I need to work faster, as well as coming up with more original angles for my column. Even he's getting bored with the concentration on deceit, and affairs.

His message hits a nerve. He's right, as I'm also bored with my column. I don't know how much longer I can keep at it. I can't afford to lose my job yet, not with everything going on, and a baby on the way. But the end is in sight.

One thing I do know is that after this week, I'll only be printing genuine readers' letters. This will be the last letter personal to me. Future content mightn't be so dark, but there's always plenty of letters on pet problems, Dignitas, gardening pests, and allergies.

I spend the rest of the day preparing supper. Roast dinner with all the trimmings, Jed's favourite. I don't feel like cooking anything for him, I'm so hurt and angry, but I need his guard down, no hint of suspicion that anything is up. The smell of his favourite meal should do the trick.

Then I've got two things to tell him when he's sitting down.

The kitchen is certainly spotless, although the cleaning agents have given the place the stench of a hospital ward. I opened all the windows, and hope the smell of roast dinner will come out on top.

He gets home earlier than usual. I'd been building myself up to six o'clock, but it's only 5.20 when I hear the door.

'Yoo-hoo. It's only me. I'm home.'

He yells the same thing every day in a full-on happy tone.

I freeze. Although I've been waiting for him, the reality of what I'm going to tell him fills me with dread.

'In the kitchen.'

Jed and I aren't yellers by nature, but we're talking so loudly, I think of actors enunciating for an audience.

'Something smells good.' He appears in the doorway, sniffing, before a bout of coughing turns him puce. 'Goodness, you've been cleaning,' he croaks. 'Wow. The place is spotless.'

'It is, isn't it?' I wander to the cupboards under the island and throw wide the doors. The shelves are gleaming, as are the doors and handles.

'Amazing. Well done. Come here, you.' He flaps a hand against his wheezy chest, before throwing open his arms. He wraps me up, and I close my eyes. The contours of his body are so familiar.

I could stay here forever. But when the baby squirms, I jump back. It's not as if Jed could feel anything, but it's kneejerk.

I give him a quick kiss, and start busying myself with futile tasks. Like fiddling in the cutlery drawer which is now devoid of crumbs and mess.

Then, out of the blue, I blurt it out.

'Okay. I'll be honest. It wasn't all my own work.'

I hold my breath, and grit my teeth. Time seems to stand still.

'Oh. What do you mean?' He steps to the side, and starts coughing again.

'Are you okay?'

He nods, and gasps for air at the same time.

'I had help,' I say.

'Who from?'

He tugs at his tie, pulling it sharply to the side. He's sweating, and beads of moisture are pooling on his forehead.

'Remember the lady who was cleaning for Blanche before her accident? Madison?'

He keeps on yanking at his tie, trying to get it over his head. I think of a hangman's noose.

'I bumped into her brother Adam, asked where she lived and then popped by to see her. She lives in the centre of town.'

He's unlikely to check this with Adam. Too late, now the horse has bolted.

'Couldn't you do the cleaning yourself? For God's sake, we don't have any extra money.'

He finally gets his tie off, and chucks it across the room. He's furious, I can see it in his eyes.

For an awful moment, I think he might explode. He usually swallows back emotion, holding himself in check, and only occasionally does he let rip. When he does, his anger gets targeted and hurtful, but he's never hit me. Not yet anyway.

I keep a distance as he stares me down. I can hardly find my voice.

'I'm under pressure with my column, and Grayson wants me to take on more work. I can't do everything.'

My eyes start to cloud over, and tears prick the corners.

His shoulders slump, and he looks concerned. He's like Jekyll and Hyde. Who is my husband really?

'But a cleaner? This isn't *Hollywood Wives*.'

I flop into a chair, and let the tears flow. I don't want to cry, but it's such a struggle. I'm battling both myself and Jed.

'Are you okay? Is there something you're not telling me?'

Concern has overcome his anger, and he sits down beside me.

'You're not ill, are you?'

Why would he ask that? I look peaky, I know, but he looks worse.

He's waiting for me to say something. Does he know what I'm about to say? Is he trying to drag it out of me?

'No. I'm not ill. But...'

'But what?' He wrings his hands together.

'I'm pregnant.'

70

Silence hangs in the air.

He grips the edge of the table, and appears to have difficulty speaking.

'Pregnant? How? When?' He slurs his words.

'What do you mean *how*? We used to make love, remember?'

Now I'm really scared. What if this is it? What if he tells me he doesn't want a child? I tremble, and curve my hands around the bump.

'The little blighter's already squirming.' I look down, giggle nervously.

Jed looks shocked, as if I've told him I've got a terminal illness, and he's having trouble taking it in. I see horror on his face, shock and horror. Did he really not guess? Or even have an inkling? Or is it another pretence? I think of Hawkeye. If Jed was Hawkeye, surely he'd have already guessed I was pregnant from my recent column.

Or else he's an A-list actor.

'How many weeks?' His voice quivers.

'Twelve weeks.'

'Twelve weeks?' He speaks so quietly, it scares me.

'I didn't want to tell you until I was confident this one might be a keeper.'

I force a smile, with a whimper of apology in my tone.

'Are you sure?'

'Of course I'm sure.'

'Have you had a scan yet? I mean twelve weeks is getting on.'

After the miscarriage not long after we got married, we parked the idea of trying again. *It'll happen if it happens* was our motto. I remember thinking at the time that Jed couldn't hide a sense of relief that he wasn't going to be a father... not yet, at any rate. Little did I know then that he was already well on the way to becoming a father with someone else.

'My first scan is booked for next Friday.'

'Next Friday? I'm up in Edinburgh again next Friday. Why did you book it for that date? I'm not due back until Saturday.'

'It's when they could fit me in. It's not a problem. I know it's a shock, but I can go on my own.'

If my plan comes together, he'll be coming back early. But first things first.

I had no idea how he'd react when I told him. If he'd guessed already, surely he wouldn't look so stunned.

My tears explode in large blubbery sobs. It's all too much. He might tell me he doesn't want the baby when it sinks in, and he's gone really quiet.

After what seems an eternity, he lets out a whoop of joy, and punches the air with his fist.

'Oh my God. We're going to be parents.'

He grabs me, swings me round and round. When I beg him to stop, I notice his own eyes are welling up.

He pulls me onto his lap when he sits down. Soon he's cradling the baby's piddly bump.

He rocks back and forth, nestling his head on my shoulder. His breathing is ragged, but it's a weirdly perfect moment.

'I can't believe we really are going to be parents.'

We sit locked together, ignoring the ping of the oven timer.

'I'll not go to Edinburgh. I can't miss the first scan.'

He suddenly coughs again, violently.

'Bloody cleaning agents. You know I'm allergic to bleach.'

'Sorry. I'll make sure she uses milder ones next time.'

'Next time? She's not coming again, is she?'

He nudges me slightly forward.

'She's only helping with a spring clean. It's not permanent.'

'I hope not. I'd prefer a messy house than being asphyxiated.'

He tries for levity, but the mood has been broken.

I get off his lap, and plant a kiss on his forehead. I'm bereft that the feelgood moment has passed.

We don't talk much during supper, but there's a celebratory glow in the air. It's muted, but it's there.

Jed suggests we get an early night.

'Too much excitement for one day,' he says as he loads the dishwasher with an exaggerated yawn.

Despite his excitement, he can't mask how bad he still feels. A breakout of worry spots has erupted on his forehead, and he has a burgeoning cold sore on his upper lip.

'And too much wine,' I add, peering through an empty bottle.

He yawns again, and we laugh when I join in.

'Come on.' He lingers by the door.

I turn out all the lights, and for the first time in as long as I can remember, we link fingers and climb the stairs together.

We crawl into bed, and Jed cocoons me and the baby in the longest of arms, and in the firmest of grips.

'I love you to heaven and back,' are the last words he utters before he drifts off.

He whistles in his sleep while I gently uncoil his arms, and turn on to my back. I stare up at the ceiling. I've no idea where Jed's dreams will take him, but mine will be like a train wreck.

I'm jealous he can sleep. My mind is tortured with all sorts of gruesome imaginings. I wonder if he'll tell Madison that Benjamin is to have a sibling, and if he'll share with her before he shares with me.

He's no idea what's to come, but he and Madison have a lot to answer for. My life will never be the same again.

* * *

In the morning, I'm up first. Ten minutes after I've got to the kitchen, I hear Jed up and about overhead.

Soon the shower cranks up, and when the water stops, I hear the creak of floorboards. He's pottering in the bedroom, getting ready for work. As he does every day.

Soon he's alongside me, zooming in for another load of kisses. A couple on the lips, followed by a dozen on baby's bump.

'How are my two favourite people in the world?' He smiles like a sunbeam.

'We're both great,' I lie.

I'm far from great, terrified of what's to come. I'm torn between relief and fury. Relief that he's thrilled by the news, and fury that it's all a sham. He's owned up to nothing.

My stomach is in knots, wondering if he'll tell Madison the news today. By phone. By text. Or perhaps in person. How will she react? Every thought makes the sickness worse.

If Madison wasn't in the picture, I'd have all I ever wanted. Jed, and our own little family. She's to blame as much as Jed, my anger split in two.

'Listen, don't cancel Edinburgh next week, please. I don't

want anything to jinx things. I'll go to the scan on my own, and make sure to get copies of our little guy.'

'Guy? Is it a boy?' His eyes widen. Is he curious, relieved, disappointed? I've no idea. The thought that he might be hoping for a girl this time round sets my teeth on edge.

'No idea. Let's wait and see.' I'm chirpy but firm.

'Okay. If you're sure, but I want a copy. Make that several copies.' The sunbeam expression is stuck firm.

I'm relieved when he finally heads for the front door. I wonder, if he didn't already have a child, if he'd be more insistent on not missing our baby's first scan.

'Oh, I nearly forgot. Will you be okay to make a start on clearing Mum's things? You were going to make a start next Friday. The day of the scan. If you don't feel up to it, we can do it together at the weekend.'

He rakes his fingers through his hair, concerned that he's only just remembered. I offered to go through Blanche's things when he said he couldn't face it.

'I'll be fine. Remember I'm pregnant, not sick.' I throw my hands on my hips. 'It's already on my do-do list. Now go.'

'Well, don't be lifting heavy boxes.'

I don't tell him I've already earmarked Madison to help. Friday week is in the diary.

'You know there's a storm predicted for next Friday. Storm Margarita or something. Supposed to be nasty. Anyway, must dash.'

I didn't know about the storm. The mention makes me tingle, as if it's an omen. Especially as it's Friday the 13th. I think back to the night I confessed all to Jed. It was a windy night then too, but nothing like the storm that raged on the night I killed Dad. That was on another Friday the 13th.

When I told Jed, he held me tight. So tight I could hardly

breathe. Although Teagan tells me, over and over, I didn't murder Dad, I've always felt I did. I was the person responsible.

As Jed heads out the door, I remember what he said that night.

'I wouldn't care if you were a cold-blooded murderer. You're mine, and I'll never let you go.'

'Bye.' I blow him a kiss.

'Au revoir, ma chérie,' he yells, before slamming the front door.

Shortly after he's gone, I dress up warm, and pull on my knee-length button-up raincoat. Despite the layers of clothes, I feel chilled to the core.

Outside there is a coating of frost everywhere, and the driveway is like an ice rink.

It takes several tugs to open the door, and even more attempts to get the car going. I let the engine run, and set to de-ice the windows with a scraper. The windscreen inside is so fogged up that I swish a soggy cloth across the glass to help it demist.

The roads are treacherous, and the thought of danger to the baby in my bashed-up car makes my blood boil. My new car, the one Jed will buy me, come hell or high water, will be top of the range. A solid brand-new four-wheel drive, with brakes that work.

I drive at a snail's pace, gritting my teeth on every corner. I should have stayed in, but the house feels too much like a prison cell.

By the time I've parked up and walked to Angelo's, the place is already busy. The noise and sight of so many people make me jittery, but I can't face going home.

At least the window seat is free. I dump my stuff before heading up to face Candy. She turns her back, and passes my order to a new girl. But I no longer care about Candy. She's the least of my worries.

It's hard to see through the café window, the glass as misty as in the car. I rub my sleeve across it, making a circle to see out. People are wandering up and down, heads bent against the chill. There is no sign of Madison. No sign of Jed. Nothing to get me even more uptight.

Today I didn't bring my laptop. There's something I need to do before I can concentrate on work. With only a week before I face the music, I'm after as many pieces as possible of the puzzle. The more I know, the more I'll be prepared.

I sip the warm milky liquid, relishing the comfort, before I pick up my phone. My stomach knots as I begin to type. I reread the message several times before sending.

> Hi. Fancy meeting up for that drink sometime?
> Izzy

In less than five minutes, Adam's reply bounces back.

> Thought you'd never ask. Tonight any good?

I'm thrown by the speed of his response. I glance over my shoulder, fearful someone might be watching, and guess what I'm up to.

Funny, I was half-expecting him to come up with an excuse. With Blanche dead, Adam no longer has anything to gain from knowing me. He doesn't need my help in moving things along, nudging Blanche to move out. Or using the fact I'm Jed's wife to help persuade my husband into taking action. Adam will soon get the green light to demolish the whole terrace, once Jed has accepted their offer.

I get goosebumps when I think he might actually like me.

Maybe this is how deceit starts. With one small move. I'm doing nothing wrong, the end justifying the means. Jed would go crazy if he knew I'd texted Adam, or any man for that matter, but I'm running out of options. As well as time, to complete my puzzle.

> Okay. The Fox in Shepley? 7 o'clock?

I watch the screen, and see he's typing.

> Perfect. I'll meet you there

I reply with a single thumbs up.

* * *

Adam will likely guess why I've chosen a pub miles from anywhere. He knows I'm married. I cringe that he might think I've fallen for him.

My agenda is to find out how close he is to Madison. How much she's told him. Does he know about Benjamin's father? Does he share his property plans with his sister? How far would she go to help him?

Is there any way he could have killed Blanche?

While I have an agenda, I wonder why he's so keen to meet straightaway. He's definitely flirting, but why me? He could have any woman he wanted, from what I've seen. Men like Adam Finch don't look at mousy girls like me.

Although this doesn't stop the butterflies in my stomach.

I'm about to make a move when I notice Candy's reflection in the window. She's standing behind, still as a statue. Just staring at me.

If looks could kill...

73

I go home for a few hours, tidy up, and prepare Jed's supper. I've put work on the back burner, as there's no way I could concentrate.

I text him, telling him I've decided to work in the library tonight. I've so much to catch up on, and I need a change of scene. Hope he doesn't mind.

I send a second text soon after in case he wonders what I've been doing all day.

> Home-cooked Cottage Pie in fridge. Heat for 5 minutes in microwave. See you later X

Instantly a text pings back.

> Missing you and the baby already. Till later. Hugs and kisses. XXXX

Telling my own lies doesn't come easily, but after Jed's whoppers, I don't feel half so guilty.

* * *

I leave in plenty of time, dressed casually in jeans and a sweatshirt, and sturdy shoes. Although I convince myself it's not a date, I can't quash the nerves. I'm excited, the way I used to feel when dating Jed.

The Fox pub is dark and smoky. Oak beams crisscross the low ceiling, and an open fire blazes in a stone hearth. It's only 6.45 when I arrive. I squeeze into a quiet corner near the heat, and spread my bag, coat and gloves along the wooden bench so that Adam's only option is the chair opposite.

He arrives ten minutes letter, scans the bar right and left, then right again until he spots me. He looks so handsome that I momentarily regret my lack of effort. I've glossed over my lips, but that's it. Jed doesn't like make-up, saying he prefers the natural look. He tells me all the time it was my dark eyes that attracted him. The windows to my soul.

Adam is the sort of guy I'd never have looked at twice because he'd never look at me. Dad's drunken criticism of mine and Mum's wan appearances did its damage.

'Hi. You're early,' he says, towering over the table.

I don't get up, embarrassed he might offer up a kiss.

'I'm always early,' I say, my cheeks inflamed.

'What's your poison?' He jiggles his wallet.

'Lime and soda, please. I'm driving.' I roll my eyes.

'Coming up.'

Adam is tall, over six foot, and I think of Madison. I wonder which parent was so Amazonian. Adam is much taller than Jed, and walks with confidence. The barmaid, pretty, bubbly and not unlike Candy, paints on her brightest smile. He's that sort of guy.

He comes back with my drink, and a lager for himself, before stretching his long legs towards the fire. He rubs his hands in front of the fire.

We make small talk about the weather, and the approaching

storm. About Hinton, the town we both call home. But in less than ten minutes, I steer the conversation round to Blanche, and what happened.

He repeats again how sorry he is.

When I say he'll be able to start the development soon, he sighs.

'I hope so. But I'd rather she'd moved out than fallen to her death.'

He seems genuine. Maybe it's the heat, and the cosy atmosphere, that swallows back the doubt. He's so relaxed. Could he really have pushed Blanche down the stairs? He was around when I found her. He could easily have slipped in earlier if he had a key. Or perhaps Blanche opened the door to him.

'Do you think your husband will agree to our offer?'

The question throws me. Jed told me he's no choice now but to accept the developers' lowered offer, but I thought he'd already done so. I'm not sure why Adam's question unsettles me, and I can't help feeling disappointment that this might be the real reason he's here.

'I thought he had already. I've been tasked with clearing out his mother's stuff next week, as he's keen to get it done.'

'Maybe Madison can help you. I hear she's helping you out at home.'

A line of foam has collected on his upper lip, and my finger itches to rub it off.

'I was thinking of asking her. She's doing a great job, by the way.'

'I bet. She's good in other people's houses, not so her own. Her flat's a mess.'

This is my chance to manipulate the conversation.

74

'You're pretty close, I guess.'

'We get on okay.' He shrugs.

Suddenly he leaps up when a spark explodes from the fire and lands on his thigh. He wipes frantically.

'Living dangerously,' he laughs, scraping his chair further back.

I giggle, but carry on.

'Can you help Madison out with money?' I ask. 'She says it's hard making ends meet, being a single mum.'

I put on my caring face, trying to draw him out.

'I was doing, but business is tough. We need to get cracking on the terrace and can't start properly until we knock the whole row down.'

'At least with Blanche gone, the wait is nearly over. Once you've sorted out things with Jed, I suspect you'll be able to start work proper.'

I listen to my voice. It's as if someone else is talking, someone at home making easy conversation. I sound so relaxed, not a care in the world.

'That's what I'm banking on,' he says.

He sounds even more relaxed, sipping languidly on his lager. Could he really be so chilled if he'd pushed my mother-in-law to her death?

'Does Madison see Benjamin's dad much?'

I've been patient, waiting for the right moment to ask this question.

Adam doesn't look fazed when I take the conversation back a few steps.

'He looks after them, financially I think, but that's about it.'

Maybe it is only about the money. Maybe Jed made one silly mistake. The thought should make me feel better, but it doesn't. It's all the lies.

'Where did she meet him?'

Adam takes a moment, as if he's thinking about it. I'm not sure if he's thinking about where they met, or whether he should tell me at all. Does he know that Benjamin is my husband's child? Perhaps Madison never told him.

'In Ibiza. She worked there. It was a one-night stand, I think.'

Fizzy drink gurgles back up my throat, and at the same time the baby squirms. Adam looks concerned when I flap a hand over my mouth.

'Are you okay?'

The nausea hits me in waves, and I have to make a dash for the ladies'.

I throw water over my face, and try to collect myself. I don't want to tell Adam I'm pregnant, as it wouldn't feel right.

When the sickness abates, I go over our conversation in my head. There's no doubt in my mind that Jed is definitely Benjamin's father. But from Adam's demeanour, I don't think he knows this. Likely Madison never told him. If she did, he likely doesn't care that much.

I get the sense that Madison and Adam aren't that close.

When I finally reappear, Adam is standing up, concern etched on his features.

'Are you okay?'

His fingers caress my arm, and send a shiver down my spine.

For a single moment, Adam and I could be the only two people in all the world.

75

I don't dwell on the evening with Adam. I feel guilty even thinking about him. That said, it doesn't stop his image invading my dreams. And my nightmares.

At least I got what I wanted; confirmation of my suspicions about Jed and Madison. Although I was certain after Jordan's revelations that Jed met Madison in Ibiza, I've got confirmation from Adam.

Although I had good reason to meet up with Adam, I'm finding it hard not to think of him. I'm constantly reminding myself that I've done nothing wrong.

Jed is in good form, humming, whistling, and talking incessantly about the baby. He's over-the-top excited about the scan, but sulky he won't be there. His mood lifts when I promise we'll book the next scan together.

His worried face returns when I remind him I'm starting on Blanche's stuff on the evening of the scan. I'll not lift anything heavy, I tell him. It'll keep me busy until he gets back. Only one more week to go. I should be relieved, but inside I'm in bits. As if the world is coming to an end.

When I wake on Saturday morning, I'm filled with dread. Responses to my column will start coming in, and I don't think I can face them. I now wish I hadn't used my column at all to weave through my own story, but at least today is the last time I'll have to worry.

I leave Jed whistling in his sleep. He's slept like a log since I told him about the baby, as if the news has fed him hope for the future. I've no idea how he can put the Madison saga to the back of his mind, as I can't rest at all.

I leave a note for him, this time on the bottom stair.

Will be in the library until lunchtime. Catch up later. Kisses from baby and me XX

I forgo Angelo's, desperate to get to the library as soon as it opens. I wander round town, look in windows, pick up a hard copy from the newsagents, and check the time every few minutes.

When I reach the library, I wander back and forth trying to keep warm. I turn my face upwards, and feel a few flakes of snow. It's only November, but the temperature has plummeted, with Storm Margarita forecast for the end of the week.

On the dot of eight, Hubert the manager unlocks the doors and mumbles, 'Good morning,' as I follow him through.

There's no one else around, not even another member of staff. The place is deserted.

I climb to the first floor, strip off the layers, and sit in my usual spot.

The clock on the wall is ticking. In the silence, if I listen carefully, I can hear the clunk of the hand. Every second that passes, my stomach clenches tighter. Baby is very quiet. Too quiet. I prefer the company of its blips and flips.

'Everything will work out. I promise.'

I bend my head and whisper. If anyone is watching they'd think I'm mad. But a little rumble makes me smile, letting me know baby heard.

Before I open my Facebook page, I reread the fictitious letter and my response.

I cringe on rereading. I'd never have asked Madison and a husband or lover to dinner with Jed and me. Even as revenge with a twist. It now seems ridiculous, but readers want ridiculous. The more far-fetched the better. *Humdrum doesn't sell.*

I open my Facebook page, and start the countdown: 9.00. 9.05. 9.10. 9.30. 9.45. The minutes are like hours.

Then the first reply comes in.

> Oh. I think it's a great idea to have your husband's mistress round to dinner. Will serve them both right. Well done. A great idea. Can't wait to hear how it goes.

This message is soon followed by a couple more. One telling me (well, telling the fictitious 'Betrayed') that she must be mad.

> Leave the prick. Do you really want to be bothered? Revenge not worth the aggro. Been there. It never ends well.

Another one simply wishes Betrayed:

> Good Luck, and Go For It!

It's 9.55. 10.00. Then I see it. 10.05. The message from Hawkeye1234.

A message for Betrayed. Bringing your husband's mistress into your home? Are you crazy? Aren't you scared of what she might be capable of? She could be a bunny boiler. She might want revenge of her own. WATCH THIS SPACE. While you're planning revenge, just imagine what your husband's fancy woman might have in mind. Can't believe you're prepared to take the risk. You'll likely end up dead.

My eyes freeze on the screen. I can't look away. It might be my sick paranoia, but this is not a random response. It's too emotional, too over the top. I take a screenshot, and immediately delete.

I hear muffled footsteps coming up the stairs, and the approach of whispering chatter. I sense danger behind me, and I hear voices in my head.

I'm so afraid. All the logic in the world can't make it better. Of course no one is going to kill me in the library. Even a bunny boiler wouldn't choose a library. My mind is skittering in all directions, and I'm scared I'm going to start screaming. Like the day Dad died. The screaming is all in my head, but I don't think I can bottle it up much longer.

I can't take any more. No more work. No more Facebook page. No more.

One more week, and it'll all be over.

76

I head home, relieved to have made the decision to forget work. If Grayson fires me, so be it.

For the rest of the weekend, I want to spend time with Jed. It might be our last weekend together. The thought is like a knife to the heart.

Jed spends Saturday afternoon and all of Sunday following me around. He asks every half hour if I'm okay, and why I'm so quiet. He asks if something is bothering me, as he's worried for the baby.

'Is it work? Izzy, tell me what's up.' He can't relax.

'Nothing. Nothing's up, now stop asking.'

My snappy responses get harsher, forcing him to stop.

I suspect he guesses what's really up, and that I know much more than I'm letting on. The charade is pitiful, but at least it'll soon be over.

Although he's agitated, worried about how tired I look, and how quiet I am, deep down he seems happier than he has in months. I'm swamped by guilt, no idea why he doesn't feel the same.

* * *

Monday morning comes around, and he sneaks out of the house early. His excuse is that trains are busier on a Monday, and he needs a seat. His body is still achy, his back grumbling.

Of course, I know the real reason he's in a hurry. It's because Benjamin is enrolled in breakfast club, and Madison is starting at eight.

At Jed's request, I've pinned her schedule under a fridge magnet. I catch him checking it when he thinks I'm not looking. He's petrified of missing any changes. The last thing he wants is to bump into her when I'm around.

The fact he keeps checking makes me think he mightn't have been in contact with her since she started cleaning. The thought should cheer me up, but I'm past that.

It's 7.59 on the dot when the doorbell rings. Like Jed and me, she's punctual to a T.

'Hi. Come in.' I open up, and usher her through.

She's wearing smart tailored trousers, and a flimsy blouse. Her lips are glossed in a luscious red, with her shapely nails painted to match. She couldn't make me feel more dowdy.

'Morning. Hope I'm not too early.'

'No, of course not. I'm an early person anyway.'

I don't share that because of her, I can't sleep.

'Where would you like me to start today?' she asks, setting her clunky cleaning basket on the island.

'Fancy a coffee first? There's no hurry.'

She hesitates for only a second.

'If you're sure you don't mind. Yes, please.'

She sits loosely on a stool, long legs dangling, while I make the coffee. Her black pumps caress the tiles. I can't bear to look at her. She's ridiculously at home, as if she's popped into a friend's for a catch-up.

I set the mugs down, along with a couple of almond croissants, and sit beside her.

I've a list of things I want to ask, but she speaks first. Her easy manner reminds me of Adam. She seems nice, not unlike her brother, but I hate her. For how she's ruined my life, and likely Jed's too.

It's hard to bite back the loathing, but I need to keep my blood pressure in check. The only thing that helps is knowing that it'll soon be over.

'Have you always lived here?' she asks. 'It's nice.'

'It is, isn't it? Jed and I moved here when we got married.'

'Do you have family close?' She sips at her coffee, puffing her luscious lips to cool it down, and leaves a red stain around the rim.

'No. My parents are both dead, and neither Jed nor I have brothers or sisters. You're lucky to have a brother.'

I'm curious about her relationship with Adam, and wonder what she'll tell me.

'Adam. Yes, I suppose I am.' Her cheeks flush, and she fiddles with her perfect hair. She could have come straight from the hairdressers. I run a hand down my lanky, unwashed strands. Hard not to see why Jed was tempted, even if it was only the once. The thought curdles my insides.

'He seems nice.' I raise my voice in the tone of a question.

'Oh. You know him?'

She looks agitated, as if she's missed something.

'I met him at Blanche's. He was there when she died.'

'Of course. I forgot. He did tell me.'

She's definitely flustered by the conversation. Could it be

because I reminded her Adam was at the scene of the crime? Or is it something else?

I don't tell her Adam and I have shared coffee and drinks, as I can't risk it getting back to Jed.

'Adam's got his good and bad points,' she mumbles, as if lost in private thoughts.

'Don't all men?'

She nods, and lets out a nervous giggle. I drum my fingers on the worktop, willing her to carry on.

'Adam is two years younger than me. He was always so handsome, even as a little boy.'

She pauses, as if wanting confirmation that her brother is still handsome. But I say nothing, and let her continue.

'He's one for the ladies, such a dreadful flirt.'

She coughs nervously, not at ease talking about him. From her demeanour, it's hard to tell if they're close or not.

Perhaps she knows I went for drinks with her brother. Maybe he told her, and the thought makes me panic. The last thing I need is for Jed to find out.

I look up at the clock. It's already 8.30.

77

Madison sets her mug down.

I'm not ready for her to get up yet, as I feel I'm on to something.

'Here. Have a croissant.' I nudge the plate towards her. 'They're delicious. From the bakery in Sun Street.'

'I should get to work.' She checks her watch.

'Another five minutes. It's nice to have the company.'

It's such a lie, as I'm craving silence. But this might be my last chance to get her to talk. After Friday she'll not be back.

'They do look yummy. If you're sure.'

She breaks the pastry into pieces, and nibbles with her perfect teeth. I leave mine, as I can't stomach food. How can she be so relaxed in my home? Mine and Jed's home.

'It's nice to talk to someone other than Jed. He's not much of a talker.'

Rather than pop more croissant into her mouth, she sets it back on the plate. She's thinking about what to say, when her phone pings.

She lifts her mobile, and checks the screen. A few seconds later, she turns it off, and pushes it to the side.

Perhaps it was Jed checking up on her. Or demanding she finds work elsewhere. Maybe he's threatening her. Who knows? Whenever I mention Madison's name, he goes off on a rant. The thoughts swirl around.

'Men don't talk. You're right there,' she says, swivelling her stool. 'Adam is no different. I can't get him to talk about anything.'

I will her on, biting back a reply. She flicks a few pastry flakes off her blouse, and rounds them up on the worktop before drizzling them back onto the plate.

'He came to live with us when his mum died. He was only four, but even then he was so shy. He talked even less than he does now.'

She could be talking about anyone other than Adam. When I'm with him, he chats for England.

But that's not what's caught my attention.

'Sorry? Live with you?'

'His mum was my mother's best friend. Cancer. They made a pact that Adam would come to live with us after she died.'

The milk jug slips from my hand, and shatters across the floor.

'Shit.'

'Here. Let me help.'

She goes to start picking up the crockery.

'Don't worry. I've got it,' I snap.

As I frantically brush up the shards, she carries on talking. I need her to stop, as I've heard more than enough.

'He's always been handsome, even as a little boy. We used to get on so well. Until more recently.'

I swish a cloth across the spilt milk, avoiding her gaze. She needs to be quiet. A couple of minutes pass before she gets the message.

'Thanks for the coffee. I'd better get to work.'

I haul myself up off the floor, chucking the cloth in the sink.

'Okay. Follow me upstairs, and I'll show you what needs doing.'

I want her out of the house, tempted to tell her I don't feel so good, but instead we trudge up the stairs together.

Her words ring in my ears. *He's such a flirt. One for the ladies.*

A rogue thought hits. What if he couldn't help himself with Madison? After all, they're only brother and sister in name.

They're not blood relations.

78

When Madison finally leaves, I slam the front door, and slump my back against the wood. At least she'll not be back.

I've been worried she mightn't agree, after I cancelled her Wednesday slot, to help me clear out Blanche's things on Friday evening instead. She's so desperate for the money that she didn't hesitate.

This evening when I tell Jed she won't be back he can't hide his relief. But when I say she's helping me clear away Blanche's things, he growls.

'What? Can't you do it yourself? Or wait until the weekend when I can help?'

'I want to get it done, and you said you didn't want to be involved. Madison is strong, and can lift the heavy boxes. Especially up from the cellar, while I do the sorting.'

He sighs, comes up to me, and grips my shoulders.

'Okay, but after Friday, that's it.'

'I'll tell her I won't need her again. I promise.'

His relief is not hard to miss when a smile erupts across his face.

He's leaving for Edinburgh straight after work tomorrow night, not due home till Saturday lunch time.

'Will you miss me?' he asks, for the millionth time.

'Yep. We'll both miss you.'

'And you'll be careful?' His face puckers.

'Of course I'll be careful. Now stop worrying.'

* * *

Jed's concern is suffocating, and by the time Thursday comes around I'm desperate for him to leave.

I watch him limp down the path as he heads off. He's getting the early-evening train up to Scotland, and leaves home clutching his Gucci overnight bag. Everything has taken its toll, and my Jed of old is hard to recognise. He waves weakly as he rounds the corner, blows me a kiss, and disappears from view.

I've got the day mapped out. The last day of my old life, the life I'm scared to leave behind. Fear of what is to come overrides my relief at facing the music. It feels like the calm before the storm. Quite literally.

I turn on the TV, and Storm Margarita is headline news. The alerts make scary listening. The storm is already building out in the Atlantic, and due to reach the South-East sometime late on Friday. It's like a premonition, a bad omen. I say a silent prayer, for the baby and me, and cup both hands around my stomach. At least the scan is booked early.

I shiver when I listen to the forecast. Torrential rain, gale-force winds, possibly flooding, and *a real threat to life*. Although it's only Thursday, a reporter is zooming in on a scene where birds are already circling, squawking, and gathering in swarms. They sense a threat.

When I've heard enough, I turn off the news and head

upstairs. I pull on warm clothes, before rubbing rouge on my cheeks, and rosy gloss across my lips. I look ill, rather than pregnant. I don't usually worry about my appearance, but the mirror confirms I look like death.

My once-healthy hair has weakened, the ends brittle, and as I brush the length a small clump of strands breaks away.

After the weekend, I'll take my appearance to task. I'll sort out my hair with a new cut, a new style. Maybe I'll grow it out, or get extensions. Then I'll treat myself to a new wardrobe. I deserve a treat after all I've been through. Whatever happens, I'll be making some changes. Teagan promises to take me out, spoil me, if I confront Jed and put an end to it all. She says no matter what, she'll be there for me.

Today I'll not be working. I leave my laptop at home, knowing that concentration would be futile. And who knows? Perhaps after the weekend, I'll chuck it all in.

Outside, there's an eerie feel in the air. I shiver. Funny how humans, not unlike the birds, can sense approaching danger.

As I walk, my mind replays the night Dad died. That night there was a storm. Torrential rain lashed against the windows, and sloshed through rotting timbers. When he fell, I'm not sure if he even made a noise. The crash of thunder, along with my screams, were deafening.

But I do remember the lull after the storm, and the silence that followed. I gripped the handrail, and stared down at his distorted body. You could have heard a pin drop, as time stood still. I couldn't move. I never meant to kill him, but I was responsible, and still can't separate the two.

I arrive at Angelo's, but linger on the pavement longer than usual. I look inside, and wonder why the place feels different. It no longer feels warm and welcoming. Once a cosy haven, it's lost its sheen. Even when I watched Jed and Madison, I felt cocooned and camouflaged from all the angst.

But it's all been an illusion. The place now seems bare, lifeless, and Candy's sour face and dagger looks are threatening. The homely welcome has flown.

Candy is dressed today in black, like a Goth rebel. Her pink sparkly trainers have been replaced by black sturdy boots. I wonder, if she had dressed like this weeks ago, if I'd have been so keen to come.

One last time, I get my coffee and sit by the window. When I notice a red lipstick stain round the rim of the mug, I grimace. Even when I rub with a serviette, it won't quite disappear.

Perhaps on Monday I'll try somewhere new. There's a place just opened at the end of Bakehouse Street. El Paradiso. It's Spanish, serving cortados, *café bombón*, and *café con leche*. Who knows? Perhaps I'll own up to Jed that I've moved on from Starbucks.

Then again, perhaps not.

79

It's Friday, and D-Day is finally here. I haven't slept a wink, and whenever I did close my eyes, all I saw were ghosts.

Jed arrived safely in Edinburgh late last night, and has been texting constantly. He's already fed up, wanting to come home, and devastated to be missing the scan.

I texted back before I went to bed, reminding him that his client is important, and hopefully will sign a new contract. Jed used to boast how much he could make, but now commissions are hardly mentioned. He no longer shares what was once an infectious enthusiasm.

I need him to stay in Scotland. Well, I need him to think he's staying, until I phone him later. He has no idea.

Despite all of last night's messages, he calls this morning before he starts work.

'I just needed to hear your voice,' he says.

I speak quietly, with a quaver in my voice, so that he'll pick up on my anxiety. I pretend it's all about the scan, but he has no idea that's the least of my worries.

'Be careful in the storm. If it's too bad, don't go out.' This is the last thing he says before hanging up.

'I will,' I mouth into the air.

As the kettle boils, I turn on the TV. Storm Margarita is nearly here. The forecaster throws in a risible comment, reminding viewers it's Friday the 13th.

'Batten down the hatches,' he says. I shiver. The date is etched on my mind.

A couple of hours' work might help pass the time, and keep my mind off things. I've already picked out a letter on euthanasia, emotive but not too dull.

However, when I try and boot up my laptop, it sticks. I flick it on and off, holding the button for twenty seconds, hoping it will reset. But the screen is completely blank.

'Shit. Shit. Shit.'

Suddenly there's a knock on the front door, and I freeze. Who the heck? It can't be Madison as she's not due this morning. I imagine the police. Friday the 13th. The horror of what happened is always there. I sit very still, willing them to go away.

The knock repeats on a loop. Three or four more times. I tiptoe along the hall, and press my eye to the peephole. It's Teagan, holding up a bunch of flowers. She never forgets the date.

'Izzy. I know you're in there. It's only me. Teagan,' she yells up close.

I unpin the chain, and let her in.

'Teagan. Sorry, I was upstairs,' I lie. She doesn't deserve the lies as she's my only friend. Through thick and thin she's been there.

'It's okay. I knew you'd be at home.'

She zooms in for a hug. It feels so good, and I'm close to breaking down when she disengages.

'Come on. Aren't you going to make me a coffee?'

She's like a beacon in choppy seas.

'Of course. Sorry, I've been miles away.'

She sits at the kitchen table, and looks at me strangely.

'You look dreadful. Are you okay? You've lost weight, and you're so pale.'

No idea why I tell her I'm fine, as I feel every bit as bad as I look.

'Izzy, I've been reading your column,' she says.

'Oh. It keeps me busy.' I snap the kettle on, keep my face averted.

'It's me you're talking to. I know you, Izzy. You've been putting your own story into print. Right?'

'Sort of.' I can't kid Teagan. She's like my mother.

'Have you confronted Jed yet? Did you have his mistress to dinner? And...'

'And?' My voice wobbles.

'Are you really pregnant?'

It's then I start to cry. Really cry. Large choking sobs. When there's no let-up, Teagan looks set to call an ambulance.

'Does Jed know?'

'Yes,' I manage. 'The first scan is today.'

'Is he coming?' She looks even more concerned than she did over the choking.

'It's okay. He's in Edinburgh on work. I told him not to cancel.'

'Oh, Izzy. Come here.'

I collapse into her, and start wailing all over again. The last few months of bottled-up secrets finally erupt.

When she asks me how much Jed knows, how much he's told me, about Madison, their son, I don't know where to start.

'Teagan. I'm confronting him tonight. He's coming back early.'

I'm assuming he'll come back early when I call him.

'Promise?'

'Yes. And I'm confronting his mistress at the same time.'

'Oh?' A raised eyebrow.

I've no idea if she's shocked or thinks it's a good idea. It doesn't matter because that's what I'm going to do.

After today, I'll never lie again. Certainly not to Teagan.

80

After Teagan leaves, I feel buoyed for having let off so much steam. We didn't talk about what happened on Friday the 13th all those years ago. It's an anniversary I've spent my life trying to forget. The flowers let me know she understands.

Now I need to get to work, kick my brain into gear. For a minute I forget that my laptop isn't working.

It's 10.30, so I message Jed to get back to me. ASAP.

At 10.40 on the dot, he calls.

'Izzy? What's up?' He sounds breathless.

'I'm fine. Just my laptop isn't working. Can I use your old one?'

I hear a laden sigh of relief.

'Of course. It's in the bottom of my sock drawer. I didn't want you throwing it out when you tidied up.'

'As if.' I tut. 'Thanks. I'll call you later.'

'I'll be waiting. Don't forget.'

Before he says anything more, I disconnect. I'll definitely be calling him later, but with more than news about the scan.

I skip up the stairs, my heart lighter. Maybe things will work out. When everything is out in the open, perhaps Jed and I can manage together. Like we did before. He'll explain everything, and hopefully it'll make sense. I might even forgive his one-night stand. I don't mull on the lies, as now isn't the time. Who knows? Perhaps he'll beg me to understand why he lied, explaining that it was all one big mistake.

Baby flutters. A little warning.

'It's okay,' I repeat for the millionth time in a soothing tone.

The drawer is stuffed with pairs and pairs of socks. I chuck at least twenty pairs onto the bed before I locate the laptop. Typical Jed, the charger is wrapped inside a single sock. I hum, keeping myself company the way I used to do.

When I'm back in the kitchen, I open a carton of chicken soup. The label says it's home-made (in a factory somewhere, Jed laughs), but it's packed with healthy ingredients.

My stomach is seriously gurgling, and I have the first pang of an appetite in I don't know how long.

Outside is getting darker, and darker. It's pretty creepy, as the tree branches are starting to sway. The clouds are building and there's a real eerie atmosphere. At the far end of the garden, the apple tree is bare, the abundance of fruit long gone.

The morning sickness eases after a few mouthfuls of soup. Once I've cleaned the plate, the old laptop should have enough charge to use.

As I watch the screen, I mull over how much longer I'll work for the magazine. After all the angst, I don't think it'll be long. The library is recruiting, so that is likely to be my first stop.

I mentioned to Jed not so long ago that I'd been mulling over a new career. One that might make us millions.

'Oh. What's that?' he asked with a wry smile.

'I might write a book.'

'A book?'

'Why not? A thriller. I'm starting with the title.'

'Hit me,' he said.

'I've got a few possibilities. *The Quiet Family. Bodies in the Basement. The Girl Who Couldn't Speak. A Pack of Lies.* What do you think?'

'I think you're crazy.'

His unease was hard to miss. He got up, feigning cramp, and circled the lounge. I thought of a caged lion. My title suggestions certainly hit a nerve. Several nerves perhaps. But he didn't say any more, and hasn't mentioned the idea since.

When I try to get into the laptop, I realise I haven't got the password. Jed changes passwords on all his gadgets at least once a month. Weird. He thinks it will keep the hackers out.

I text him, asking for the password. A second later, he sends it through. Perhaps he didn't immediately twig, because a second later he deletes the message. But not before I've got it down.

Hawkeye1234.

Perhaps a better title would be: *A Liar and a Cheat.*

81

No idea how I make it to the scan as I'm all over the place again.

I now know Jed has read all my letters. All my recent *personal* column letters. The ones about cheating. The one about elderly relatives living on their own. And... the one about the reader being pregnant.

He knew all along. As I sit in the white-walled waiting room plastered with pictures of bouncy, cherub-faced babies, I'm sick to the core. Why did he respond to my column? Did he want me to know he was on to me? Why didn't he say? We could then have had it all out in the open. He must have known he wouldn't get away with it forever.

I try and justify his reaction when I told him I was pregnant. He must have guessed from my column, but likely wasn't certain. Otherwise he couldn't have been so over-the-top thrilled when I told him. Could that also have been an act?

I check my screenshots for the replies he sent in as Hawkeye1234. Each one was warning me off rocking the boat. *Be grateful for what you have. Leave well alone. Crazy idea having the mistress to dinner. Stick by your husband. He's still with you. Leave the guy alone.*

Then I reread the text message from an anonymous caller, warning me that staying with my husband might be the wisest move. I'm now guessing Jed has a burner phone stashed away somewhere too.

What I don't get is, that if he was on to me, why didn't he confront me? Could we really be so much alike, that he's no braver than I am to face the music?

By the time I'm lying on the midwife's couch, my blood pressure is sky high.

The nurse tells me I need to take it easy. High blood pressure can lead to all sorts of complications.

She checks my records, and looks concerned when she sees I suffer generally from very low blood pressure. The sort of reading that can make you dizzy.

I promise her I'll buy a home monitor, and keep an eye on it. What's the point in telling her the real reason for my racing heart and rocketing blood pressure?

At least I've now got a convincing reason to phone Jed. It's not a lie. He'll be home like a shot when I tell him how worried I am.

Meanwhile baby is booming. Its little heartbeat sounded like a kettle drum. Loud and strong. The feeling of love is overwhelming, and I wonder what Jed will say when he learns it's a boy.

It's nearly one by the time I get home. Once I'm safely inside, I kick my shoes off, and collapse onto the sofa.

There have been four texts from Jed, wondering why I haven't got back about the scan.

How did it go?

Is everything okay?

Where are you?

I'm really worried. Call me. Please xx

He's likely back in meetings, but I pull up his number, and press dial. I'm shaking like a leaf, praying that he'll bite. I know Jed. Well, I thought I did, but this time at least I'm confident he'll play ball. He picks up straightaway.

'Jed. It's me.'

'Izzy. What's up? Why haven't you got back?'

'I'm okay.'

'The baby? Is it the baby?'

Somehow I let the tears come. I'm not even sure if they're theatrical, or real. But I feel so shit, they flow easily.

Jed is quick to pick up on my distress.

'Izzy?'

'It's just my blood pressure is sky high. I'm scared, Jed. Baby is fine, but it's a danger. I don't like to ask, but...'

Another sob, and he starts to freak out.

'But what? Tell me. What's going on?' His words speed up. It's as if I'm about to tell him I'm dying.

'Can you come home? I'm really anxious, and need you here.'

Without hesitation, he says, 'I'm on my way. I'll get the next train, and I can be there by seven.'

'Thanks.'

'Don't thank me. I love you, Izzy, and I'll always be there. Sod the bloody client.'

I hang up.

The plan is to tell him, when he texts from the train, that I feel a lot better, and am going to go to Blanche's as agreed. I need to keep busy. I'll tell him Madison has cancelled, and ask if he'll meet me there and help out instead.

When he gets there, I'll show him the scan.

After he and Madison have told me everything.

82

I'm ready to leave home shortly before six. I need to be there before both Jed and Madison.

Madison is likely to be there first, as the trains are running late, and Jed keeps texting, begging me not to leave the house. He'd rather meet me at home.

I hear the storm rampage through the house, as if it's inside. It's so loud. Thunder, lightning, rain. It couldn't get any worse.

I must be mad, but I can't pull out now. Jed will have no choice but to come to Blanche's if I'm there.

> I'm on my way to Blanche's. Stop worrying. See you there soon X

I keep it simple.

I slip my phone in my bag, pick up the keys, and dare to open the front door. It nearly flies off the hinges. I know I should pull out, go back inside, but I don't. Ten minutes, if I drive carefully, I can be there.

It's even worse outside than I could have imagined. The rain is blinding, coming down in sheets. Weirdly, the car starts first go, and I take it as a sign to carry on.

I drive at a snail's pace, and somehow make it to Miners' Terrace. The car buffets from side to side as I try and park up, and the wind howls like a banshee, rattling the windows. There's only one tree left in the whole street, in the garden next to Blanche's, and it's bent double.

A streak of lighting sears through the sky, followed by a clatter of thunder. I thrust my hands over my ears, the noise terrifying. I'm tempted to stay in the car, but as rain is pooling heavily on the street, I reckon I'll be safer in the house.

Somehow I struggle out of the car, and make it to the front door. My trainers are drenched, and even under my coat, I can feel my clothes are sodden. I drop the keys a couple of times before I find purchase in the lock.

As soon as I get inside, I slam the door behind me, but leave it unlocked for Madison. And Jed.

There's a spooky silence in the hall. The thunder is still crashing, but inside is seriously creepy. The floorboards creak as I stumble a few steps to find the light switch.

Shit. The light comes on for a couple of seconds, fizzes, then everything is back in darkness.

I pull out my phone, turn on the torch and inch towards the cellar. I think the fuse box might be in the basement, but I'm not sure. I try the switch at the top of the stairs, the one that lights the dangling bulb, but there's nothing. Likely a single fuse has tripped the whole circuit.

If I can't find the circuit board, I'll have to bring up some candles. Blanche kept a stash for emergencies, and they're in the cupboard right at the bottom.

I gingerly pick my way down over the stone-flagged steps. It's like entering an ice cave, it's so cold. My heart is seriously racing, and my blood pressure isn't doing much better. I can feel it rising even higher.

Water has started to collect over the flagstones, where it's seeped in from outside, and it's now puddling around the log stash. At least there is some dry wood upstairs, as my plan is to light the burner.

I yank open the doors of the cupboard and find a whole stash of candles, as well as a box of matches. I scoop the lot into the end of my hoodie, and somehow make it back to the top in one piece.

I dump them by the log burner, and am just about to light a couple when there's a clattering outside. I freeze. Before I go to see what's happened, the front door sweeps open.

And Madison appears.

I check my watch, no idea how it can already be seven o'clock.

83

'Madison,' I scream. Her sudden appearance makes my hairs stand up, and I have to steady myself by gripping on to a chairback.

'Hi. I tried to call you, but I couldn't get any reception. I did text though.'

I don't tell her I got the message, but there was no way she wasn't coming. Tonight is the end of the line, and if I made it, so could she.

'I'm so glad to see you. It's scary here on your own,' I laugh, sounding weirdly like a squealing hyena.

I point the torch at her face, and the shadows make her look strange. I can't see if she's smiling, her features look so distorted.

'I wasn't sure if you'd be here,' she says, tugging off a long red coat. How can she look so glamorous in this weather?

I swallow back the nausea, knowing I've got to hold it together.

'I'm sorry, I've muted my phone,' I lie. It's not muted, as I'm desperate to hear from Jed. The trains are delayed, and he's not sure of his exact ETA.

'It's dark,' she says, spinning her head in all directions.

'The lights have fused. But listen, I've got loads of candles.' I point towards the log burner. 'If you help me, we can light the place up. It'll be fun,' I quip. 'May as well get to work now we're here.'

'Of course.'

'Maybe by the time we're done, the storm will have calmed down.'

Then she does a strange thing. She extends an arm, and hands me a carrier bag.

'What's this?'

I peek inside. It's a bottle of wine, and a box of expensive-looking Hotel Chocolat chocolates.

'For you. Izzy, I need to talk to you.'

'Oh.'

I stare at her, what I can see of her. What is she going to tell me? What does she want to talk about? I'm the one who is going to ask the questions.

For an awful second, I imagine the gifts are in exchange for my husband. To say sorry. To thank me, and to tell me her and Jed are now a couple. My mind is spinning with ludicrous notions.

'Shall we light the candles first, and then maybe have a chat before we get to work?'

I set down the wine and chocolates, but first go and lock the front door. The catch is loose, and we don't need it flying open. Jed will have his own key anyway.

For the millionth time I look at my phone. Nothing more from Jed, and it's already 7.10. His train was due in ages ago. Now I've no choice but to listen to what Madison has to say. I was hoping I'd make them both talk and listen at the same time. Look into the whites of both their eyes.

We set to lighting the candles all around the living room, keeping some for the route through to the cellar where all the heavy boxes are stored. Madison says she's happy to bring them up one by one.

'Thanks. I'm wary of lifting anything heavy,' I own up, and pat my stomach.

'You're pregnant?' she asks. She doesn't look surprised, as she's likely been reading my column too, or perhaps Jed shared the good news.

'Yes.'

'I did wonder,' she continues, 'as you've been feeling so nauseous. I recognised the symptoms.'

'I'd no idea it was that obvious.'

I can't look at her. What is her game? She's acting as if we're best friends.

'Congratulations,' she says.

'It's a boy. Benjamin will soon have a half-brother.'

She pauses as she's about to light another candle. Luckily Blanche has loads of metal candle holders, the sort the Victorians took up to bed. Madison strikes the match, lights up, and sets the holder down. Already the room is getting brighter.

'That's what I want to talk to you about.'

I'm not sure if she's flushed, red in the face, or if it's the half-light. She's staring at me, willing me to pick up on the importance of what she wants to tell me.

I'd love to run a mile, but I have to listen. I've waited long enough, and can't turn back now. I know most of what she's likely to say, but it's the gaps that need filling in.

I bend down, move the logs around the burner, and put a match to one of the kindling sticks. I stay hunched down until the fire starts to spit, and hiss.

'Let's light a few more candles first.'

We work for several more minutes in silence, until we finally sit down opposite each other.

With a sour expression, I watch as she fiddles with her hair. Her hands are shaky, as she stares into the fire.

'Shall I start at the beginning?' she asks.

'Where else?' I ask.

It looks as if I might finally get some answers.

84

'I know you've been watching me and Jed from Angelo's.'

I wince at her opening words, as they suggest accusation. But I let her carry on.

'I can see down onto the street, the way you can see up. I never said anything to Jed, as I didn't twig for ages who you were.'

'Go on.'

'I met Jed about two and a half years ago. I was working in Ibiza.'

'Lap dancing, I think.'

'Yes.' She looks at me quizzically. 'Truth is, I targeted Jed. None of this has been his fault.'

She takes a swig from a bottle of water.

'I hadn't long been in Ibiza. I'd left England in a dreadful state.' She takes a deep breath. 'Anyway, that's another story. The night we met, I was playing the room, eager for tips.'

'Bet they were good.' My sarcasm makes her flinch, and she takes a moment to compose herself.

'I needed the money. When I spotted Jed, he was sitting aloof from his mates. He was the only one not knocking back cheap champagne. Even in the dark seedy bar, I sensed his unease. I guessed it was his stag do.'

She guessed the man she targeted was about to be married. I want to put my hands over my ears, and scream. She targeted my fiancé so that she could get pregnant. At least it wasn't love at first sight.

'One of Jed's friends got up on the table, waved his arms in the air and chanted. *Jed. Jed. Jed.* I felt sorry for him.'

If she's after points for caring, she hasn't got a chance in hell.

'Go on.'

'Jed didn't want to spoil their fun, but you could see he was uncomfortable. He eventually joined in, and began knocking back the champagne. That's when I shimmied closer. I flicked my knickers back and forth, like we were told to do, until they were filled with notes. The other girls urged me to keep going until walking became difficult.'

As the fire burns brighter, I can see her features better. Small teardrops leak from her sad eyes.

Something about her demeanour and discomfort tells me that I could be about to hear the whole story. No stone unturned.

'I winked at Jed when he handed me a twenty-euro note. His friend, Jordan, I think it was, yelled at Jed to rip my knickers off. I remember wondering how Jed had him as a friend.'

'No idea.' I'm with her on this. 'And... I'm all ears.'

'Sorry.' She wipes tears away with her hand. 'I kept an eye on Jed, and when he got up, I took my chance. I moved quickly, guessing he was heading for the gents', and blocked the entrance when he got there. I leant provocatively up against the door.'

I can visualise her, half-naked, bathing in Jed's discomfort. In this moment I hate her as much as I did Dad. My level of loathing is frightening.

Yet as I listen, I still wonder why Jed fell for it. Why did he let his guard down? I've gone over it again and again. Even when drunk he maintains a steely control.

As her words tumble out, I wonder if I ever really knew him at all. If he was so easily seduced, then perhaps our life really has been built on one enormous lie.

She then tells me what happened next. How they talked, how miserable he looked, and how she used this to her advantage.

'I said I could do with the company if he fancied a change of scene. I suggested we go somewhere and grab a coffee.'

'Let me guess. He said, "Why not."'

85

Suddenly there's an almighty crash outside. I yelp, and Madison jumps.

'It sounds as if something has flown off the roof,' she says.

From where I'm sitting, it sounds as if half the roof has collapsed. But I don't care. If the house caves in on us, it might be the best thing that could happen. All the misery would get buried alive.

The storm is still raging, and it looks as if Jed might not have made it back yet. There's been no more messages, and likely he's also lost reception. But I'm confident that if he knows I'm here, he'll brave the storm. Perhaps he's popped home first to check.

But none of that matters now. Madison has started her story, and I need her to finish. Jed will likely have nothing left to add. Perhaps it's best he doesn't make it.

The door rattles, the windows shake, and water has started to drip through a gap in the roof. Dangerously near an electric cable.

Despite another almighty bang, and the dangers all around, the only thing that matters is to hear the end of Madison's story.

'Listen, Izzy. I'm so sorry.'

She's at it again. My understanding. My sympathy. My caring. But I feel numb, drained of all emotion.

Perhaps she really does believe she'll get out of it all with an apology. She might feel better confessing, and getting it all off her chest, but I couldn't feel any worse.

'What are you really sorry for, Madison? Ruining mine, or ruining Jed's life?' My hiss mingles with spit from the fire. 'Is it forgiveness you're after?'

'The truth is nothing happened.'

'So Benjamin is just an illusion.'

It's hard to shout with effect, as the storm orchestra is relentless.

'Jed did come back to my room. It was in a cheap hotel where all the girls stayed. He fell asleep on the bad. That was it. Nothing actually happened.'

I'm seriously close to hurling the metal candle holder across the room. She must think I'm crazy if she thinks I'm going to fall for it.

'I've already heard he woke up naked in your bed.'

I lift the poker, wave it in her face. She looks terrified that I might smack it over her head. I'm sorely tempted.

'I'm sorry. I'm really, really sorry. You've got to believe me.'

She starts to cry, tears rolling down her cheeks.

I stick the metal poker in the fire, prod violently at the embers, and add a couple more logs. I know she hasn't finished her tale, but I'm dreading what's to come.

Minutes tick by as we sit beside each other like a couple of actors in *Waiting for Godot*.

I feel sick to the core, and wonder why I don't just drag her out into the storm. Hearing her confirm my worst fears, I doubt I'll ever be able to forgive Jed. Even if he does admit the truth.

'You see, I was already pregnant when I met Jed.'

She chokes on the words, and I wonder if I've heard correctly. Until she repeats herself.

'Benjamin isn't Jed's. Your husband and I never slept together.'

86

When a sudden cramp attacks my calf, I have to get up and walk about.

Madison looks concerned, doubtful because of the pain, more likely because I haven't responded to what she's said. Likely she's expecting a barrage of questions, or perhaps an onslaught of abuse.

It's hard to take it all in, and I walk round and round trying to get my head straight. If she didn't sleep with Jed, and Benjamin isn't his, who the hell is the father?

Presumably she's used Jed to get support for Benjamin. *A single mum. It's tough on your own.* How many times has she said this? But why Jed? More to the point, why did he pay her? Couldn't he have done a DNA test? Perhaps he fell in love with her.

I check my phone. More for something to do than anxious to hear from Jed. I've given up hoping that he's going to show, and now want to hear the end of her story without him around. He might try and make her stop talking.

Madison doesn't comment when I go to the kitchen for a

glass of water. She's sitting up very straight, sipping relentlessly from her Evian bottle. I'm like her father confessor, and wonder how long she's been wanting to tell me. Perhaps Jed threatened her to silence, but she can't hold it in any more. I can't help wondering, *why now?*

It's eight o'clock. I can hear noise all around, as if Blanche is listening. There's a creak, a rattle, a thump, as if her ghost is haunting us.

'Can I finish the story? Please.' Madison speaks even before I've sat down again.

'I'm listening.'

'I fled England when I knew I was pregnant. Adam tried to dissuade me. He called me a tart, a whore when I told him I was going to work in a lap-dancing club.'

Adam's name is making sense. He could be the key to the whole mess.

'Adam?' I ask, as if I'm curious.

'He wouldn't speak to me for days when I told him I was off. We were so close. Too close. Funny, it's all right for a guy to sleep around, but not for a woman.'

I visualise Adam, his broad shoulders, his good looks, his easy manner. He could have his pick of girls. Now I feel uneasy when I remember the butterflies in my own stomach.

'He dropped me off at the airport, and as I wheeled my case towards the terminal, I didn't look back. He still has no idea why I really left. And certainly not what my plan was.'

A spark springs out from the fire, lands on the rug. I trample it frantically with my foot.

'I'm now guessing he's the father.'

It's starting to make sense. But not quite.

'Yes. Adam is Benjamin's father.'

I can't bear to hear the end of the tale. Tinnitus has started to play havoc with my ears, as a loud ringing won't let up.

But it's not over yet. The questions just keep coming.

Why didn't she tell Adam that she was pregnant?

Did Jed really think he'd slept with her?

How did she persuade Jed that he was the father?

And why did Jed go along with it?

Why is he still going along with it?

Half an hour is all it takes for me to have the answers.

It was all to do with love. Madison has always been in love with Adam, ever since he moved in to live with her. Her feelings grew as they got older, and only once did he sleep with her. She made it easy for him, and he instantly regretted it and told her it must never happen again.

He's never felt the same for her as she has for him. She's still living in the hope that perhaps, one day, he will. If she had told him about being pregnant, he'd have made her have an abortion. She couldn't risk him never speaking to her again. When

Benjamin was born, she loved having Adam around to play with him. By then it was too late to own up to what she'd done.

Her eyes glass over in the telling. She's still in love with him.

'How did you get Jed to sleep with you?'

'Oh, Izzy. I'm sorry.'

She's like a stuck record with all the *sorrys*. I have to bite my tongue.

'What did you do?'

'Rohypnol. What else? I drugged his coffee, and he went out cold. He had no idea I undressed him. Not an easy task.' She rolls her eyes, tries to make light. 'When he woke, and saw the scene, he put two and two together. I was on the other side of the island by then.'

'Why didn't he do a DNA test? How did you track him down?'

'He was easy to track down. I made sure I knew where he lived. I followed him to Hinton, and when I presented Benjamin as his, he had no choice but to support us.'

'Did he have feelings for you?'

I don't know why I ask this, but why didn't he tell me? It was all one big mistake. One huge lie that Madison concocted.

'No. Jed doesn't have feelings for me. We get on. He loves Benjamin, and has been a great dad.'

'Why? Why did he accept your word for it?'

'Don't you know?'

Then it comes back to me. The one sentence I said to Jed that has sealed so many of our fates.

It was just before we got married. He asked what I'd do if he ever strayed. I promised, over my dead body, that I'd leave him. I'd never be back. Even if it was only a one-night stand.

Jed has always trusted me with his life. Why would he have doubted me then?

'Jed loves you so much. He said if you ever found out he'd so much as had a one-night stand, you'd never be able to forgive him. He could never risk losing you.'

'But he didn't sleep with you?'

'No. But he doesn't know that.'

———————

88

At last I've got my jigsaw completed. It sort of makes sense in a convoluted way.

Money and love. They make the world go round. Maybe I played a part with my wild throwaway comment. I wonder, would I really have left Jed if he'd had a one-night stand? It was before we were married, so perhaps I'd have stuck by him. We'll never know.

I feel a weird sense of relief. Outside the storm is quietening down, the wind no more than a whisper through the cracks. An occasional streak of lightning passes by, the thunder no more than a faint rumble.

Funny, I should be furious with Madison, but she looks so sad, and as if she's genuinely sorry. Once Jed finds out, I wonder how forgiving he'll feel. Whether it's Madison or me that tells him, it won't be easy.

Although it's been tough for me, I dread to think what the truth will do to Jed.

'Do you still want me to help you?' Madison's whisper breaks into my thoughts. Her voice is shaky, but it's tinged with relief. Relief that she's finally told me.

I smile. I might one day be able to forgive her, but I'll never forget. They're two completely different things.

'That's why you're here, isn't it? Let's get started. First, there are a load of boxes in the cellar if you could bring them up.'

'Of course. And Izzy. I really am sorry.'

I ignore the repetition.

'I'll start clearing upstairs if you can bring the boxes up from the cellar.'

We stand up at the same time, and she awkwardly nudges past.

I head towards the stairs, and suddenly the lights flicker to life. Well, the two lights I tried to turn on earlier.

'At least you'll be able to see what you're doing,' I yell after her. But there's no reply.

The light in the cellar should have come back on. I hover on the stairs, halfway up, and watch as she walks slowly towards the top of the cellar stairs. I never closed the door.

If I lean close against the wall, I have a good view. Her shoulders are rounded, her gait uncertain. It's taken her a lot of effort to tell me.

I know how much I loved Jed. It all makes sense if he loved me as much as I did him. If only he'd told me the truth. So many lies, so much subterfuge.

Yet I feel a little glow inside. If it was all because he loved me, too scared that I'd leave him, perhaps we can move on. Who knows? Maybe I'll do one last column. Telling the world about forgiveness.

All of a sudden I freeze. I push my back hard into the wall. I come over hot, and feel as if I'm suffocating. In an instant my life flashes before me. The night Dad died. Images of Blanche's fall down the cellar steps. I want to scream out. Tell Madison to move away.

Before it's too late.

The warning sticks in my throat, and my yell won't come out. I lean across, grip the handrail, and sway back and forth. No. No. No. I take out my phone. This time I don't use the torch, but set the video rolling.

Later I wonder why I did. I guess I knew in my heart what was going to happen.

I can't hear what's being said. But I sense the heat from here. I'm shaking like a leaf as I watch an outstretched arm push Madison. It's a gentle nudge at first, but then with an almighty thrust, using both his hands, she's catapulted down the stone stairs.

Tripping over my feet, I somehow make it as far as the landing. I stumble into Blanche's room and collapse onto the unmade bed. My heart is thrashing in my chest.

Jed must have come through the back door. I locked the front door, but didn't he have a key?

Maybe it was the noise from the storm. Maybe he tiptoed, stealthy as a ninja. But we didn't hear him come in.

It looks as if he might have heard it all.

89

From the bedroom, I can hear the back door slam. Has he left? Is he pretending that he wasn't here? No one would have seen him come in. Not in this weather, and not round the back. Is he already working on an alibi?

My mind careens along. But I need to check on Madison. How am I going to be able to go into the cellar and face my nightmares all over again?

'Izzy? Izzy? It's me. Where are you?'

Jed yells at the top of his voice. He hasn't gone. It looks as if he might pretend he's just arrived, and has slammed the back door to let me know he's arrived.

I don't reply, until I'm out on the landing.

'Jed? I'm up here. Coming.'

Then he screams. As if he's looked down, and noticed the body for the first time. He's going to pretend all the way.

'Izzy. Izzy. Come here now!' His command is piercing. He races to the bottom of the stairs and looks up at me.

'Jed. What's up?'

'It's Madison. She's fallen down the stairs.'

'What?'

The time for honesty has gone. He really is going to pretend that he's just found her there. My Jed. My deceiver. My husband.

He looks mad. He's holding his phone, as if he's going to make a call.

'Izzy. I thought for an awful moment it was you down there.' He nods his head in the direction of the cellar.

I walk as if in a trance. Sleepwalking to the edge of a cliff. Like Mum must have done when she inched her way to the edge of the railway platform.

'Hurry. Hurry. We need to call an ambulance.'

Why we? He needs to call an ambulance.

'Are you okay? You look dreadful,' he says, as if registering properly that I'm here.

I push past him, no idea how my legs are working. They're like jelly.

'She's down there,' he says, as if I can't see.

I stare down, and there's not the faintest movement. I could be looking at Dad, or Blanche, all over again. I can see blood. It's mingling with the pool of water, and draining away under the crack in the door.

Jed makes the call, and speaks quickly, but clearly. He gives the address of where he is, his full name, and the name of the person who has fallen. Madison Finch. Thirty-four years of age. He even mentions she has a son. Benjamin.

I don't go down into the cellar, but instead go back into the lounge. My legs have lost all feeling, and I have to sit down.

'They'll be at least ten minutes,' Jed says once he's disconnected. 'I'll go and check for a pulse. See what I can do.'

My lips curl, but if he notices my eyes are blank, icy cold, he doesn't comment. He'll put it down to shock. All that's important to him is that he's taking over. He'll show me how good he is in a crisis. More brownie points for my devoted husband.

He treads carefully down the stone stairs. I hear his leather brogues take measured steps. He'll not risk falling over the slimy descent.

Everywhere now is really quiet. Quieter than it's ever been, like the lull after the storm. It's then I hear a click. It's a key. I lift myself up from the chair, crane my neck to the right, and see the front door open.

My first thought is the ambulance has arrived. Maybe Jed left his key in the front door by mistake, before sneaking round the back. Perhaps I never locked it.

Then a vision in black appears in front of me. Like a member of the Gestapo, in heavy-duty lace-up boots, and a trench coat. It takes me a minute to recognise them.

'Candy?'

'Izzy. Izzy. Is Madison here? She needs to come quickly. Ben has got worse.'

90

'Candy? What are you doing here?'

'It's Ben. He's got worse. Madison didn't want to leave him, and I can't get hold of her. He's had a temperature all day, but he's convulsing.' Candy's eyes are wide in terror.

I suspect Madison's need to get things off her chest was overwhelming, and overrode a mother's instinct.

Candy's coat and boots are drenched, and her hair sodden like a floor mop. Black mascara dribbles down her cheeks.

I jump up when Jed appears. If Candy looks like a ghost, Jed is like a vampire. The pair are like spooky ghouls from a horror movie.

'They're on their way,' Jed says. He doesn't look at Candy. I wonder if he'll pretend not to know her. Madison mentioned that Candy babysits, so Jed must surely have met her before.

Candy starts to cry, and grows hysterical. She's desperate for us to get how worried she is about Ben. When neither Jed nor I speak, she quietens, and the sobs are replaced by an uneasy silence.

I touch her arm, and lead her to the chair where Madison was sitting less than ten minutes ago. I gently press her down.

'Candy.'

'What? Where's Madison? She needs to get home. I don't know what to do about Benjamin. He has a real fever. I couldn't get a signal and had to walk the whole way here.'

Her words tumble out in a torrent of distress.

'Candy. She's had an accident,' Jed says. I was right. Of course he knows who she is.

'What sort of accident?' Candy is trembling head to toe.

'She's fallen down the stairs. We're waiting for the ambulance.'

'What? What stairs? Is it serious? Oh my God. That's what happened to Blanche.'

Her eyes are agog.

She tries to get up, but I tell her not to. She then looks frightened, as if I have an agenda she hasn't worked out yet.

'Yes, it's serious. How bad is Ben? Someone needs to get to him,' I say.

'Ben? What's up with Ben?' Jed pipes up. He stares at Candy, shock scrunching up his features. I wonder if he's momentarily forgotten that Madison said he's not the father. I'm certain he must have heard our whole conversation.

'He's really ill. I don't know what to do. Can you come with me, Izzy, drive me there? He needs a doctor.'

'Best to phone his dad. Let him deal with it,' I say.

Candy goes silent, and buttons her lips. Then it clicks. She thinks Jed is the father, and is scared to say it in front of me. Madison has told no one other than me (and Jed, by mistake) that Adam is the father.

'Phone him now. Use my phone if you can't get a signal,' I say, handing across my mobile. 'Tell him to go round straightaway. He can be there in five minutes.'

Jed watches me. He'll be wondering how I know Adam lives so close. Probably wondering if I know exactly where he lives. Jed's eyes darken in the dying glow of embers.

'Izzy. I shouldn't tell you this, but...'

'It's okay, Candy. I know what you're going to say. But Jed isn't Ben's father.'

She looks from me to Jed, and back again.

'But Madison told me in confidence that Jed is his father,' she says, gritting her teeth as she waits for a backlash. But both Jed and I are silent.

Jed's likely still in shock, but he's not going to comment now. Not with the dead body of the woman he's just killed lying cold in the cellar. His face is hard, set in stone. I knew he was a good actor, a good keeper of secrets, but a calculating murderer? Looks like I've been even more wrong about him than I could ever have imagined.

'Well, he's not. Now get a move on. You need to call Adam.'

The rest of the night passes in a blur.

The ambulance arrives, followed on closely by the police. Madison is pronounced dead at the scene, and her body is zipped up in what looks like a sturdy black binbag.

I gag as it's stretchered out, while Jed puts a comforting hand around my shoulders.

Candy is in the worst state of us all. She's in such shock that she mumbles incoherently when the police ask her questions. A medic makes her sit down, and gives her a sedative, suggesting to the police they leave further questioning until the morning.

At least she gets hold of Adam. She rambles into the phone, her words disjointed. One of the ambulance crew phones for a first responder when they hear about Ben. Candy is in such a state that I take my phone back.

I tell Adam to get round to the flat straightaway, as he needs to let the medic in, and take care of Ben. I repeat that Madison has had an accident, and like Candy, I don't use the word dead. When I mention Ben, I don't use the word father either.

Adam says, 'Of course.' Madison is his sister, after all.

Once the ambulance has left, Candy tells me in a tearful voice that it's not up to her to tell Adam that he's Ben's father. She promised Madison never to talk about his father to anyone. She really did believe it was Jed.

'Adam told me he didn't want children,' she says. 'I hoped he might one day.'

She snivels when she tells me she loves Adam. I listen quietly, and let her talk. She has a teenage crush on him, and is already more consumed about the revelation that he's a father than about the death of Madison.

I feel for her. Love is like that, all consuming. I could be listening to myself. It's how I once felt for Jed.

The police mooch around, asking random questions, confirming that tomorrow they'll be round to take full statements. We give them our address, and phone numbers. When they ask Candy for her details, she looks horrified.

'Why?' she asks.

'Because you are present at the scene of a death. Everyone needs to be questioned,' a young officer tells her.

'Oh.' She hangs her head, and sobs into a sodden tissue. Her face is almost completely black from runny mascara. 'Can I go home now?'

'I'll drive you,' Jed suggests, looking towards the officer.

'Good idea, sir. But she shouldn't be left alone.'

'It's okay. Lindsay, my flatmate, is home.'

Jed goes outside to start up my car. At least the rain has stopped, and only an occasional flash of lightning breaks through.

'Candy, may I have your key back?' I ask her.

'Sure.' She fumbles in her pocket, and hands it over.

It's attached to a broken keyring, with a snapped-off piece of a metal clothes peg.

It's the matching piece to the one I found beside Blanche's body. What seems like a lifetime ago.

91

Jed takes Candy home, while I wait at Blanche's, soaking up the fading heat from the log burner.

Jed didn't ask to see the scan, forgetting it in all the drama. I hold up the grainy image, and trace the baby's outline with a finger. My perfect little boy.

I'm so lost in thought, in the silent world of ghosts, that I jump when I hear the horn beep. Jed is back.

I fold the scan in two, and slip it in my bag. Time enough to share when we get home. It's going to be a long night.

The first thing Jed does when we get home is to offer to make me a sweet tea.

'Sugar. Good for shock,' he says.

'Sure. Thanks.'

It's still only ten o'clock, and although I'm exhausted, there's no way I'll be able to sleep.

Jed is like a robot, fiddling with the kettle, the mugs, the milk, the sugar. I wonder how I'd behave if I'd just heard that I'm not a father, and if I'd killed someone.

'Let's go into the lounge,' I suggest, carrying my mug in both hands.

He takes his time, moseying around in the kitchen. Probably trying to work out what to say. How to approach everything. I've no idea how honest he'll be, or how contrite, but I'm so worn out with what's happened that I feel numb. I'm no longer sure I care.

He sits on an armchair, while I stretch out on the sofa. Small, dimly lit table lamps mute the atmosphere.

'Izzy. I don't know where to start.'

'Perhaps at the beginning?' My voice, like me, is flat. Drained of energy.

'I think Madison told you everything. I heard it all, you know.'

'I guessed.'

He looks at me strangely. He'll be wondering why I guessed. Because I saw him push Madison to her death, or because I've worked out the timing of his appearance at the house?

'You understand why I never told you, don't you?'

He sits up very straight. As straight as his twisted torso lets him, having momentarily forgotten all about his debilitating pain.

'You didn't want me to find out. But why didn't you trust me? If you'd had a drunken one-night fling with Madison, and explained it to me, I might have let it go. We weren't even married yet.'

He blinks rapidly, as if he's having difficulty thinking straight.

'You told me once that if I so much as looked at another woman, you'd leave me. Don't you get it? I love you that much.'

He manages to wring a tear from his eye. I can just make it out in the gloaming. Perhaps he is sad, but why do I feel it's for effect? To keep me onside. On his side.

'You should have told me, Jed. I loved you as much as you loved me. Remember, I told you about Dad. My darkest secrets, and you were there for me. We could have worked through it together.'

A glimmer of hope flickers across his face.

'We still can. Can't we?' He sets his mug down. 'Now I know I never actually did sleep with Madison, and that Benjamin isn't mine.'

His eyes are wide, pleading like a puppy's.

'It's the lies. I had no idea, until I started watching you.'

'From the café? Well, you kept that from me.' He laughs. Somehow my omission of telling him I watched him visit another woman is up there with him not telling me he had a son.

'I watched you for weeks, Jed. I even saw you come off your bike.'

'I sort of guessed.'

'How?'

I wonder, if he hadn't killed Madison, if I'd now forgive him. Perhaps we might even be able to laugh about him replying to my column. Catching me out in my own game of cat-and-mouse.

'I read your column. I always read your column. Every week. You talk more through that than you ever do in person.'

'Why didn't you talk to me then when you guessed I was on to you?'

'I suppose it was because I was scared. You won't leave me, will you, Izzy?'

'It's all the lies. I wondered who Hawkeye was. I even thought it might be Madison.'

'Really?' His tone lightens. 'I just didn't want you to rock the boat. It was all a silly game.'

I find it hard to look at him. In the last few hours, he's become a stranger.

'What's up?' he asks when I go quiet.

'You haven't even asked about the scan.'

'Holy shit. I'm sorry. In all the drama I forgot. Show me. Show me.'

He's beside me on the sofa in a flash.

Surely if he really loved me, this would have been his first thought. He's been leading me away from what happened tonight, his mind skittering like feet on ice. He's all over the place, wanting to talk about everything, except Madison's death.

And making his best effort to redirect any suspicions I might have.

He really thinks he's going to get away with murder.

92

We carry on the charade, until Jed gets up, and digs out a scrap of paper from a small drawer under the coffee table. On it is a list of baby names for boys and girls.

'So I can now forget Scarlet, Susan, and Sherry,' he laughs, throwing the scrap in the air. 'Looks like it'll be a battle between Jethro, Jerry, or Julian.'

All at once, he's engulfed in excitement about the baby, about the future. His eyes are aglow.

'Everything is going to work out okay. Isn't it?' he asks.

He stretches out both hands, and pulls me up, suffocating me with kisses. I'm rigid, but he doesn't seem to notice, and carries on squeezing me to death.

I paint on a smile, but my insides churn.

It's 3 a.m. by the time we climb the stairs to bed. We both strip off, throw our clothes on the bedroom chair, and climb under the duvet. I don't even brush my teeth. The room is hot, sweltering as the heating has been on all day, but my limbs are icy.

I'll not be able to sleep, but Jed will. He's yawning uncontrollably, and he's eerily calm and at ease. That's the difference between us. He can block out any shit as soon as he crawls into bed. He's always been the same.

Tonight, I'm desperate for him to sleep. To stop talking. His words have been pouring out since we got home. Justifications for all the lies. Trying to turn the tables, and put some of the blame back on me. It crosses my mind that if he ever got caught, he'd likely try to make me an accomplice in Madison's murder. He's confident he's got away with it.

He finally turns over, and is soon snoring contentedly. I watch him. His body is more relaxed than it's been in months, as if a magic wand has zapped away all the tension.

'No more lies,' he mumbled before he closed his eyes. 'We'll tell each other everything from now on.'

'No more lies,' I said.

This is my biggest lie. I've more to tell, but it'll have to wait until the morning. The police are due around eleven, but for now I need to get some sleep.

* * *

Jed is still out for the count when I crawl out of bed. He doesn't so much as twitch when I pull on my jogging clothes, or when I close the door behind me.

Downstairs I leave another note. Likely the last one ever.

Popped out for some fresh air and a walk around the park. Will be back before 11 X

The pen hovers before I add the kiss.

I linger by the front door, look back up the stairs, and listen.

Still no sound. I don't think he's slept this soundly since we first got together. He really thinks everything will work out.

I drive into town. The roads are strewn with the aftermath of the storm. I skirt round branches and debris littering my route until I park up near the market square.

Angelo's opens at 7.30, even on a Saturday. At weekends it's quieter this early than in the week, and, as usual, I'm the first customer.

Today is likely my last visit. I need to say goodbye to a lot of things, and places, and Angelo's will be one of the first to go.

There's no sign of Candy, but I didn't expect to see her. I'm still reeling from her having the broken-off piece of keyring, but that's tomorrow's worry. Today, I've too much else to deal with.

Candy will be reeling from Madison's death, not to mention learning that Adam is Benjamin's father. Maybe she killed Blanche, for Adam's sake. Love can make you do crazy things. But deep down, I don't believe she did.

The only other person here this morning is Angelo. He froths my drink in silence, with a definite hint of reverence. No doubt he's heard what happened, as he pushes the mug gently towards me.

As I carry my drink over to the window spot, I wonder if Angelo knew Madison. He must have met her.

The quiet is soothing, a meagre balm for all the turmoil. I daren't think of what the day will bring, but for now I need to stay focused. I'm no longer looking out just for myself, but for the baby as well.

Last night, Jed and I agreed on the name Jethro for our son. Jed remembers Jethro Tull, a rock band from the sixties, as he was once into heavy metal. For me, I just like the name.

The curtains across the road in Madison's flat are drawn. I wonder where Benjamin is? I presume with Adam.

Then a chink appears as one curtain is slowly drawn back, and I see Adam. Even from this far away I see his tousled hair and sad expression. I can only imagine how he's feeling. I wonder if he knows yet that Benjamin is his son. My mind is on fire with thoughts.

He looks down, and raises a hand. I think he's going to wave, but instead he runs it through his wayward hair. My heart flutters at the sight. He turns his back, and widens his arm. Then I see him hoist Benjamin up and hold him tight. I imagine it's tight because I doubt he'll let him go again.

Angelo interrupts my thoughts, and makes me jump.

'On the house,' he says, setting down another coffee. It's the first time he's ever waited on a customer. He usually leaves that to the staff. And my first ever free drink.

'Thanks.'

I'll not be able to drink it though, not without food. And I'm far from hungry. Angelo might be upset when I leave it, but he'll likely understand.

A few customers start to filter through. I'm about to pack up and set off for the park as I need to walk and clear my head. I've got a busy day ahead, and this might be my last chance for peace.

Then I see the front door of Madison's flat open, and Adam appears alongside Benjamin. They're holding hands. Ben is clinging on as if for dear life. They start walking right, away from the town centre, in the direction of the park.

Adam must feel my eyes on him because he stops, and looks across the road. Benjamin glances up at him, eyes wide as saucers, but puffy from crying. I've no idea how the lad is coping, or what he's been told. Perhaps he thinks Mum is on holiday, and Uncle Adam is a temporary babysitter.

I watch Adam bend down, until he's level with Ben's face, and kiss him on the forehead. Then he points my way, and Ben brightens up. Perhaps mention of marshmallows and hot chocolate have done the trick. Madison told me these were his favourites.

Soon they're wandering into the café. Adam's eyes are even puffier than Ben's.

'Hi, Izzy,' he says. 'Meet Ben.'

He lifts Ben up, swirls him round, and pops him down in front of me.

'Hi, Ben.'

I've only ever seen Ben from afar, but he's really cute. Dimples, dark brown eyes, and smooth olive skin. He's more like Adam than Madison in looks. I imagine the ladies will love him too.

'Can we join you?' Adam asks.

'I was just going to walk round the park, as I've a lot to do. But you're welcome to come with me.'

Benjamin pipes up.

'Park. Swings.'

Adam and I laugh.

'Let me get the drinks and we'll take them with us,' Adam says. 'Can you look after Benjamin for a minute?'

Before I can reply, the lad has wound his arms round Adam's legs. He's not letting him out of his sight.

93

We spend about an hour wandering round the park. Adam has brought breadcrumbs to feed the ducks, and Benjamin doesn't seem to have a care in the world.

'I'm really sorry about Madison,' I say.

Adam and I sit on a bench while Benjamin shoots right and left.

'It's been such a shock. Dreadful for Ben.'

'Have you told him yet?'

'Not yet. I've said Mum had to visit a sick friend. He's been crying all night, wondering why she didn't tell him.'

'How's his fever?'

'Lots of Calpol, and the temperature was back to normal this morning. That's kids for you.' He smiles. 'Much more resilient than adults.'

There's a long silence while we both look out over the lake. Does he know he's his dad? Did Candy tell him?

I needn't have worried, because, as if reading my thoughts, he says, 'I know I'm his dad. I had no idea until yesterday.'

'Did Candy tell you?'

'No, it was Madison. She told me in the morning that she was planning to tell you everything last night, but wanted to tell me first.' His voice cracks, and he looks round. 'Did she get her chance to talk to you?'

'Yes. We talked before she had her fall.'

Tears are rolling down his cheeks. I dare to touch his arm, and he puts a hand on top of mine.

'I'm so sorry, but she loved you, Adam. Too much if that's possible. She was scared you'd make her have an abortion, or that you'd disown her completely.'

The moment passes, as Benjamin bowls up and grabs Adam's hand.

'Excuse me, first things first.' Adam smiles, and my heart melts.

'Uncle Adam. Come feed the ducks,' Benjamin squeals.

It looks as if Ben hasn't been told yet that Uncle Adam is in fact his dad.

* * *

An hour later we're strolling back. Benjamin has fallen asleep in Adam's arms, and we pick up our conversation.

'How did Jed take it, finding out Ben isn't his?'

'Upset, obviously, but almost more relieved that the truth has come out.'

'It'll not be easy for him.'

'He'll be okay. He's about to be a real father soon.'

I pat my belly.

'Congratulations. That is good news.'

Adam smiles. Maybe I'm being ridiculous, but did I pick up a slight disappointment in his tone? Whatever, I decide to tell Adam what my plans are. No more lies, or pretence.

'It's good and bad news. Thrilled about the baby, but I'm leaving Jed. There have been too many lies. There's no trust left.'

'Oh. I'm sorry.'

'Don't be.' I manage a smile when he stares at me. Benjamin fidgets in his sleep, but it doesn't stop Adam leaning across and kissing me gently on the cheek.

The butterflies are back, battering my insides. The way they did when Jed first kissed me.

Who knows? Maybe Adam really does like me.

94

Adam and Benjamin walk me back to my car, which is parked by the market square. Benjamin has woken up, but is still woozy from sleep. Adam sets him down, and his little legs plod along.

When I struggle to open the car door, yanking, tugging, and cursing, Adam leans across.

'Here. Let me help.'

I blush, his closeness like an electric shock.

As I settle into the driver's seat, and tug the seat belt across, he hits me with the curveball.

'Oh, may I have the key to Blanche's back, please? I lent it to Candy, and she says you kept it. It's just I'll need it to get in and out of the house over the next few weeks before work starts.'

He towers over me, leaning his arms on top of the car roof.

I swallow hard. My throat is so dry, the words won't come. He looks concerned, bends down.

'Are you okay?'

'Fine. It's just a touch of morning sickness, but it'll pass.'

I close the door, wind the window slightly down, and talk

through the crack. I have to grip the steering wheel to compose myself.

'Yes, I've got the key. No worries, I'll drop it off.'

'Great. I'm staying with Benjamin at the flat, so pop round for coffee.'

'I didn't realise you had a key. Jed never said.'

'We held keys to all the properties. The terrace was so unstable that we needed emergency access.'

'Oh. Blanche would never have let you in.' I give a dry laugh.

'I know, but it was a health and safety issue.'

'When did Jed give you the key? I had to get a spare cut for Madison.'

My knuckles are white against the wheel. I can't grip any harder.

There's definitely a moment's hesitation before he answers. I watch him like a hawk.

'Shortly before she died.'

He steps back a bit from the car.

I start up the engine, my questions having dried up. There's nothing more to ask.

'Bye. See you soon,' I say, unable to look at him.

'Hope so.'

His voice gets swallowed up when I rev the engine, and he slaps the car roof as I drive off.

I look back through the rear-view mirror.

Ben is clinging on to his new dad. The sight breaks my heart.

Adam was the person who had the key when Blanche died. What if Ben's new dad is a killer? Could he really have been the person who threw Blanche down the stairs?

Before they disappear from view, Adam hoists Ben back up onto his shoulders, and grips his ankles. Already they're inseparable.

* * *

I drive round and round for what seems like an eternity. I finally pull into the old church car park at the far end of town. The place is deserted.

I get out, and head for the small graveyard round the back, and halt by an overgrown plot. I bend down, pull out some weeds, and wipe away a tear.

I wonder, if Benjamin hadn't lost his mother, and Adam wasn't his father, if I'd have the same quandary. When baby flips, squirms, talks to me in gurgles, I can't imagine anything worse than him not having a mother, or a father.

Mum used to tell me, 'If you don't know what to do at any moment, do nothing. The answer will find its way.'

I kneel down in front of Mum's grave, and say a prayer.

There's nothing left to do.

95

Half an hour later, I'm parked up outside the police station. I start the countdown from one thousand. It's going to take more than courage to go inside.

I finally get out, and head for the entrance. Each step is such an effort, I could be walking towards the gallows.

When a police officer appears through the swing doors, and holds them open, I know it's now or never.

* * *

It's 10.30 by the time I get home. From the hallway, I hear Jed moving around upstairs. He's tramping back and forth across the creaky floorboards. I'm so alert, I think I can hear him breathe.

'Yoo-hoo. I'm up here,' he yells.

He sounds miles away.

I brace myself as I climb the stairs. At first, I'm not sure which room he's in, until I see the tins of paint. They're lined up outside the spare room.

'I've put everything else in the bathroom for now,' he announces when he sees me. A grin is splayed across his face.

'What are you doing?'

It's obvious what he's doing, but I'm shocked. It's as if the last twenty-four hours haven't happened. He's sitting on the floor, dabbing different shades of paint on the whitewashed walls. The walls of what will be Jethro's nursery.

'What do you think? This shade of blue? Or this one? Or what about lilac?' He points at the different options.

He's beaming like a kid with a paint set. His forefinger is white and bony. Bonier than I remember. I used to think his fingers were slim, and refined. Elegant. But now they just look skeletal.

In fact he's hard to recognise at all. He's dressed in old shorts, an already paint-splattered t-shirt, with a bandana round his head. He's like a hippy without a care in the world.

'It's too soon, Jed.'

'The time will go quickly. We need Jethro's room ready for him.'

Forget the last twenty-four hours, it's as if the last two years haven't happened.

I wish it could have been any other way. If he'd been honest from the outset, and even if he hadn't and I'd only found out last night exactly what had happened, I might have forgiven him.

But murder is something else.

I hunker down beside him, pick up a spare brush, and dip it in a cream-coloured mixture.

'Would you prefer a neutral colour? That's okay with me,' he asks. Hope is seeping through every pore.

'Jed...'

'Yes?' He carries on dabbing at the walls, overdoing the concentration on the paint.

'It's over,' I say.

'Sorry?' He blinks rapidly, before scratching his eye and leaving a daub of paint on his cheek.

'It's over. We're over.'

'What are you talking about?' He swivels to face me.

'Us. Our marriage. Everything.'

'But why? I thought you forgave me. It's all been a big mistake.'

He actually believes this. In his own twisted world, that's all that matters. That I've forgiven him.

I wonder, if he told me the truth about pushing Madison down the stairs, if I could have forgiven him even for that. He could have pleaded manslaughter. She deserved punishment, no doubt, but not to be killed. It wasn't even a crime of passion, simply a crime of payback.

I watch the stranger in front of me.

'Jed. It was the lies. You should have trusted me. We could have faced it together. We weren't even married when you thought you'd slept with Madison. I'd have listened.'

'But I was so scared. I can't lose you, Izzy. You're my life. Always have been.'

He sets the brushes down, slides closer, thinking proximity might do the trick.

'Have you anything else to tell me? Something that might make it okay? Something to help me forgive you all the lies?'

He scratches his arms, his neck, his head. As if for inspiration.

'No. Nothing. What else do you think there is?'

I get up slowly, turn and leave him on the floor.

He shoots a hand out against the wall to steady himself when he hears the siren. We're expecting the police, but it's the siren that's freaked him. The fear of a guilty man is written all over his face. The police would have knocked quietly if it was just to take statements.

Now is his last chance to tell me. That he deliberately killed Madison. It might not make a difference to the outcome, but it would show he trusts me.

He says nothing as I hover by the nursery door. I can see down the stairs and the outline of a policeman through the frosted glass. The bell rings. Once. Twice. Three times. Neither of us move.

When he doesn't say anything more, I speak over my shoulder.

'I'll now tell you why I'm leaving you. Killing Madison, pretending she fell, was one lie too many. Who knows? If you'd told me, I might have even forgiven you that.'

'How do you know I killed her?' His eyes protrude as if on stalks.

'I videoed it, Jed. I saw it all.'

'Are you handing me in? How could you? You killed your bloody father, so what's the difference? I never told on you.' He spits in disbelief.

'I didn't kill Dad. I wished him dead. There's a big difference.'

There, I've finally said it. What Teagan has been wanting to hear for years; that I didn't kill my father.

96

I opt not to go with Jed.

He changes into a pair of chinos, a clean shirt, and combs his hair. He looks as if he's off to work, perhaps hoping a better appearance might work to his benefit.

Even after he's read his rights, he looks hopeful. I wonder how he's going to try and talk his way out of this one, as it's not as easy lying to the police. And the video evidence is enough to put him away for a long time.

'I'll be back soon. See you later,' he yells, rattling his hand-cuffs up and down.

As he's led out of the house, he pauses a second. He doesn't look back at me, but adds, 'Izzy. You'll wait for me, won't you?'

But I'm already inside, and closing the door behind him.

Once the police drive off, I call Teagan. I sob into the phone, tell her Jed has been arrested for Madison's murder.

She listens like she always does. When she doesn't voice shock or horror, I sense she's not that surprised. She's cute, clever, and always has my back.

I tell her I'll meet up with her in a few days' time... whenever that is. I know she'll be there.

For now, I need to be alone.

The days pass, and soon turn into weeks. I've started sleeping under our bed in a sleeping bag, with torchlight for company. I've even dug out an old jigsaw of the Tower of London. I know there's a piece missing, bottom left-hand corner, but it makes me smile to know that.

Funny how the comfort of old habits is hard to beat. I survived once, and will do again. I've come full circle, finding the silence to be my happy place. My phone is switched off, although I'll turn it on again when I'm ready. So far, my only visitors have been the police.

But that'll do for now.

97

ONE YEAR LATER

I jiggle the handle on the buggy. Teagan tells me I'm now officially a *yummy mummy*. She babysits, mothers me, and smothers Jethro in kisses. Auntie Teagan knows how to make him giggle, and once he starts, he can't stop. He's beyond cute.

This morning I'm in El Paradiso. It's my new go-to café at the opposite end of town to Angelo's. The coffee isn't as good, but the view is becoming more intriguing by the day. I come here when Jethro has his morning nap which can go on for over two hours.

Again, I've found the most amazing window seat, with an even more amazing view. The young barista, Manuel, made a cardboard 'reserved' sign for my table. He's pretty cute, that's for sure. He plonks it on my table first thing every morning, and no one has ever dared take my seat.

The staff are young, lively, and full of fun. They know I'm quiet, but it doesn't stop me listening in to all their chat and banter.

I've started work on my novel, and have almost finished the first draft. I took paid maternity leave from *Echoes of London*, but won't be going back. I really think I might have something with this writing malarky.

Teagan didn't like the title of my novel: *A Liar and a Cheat*. She wants me to lose the anger, the vitriol. As always, she's right. But she's still not sure about the alternative I came up with: *The Dishonest Assassin*. I'm not certain either, but if I ever find a publisher, no doubt they'll change it anyway. For now, the title gives me inspiration, as I have plenty of material to include.

There's a monstrosity of new-build flats across from El Paradiso. And would you believe it? Adam is the developer.

He now drives around in a top-of-the-range Mercedes saloon. A Mercedes Benz S-Class. It's so luxurious. He made a load of money from the Miners' Terrace development, that's for sure. Most of the luxury apartments have already been bought off-plan, even though the building work is still on-going. The location is so central, it was always going to be a winner.

I can no longer complain about my transport. Jethro and I cruise around in a Mini Clubman Countryman. Lots of room in the boot for teddies and toys. After my bashed-up Fiesta, it's beyond plush. Jethro and I, at a push, could live in it.

At least I no longer have money worries. The sale of Blanche's house brought in a tidy sum, and as Jed and I are still officially married, he tells me to use the proceeds however I want. I certainly intend to. He's determined Jethro will have the best of everything.

From his prison cell, Jed is planning what they'll do together when he gets early release.

'I'll be out soon for good behaviour,' he whispers at me across the table.

He's still in denial about killing Madison, and is on a new delusional loop of lies.

It's tough to listen, as he jiggles Jethro on his knee, and tells him that he loves him to heaven and back. The way he loves Mummy.

Strange that I never realised how delusional Jed was. He assumes I'll be at home waiting for him, no matter how long it takes. I haven't the heart to tell him otherwise, or that I'm currently sorting out divorce papers. One thing at a time.

He doesn't know our house is up for sale, and Jethro and I have our eye on a little cottage in the countryside. It's in a village not far from town, with a super little nursery. I'll be able to walk Jethro there and back every morning, the way Madison did Ben. Our future is all mapped out.

Although Jed got life for murdering Madison, the video evidence irrefutable, a cloud still hangs over my head as to what happened to Blanche.

The police moved on pretty quickly after her death, putting it down to a tragic accident. It was completely different with Madison, as I had clear proof that Jed killed her.

Teagan, for a while afterwards, tried to make me talk about it. Deep down, she suspected Jed might have pushed his own mother. He needed the money, after all, but I told her there was no point discussing it, as he's already doing life.

She never suspected anyone else was involved. I never shared about the broken-off piece of keyring, or my suspicions about Adam. Too much time has passed, and I try hard to keep it to the back of my mind. With writing, and Jethro to keep me busy, it's getting easier.

Teagan has been amazing though. She always makes the world seem a better place. She's logical, loving, and the only person I trust in the whole world.

As for my new boyfriend, that's a completely different matter.

98

While I work on my novel in the café, I've started watching Adam. At least he's not going out with me because of likely benefits with regards to his latest project. I have absolutely no connection to this development.

He doesn't know that I watch him from the window of El Paradiso. He buys takeaway coffee these days, far too busy to sit in. He told me that only once did he buy coffee from El Paradiso, but couldn't stand the taste. Far too bitter. So I'm confident he'll not be back.

Perhaps one day, I'll own up that this is my new regular haunt. But then again, perhaps not. He doesn't really need to know. As there are eighteen cafés in total round the town, I joke that Jethro needs a change of scene.

Adam likes that we are a ready-made, makeshift little family. Him, me, Benjamin, and Jethro. He genuinely seems to like me, and has suggested (more than once) that we should all live together. But I'm reluctant to commit, unsure if I'll ever really trust him. Once bitten, and all that.

It wasn't easy, but I decided not to go to the police with the broken-off piece of keyring. The keyring that I know belonged to Adam, and which I found beside Blanche's body.

None of what happened was Benjamin's fault, and as I watch them together, I have no regrets. I'll never know for certain if Adam pushed Blanche, but Benjamin is so happy that I could never be the person who takes that away from him.

While Benjamin needs his father, I'm becoming more and more attached to Adam myself. I keep the broken-off piece of keyring locked away, as a personal reminder to never trust anyone completely.

This morning I'm surprisingly relaxed. Jethro is still asleep, and a rare wave of contentment sweeps over me as I sip my cappuccino. There'll be nothing much to see today, as Adam is due up in Manchester. His development portfolio is growing fast.

Suddenly my hand wobbles. Oh my goodness. Milky liquid dribbles down my chin.

I duck down in a panic behind the waxy indoor plant.

What is Adam doing here this morning? He told me last night he would be in Manchester.

I feel a chill come over me when I see him get off his new roadster bike, and padlock it to the railings. He can't park the Merc close enough to the development, so if the weather allows, he uses his bike instead.

Why didn't he tell me about his change of plans?

It's then I remember telling him that I was taking Jethro up to Cambridge today, for his first ride on a train.

Neither of us are where we said we'd be. I changed my mind when Jethro started to cough.

Hard not to smile, as it's pretty hypocritical.

That said, I need to stay alert. Adam is my new puzzle. I'm sure there's more to him than meets the eye, and that he has a few secrets up his sleeve. Even if he didn't kill Blanche, I doubt I'll ever trust another man completely.

For now, he's my new project. Another café window. Another soap opera. It passes the time, and in a masochistic way, I enjoy the drama. And the way things are going, I might get enough fodder for a follow-on novel.

I peer through the window, and watch Adam stroll across the rubble. Past the diggers...

Until he disappears from view.

ACKNOWLEDGEMENTS

After the success of *The Girl in Seat 2A*, it was always going to be a struggle to come up with a follow-on novel.

If it wasn't for Emily Yau, my wonderful editor, and only early reader, I'm not sure I'd have got there. Having someone completely in your corner is all that matters to a writer, and someone who believes in you. Thank you so much for all your sage advice and input. We got there in the end.

Also, thanks to the whole amazing team at Boldwood Books. Every single member of the team is involved in bringing an author's books to fruition, so a huge thanks to you all.

www.boldwoodbooks.com

As always, thanks to readers everywhere. The good reviews spur us on, and the negative ones are there to teach us. Keep them coming.

Finally, thanks to my hubby, Neil, my sister Linda, and my gorgeous niece, Lindsay... they are my constant supporters. Always encouraging, and willing me on.

And thanks to James, still the most wonderful son in the world... but I do wish you'd read my books!

For updates on new releases, competitions, and exclusive author news, sign up to my newsletter link below:

https://bit.ly/DianaWilkinsonNews

ABOUT THE AUTHOR

Diana Wilkinson is the number one bestselling author of psychological thrillers. Formerly an international professional tennis player, she hails from Belfast, but now lives in Hertfordshire.

Sign up to Diana Wilkinson's mailing list here for news, competitions and updates on future books.

Follow Diana on social media:

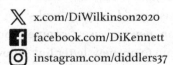

x.com/DiWilkinson2020

facebook.com/DiKennett

instagram.com/diddlers37

ALSO BY DIANA WILKINSON

One Down

Right Behind You

The Woman in My Home

You Are Mine

The Missing Guest

The Girl in Seat 2A

The Girl in the Window

THE

Murder

LIST

**THE MURDER LIST IS A NEWSLETTER
DEDICATED TO SPINE-CHILLING FICTION
AND GRIPPING PAGE-TURNERS!**

**SIGN UP TO MAKE SURE YOU'RE ON OUR
HIT LIST FOR EXCLUSIVE DEALS, AUTHOR
CONTENT, AND COMPETITIONS.**

SIGN UP TO OUR NEWSLETTER

BIT.LY/THEMURDERLISTNEWS

Boldwood

Boldwood Books is an award-winning fiction publishing company seeking out the best stories from around the world.

Find out more at www.boldwoodbooks.com

Join our reader community for brilliant books, competitions and offers!

Follow us
@BoldwoodBooks
@TheBoldBookClub

Sign up to our weekly deals newsletter

https://bit.ly/BoldwoodBNewsletter

Made in the USA
Monee, IL
03 July 2025

20452676R00193